———————— ★ ————————

A chilling scream, a woman's scream, pierced the golden afternoon air.

I paused long enough to point myself in the probable right direction. Lettie was right with me as I raced around, not up, the wide double staircase. Tessa stood at the balustrade, leaning over. She appeared to be choking. I dashed over and touched her shoulder gently, so as not to frighten her. Tessa pointed downward.

It was a sheer drop from the balustrade to a grassy slope. At the base of the slope, Amy lay in a contorted position, her head downhill from her feet. It was obvious to me that her neck was broken. She lay on her right side, her left arm behind her back. Her legs were in a sort of climbing position, but her head faced the other way. Tessa kept making choking sounds.

———————— ★ ————————

"Maria Hudgins writes a delightful amateur sleuth tale and armchair detectives will enjoy seeing Italy through Dotsy's eyes."

—Harriet Klausner

DEATH
of an
OBNOXIOUS
TOURIST

Maria Hudgins

W⊕RLDWIDE®

TORONTO • NEW YORK • LONDON
AMSTERDAM • PARIS • SYDNEY • HAMBURG
STOCKHOLM • ATHENS • TOKYO • MILAN
MADRID • WARSAW • BUDAPEST • AUCKLAND

To
Mike and Nell

DEATH OF AN OBNOXIOUS TOURIST

A Worldwide Mystery/September 2007

First published by Five Star.

ISBN-13: 978-0-373-26611-1
ISBN-10:   0-373-26611-1

Acknowledgment

I would like to thank Cynthia Riggs and Nancy J. Cohen for their guidance. I'm enormously grateful to my good friends Brian and Marie Smith and to Gordon Statzer for their suggestions and for listening to my endless prattle. And a great big thank-you to Denise Dietz for her editing and encouragement.

The Travelers

Dotsy Lamb—ancient-history professor and recently divorced mother of five grown children, she really needs this vacation

Lettie Osgood—Dotsy's lifelong friend, she's a bit scatterbrained but is blessed with an almost photographic memory

Amy Bauer—youngest of the Bauer sisters and a college friend of Tessa D'Angelo

Beth Bauer Hines—middle sister of Amy and Meg

Meg Bauer—eldest of the Bauer sisters, and a nurse with the world's worst bedside manner

Geoffrey Reese-Burton—a jovial Englishman, but no one can understand a word he says

Victoria Reese-Burton—Geoffrey's wife; she owns a bookstore in England

Dick Kramer—he's in the furniture business, but what business he has in Italy is unclear

Michael Melon—a handsome young man from Washington, D.C.

Walter Everard—a sophisticated man whose photos help to solve a mystery

Elaine King—a friend of Beth Hines. Along with Dick, Michael and Walter, she's a member of the "curious quartet"

Shirley Hostetter—a squeaky-clean nurse and mother, she's struggling to hold on to her rebellious daughter

Crystal Hostetter—a punk/goth teenager with more facial hardware than a medieval knight with braces

Jim Kelly—a Canadian dairy farmer, he loves his bovine "girls" almost as much as he does his wife, Wilma

Wilma Kelly—an environmental activist and animal lover

Paul Vogel—a mole-like little man who takes a lot of pictures

Lucille Vogel—a professional singer whose star has dimmed, she's subject to wild mood swings

Waiting for Them in Italy

Tessa D'Angelo—the tour guide; she and Amy were friends in college

Cesare Rossi—Tessa's fiancé

Marco Quattrocchi—a captain in the carabinieri, Italy's military police

Achille Santacroce—the bus driver

Ivo Ramovic—a Gypsy street vendor

Chiriklo—a teenage boy who shows Crystal about life in a Gypsy camp

ONE

"STRIP SEARCH?" Lettie slapped a cold, quivering hand on my arm. "Please, Dotsy, talk to them. This can't be happening!"

"I can't believe you had a gun in your carry-on, Lettie. Have you lost your mind?" Here we were in Milan, Italy. A whole new world. Same old Lettie.

"I was just following your suggestion, and it isn't a gun. It's a water pistol."

I threw a maternal arm around Lettie's trembling shoulders. At home, Lettie and I live two hundred miles apart, and we normally get together maybe once or twice a year. It amazes me that she manages to stay alive and out of jail without my constant intervention.

"I told you to bring a water pistol to Italy? Maybe you misunderstood me. I may have said to bring a water *bottle.*"

"No, and don't treat me like a kid. I'm fifty-umm years old." Lettie shuffled at a snail's pace toward the door the uniformed security man had indicated. He scrutinized her from his position behind a checkpoint table. Lettie eyed him as if she might try to make a break for the concourse and hide out in the duty-free shop.

Dragging her suitcase behind her like an albatross dead three days, she trudged through the doorway and disappeared behind a humorless-looking woman who shut the door with an ominous click. Welcome to Italy.

I wasn't about to let this ruin my day, let alone my trip. I could already see myself laughing about it at Christmas parties next winter. I slipped out my passport and ran my finger lovingly over the brand new stamp. My first passport stamp. My first passport.

"Dorothy Lamb?" I jumped at the sound of my legal name and located the source, a pretty young woman with tousled auburn hair shoved back with a pair of large sunglasses. "I'm Tessa D'Angelo, your tour guide. Welcome to Milano."

"Please call me Dotsy."

"And this is Amy Bauer," Tessa said, turning to her companion.

Just behind Tessa, a tall woman who could easily have been a model—she was gorgeous—stepped forward and extended her hand toward me. The extending of the hand, I think, caused her purse to slip off her shoulder and bounce into the crook of her arm. A slip of paper popped out of the purse and drifted, perhaps caught by a tiny air current, toward me. As it landed near my left foot, I bent over to pick it up for her.

Amy Bauer lunged forward so fast and so awkwardly—it would be no exaggeration to say she pounced on it—that she fell, head first, onto the top of my lowered head. The inside of my eyes were immediately treated to a psychedelic light show. I heard a crack which could have been either Amy's barrette or my own skull, and my sinus cavities imploded, as if I had just dived off the high board and hit the water, chin first. I grasped the paper, but Amy snatched it away before I could even yell, "Owww!"

She apologized profusely, and I, in an attempt to get this relationship off on a smoother footing, changed the subject. "You must be Beth Bauer's sister. Lettie is dying to meet you. She says the last time she saw you, you were about six."

"If she says so, I'll take her word for it. Beth has told me so much about her old friend—oh, I didn't mean…"

"That's okay. I know you meant old in the good sense of the word," I said. *What the hell is the good sense of the word "old"?* I wondered. If Lettie was old to Amy, what must I seem like to her? I'm five years older than Lettie.

"Is that Letitia Osgood you're talking about? Where is she?" Tessa scanned the printed list she held clamped to a clipboard.

"Well, at the moment, she's being strip-searched. She ran into a spot of trouble at the immigration gate." I explained the whole thing while Amy's and Tessa's mouths dropped closer and closer to their collarbones.

"Why didn't she get caught in Washington?" Tessa asked. "Security should have caught that before she got on the plane."

I shrugged as the door swung open and Lettie, now pushing her luggage ahead of her, sort of oozed out with her head down, as if she thought everyone in the airport had just seen her naked.

"I hate Italy. I want to go home." Lettie's chin tightened up in that way it always did when she felt vulnerable.

Tessa whisked us out of the airport so quickly, Lettie had no further chance to dwell on her recent unpleasantness. A blast of heat hit us as we dashed out and through a parking area to the six-passenger SUV Tessa had borrowed from her tour company. She heaved our luggage into the back. "We have to pop over to Linate Airport on the way out of town. There's a couple coming in on a ten o'clock from England to join us, and that, I believe, will be everybody. The others are already at the hotel in Venice."

Lettie and I hopped in behind Tessa and Amy. "I'm at a total loss to think what I said that made you bring that water pistol, Lettie," I said.

"You said, 'it's fun to meet children when you travel, and one way is to have a toy to show or give them.'"

"I meant something like a balloon or a finger puppet."

We stopped in Verona for lunch. Now *this* was Italy; or my image of Italy. Milan had struck me as being no different from any city anywhere. It could have been Cleveland, for heaven's sake, except the signs were in Italian. Milan seemed to have more than its fair share of furniture stores and factories. Where were all those exclusive boutiques I'd heard about?

Verona, by contrast, sang with color and whimsy. Frescoed walls, crumbling corners, Roman ruins. Flowers cascaded from every window. The windows served as box seats from which small, frizzled women watched the pageant of street life below.

We ate at a sidewalk café on the Piazza Brà, overlooking the Arena. The Arena di Verona looks, for all the world, like the Coliseum in Rome, but in much better shape. Several huge sphinxes and lotus-shaped columns littered the eastern side of the piazza, testaments to the Arena's modern use as an opera house. They were apparently doing *Aïda*. In spite of my jet lag and the headache left over from my collision with Amy, I began to get that giddy feeling that comes over me when I plunge into totally foreign territory—like when I water-skied for the first time and the night I bought moonshine from a bootlegger.

"Juliet's house is just a few blocks from here." Tessa signaled the waiter for menus.

"Juliet? But she wasn't a real person." I laughed. "How could she have a house?"

"You're not supposed to think like that. You're supposed to be a tourist."

The Reese-Burtons, the couple we had picked up at the Linate Airport, seemed like a jovial enough pair, but the problem was, I couldn't understand a word the husband, Geoffrey Reese-Burton, said. He looked like the prototype of the English colonel, retired from Her Majesty's service in India. He blustered out sentences in a sort of guttural word purée. He plopped his well-padded bottom beside Tessa and said something like, "Yawf tendop heh?"

"Pardon?" Tessa asked.

"Don't worry if you don't understand a word Geoffrey says," Victoria Reese-Burton offered, glancing around at all of us. "I can't understand him myself, half the time. But what he said just then was, 'Have you ever attended an opera here?'"

Amy glanced toward me and grinned. Tessa said, "Oh, sure. I've been to performances over there. It's marvelous. The acoustics are…" She kissed her fingertips in a typically Italian gesture.

Tessa, Amy and I had kept up a light-hearted chatter in the car, between Milan and Verona, and slowly Lettie had climbed out of her blue funk and joined us. As she studied the menu, she nudged Tessa. "You'll have to help me with this menu. I need to get something easy to chew." Lettie put the back of her hand up to the side of her mouth in a sort of stage-type aside.

It was such a uniquely Lettie-quirk, that I could have spotted her in a jam-packed stadium if she only did that little thing with her hand. It was as if she was telling a secret, but she always did it while talking in a normal voice.

"You see," she said, "I've been having some dental work done, and temporarily, I have to wear this partial plate which I cannot get used to. So what would you suggest?"

Tessa suggested the eggplant Parmigiano, and the rest of us shared two pizzas. I said, "You haven't even a trace of an Italian accent, Tessa. What's your first language, English or Italian?"

"Both, actually. I grew up in Pennsylvania, but my mother immigrated to the U.S. after she and Dad got married."

Amy butted in. "She and I were buddies in college."

"Anyway, I grew up speaking English everywhere but home. At first, my mom tried to learn English, but then she…well, I have a younger brother who is mentally challenged…my mother would never let anyone care for him but herself, and he had to be watched all the time. So, after he was born, she hardly ever went out, and therefore, hardly ever practiced her English. I grew up speaking Italian with her and English with everybody else."

"And after you moved here?" I tried to imagine the loneliness of the poor woman, housebound, in a foreign land. "Has she been here to visit?"

"No. Mama died a few years ago. Then my brother had to be put in a nursing facility, anyway, in spite of how hard Mama had worked to avoid that very thing." As if to turn the conversation in a happier direction, she touched Amy's hand lightly and said, "But my ol' buddy, Amy Perez…whoops, Bauer, I mean, has finally come to visit. Amy and I hadn't seen each other since we were in college and then we bumped into each other at a travel convention this spring. I talked her into this trip, and then she recruited her sisters to join us."

Beth and Meg, as I well knew, were Amy's sisters. Like everyone else in the world, I had already asked Lettie if they had another sister named Jo, and Lettie had informed me that, of course, they didn't. They had a brother named Joe.

"And then Beth talked me into coming," Lettie said. Lettie and Beth were sorority sisters.

"And then Lettie talked *me* into coming," I said.

"And Meg has also talked a few acquaintances into coming," Amy added.

"Just like old home week!"

"Oh, dear. Geoffrey and I are like interlopers." Victoria peered over her sunglasses with questioning eyes.

"Not at all. When we get to the hotel, you'll find we have people from all over." Tessa signaled for the check. "Speaking of that, I've run off copies about the folks in our group for each of you. Remind me when we get back to the car."

As we headed for Venice, Tessa drove, and the rest of us studied our copies of the list she had given us. It was arranged, she said, with roommates listed together. I read mine, mentally matching up spouses, siblings, friends and parents with children as well as I could:

Amy Bauer—Philadelphia, PA
Margaret Bauer—Baltimore, MD
Elizabeth Bauer Hines—Baltimore, MD
Richard Kramer—Silver Spring, MD
Michael Melon—Washington, DC
Letitia Osgood—Fredericksburg, VA
Dorothy Lamb—Staunton, VA
Shirley Hostetter—Philadelphia, PA
Crystal Hostetter—Philadelphia, PA
James Kelly—Newbury, Ontario
Wilma Kelly—Newbury, Ontario
Walter Everard—Washington, DC
Elaine King—Washington, DC

Geoffrey Reese-Burton—Woodstock, England, UK
Victoria Reese-Burton—Woodstock, England, UK
Paul Vogel—Arlington, VA
Lucille Vogel—Arlington, VA

I decided that Shirley and Crystal Hostetter were mother and daughter, rather than sisters, based purely on their first names. I knew a lot of Shirleys my own age, but hardly anyone over twenty-five named Crystal. I knew that the first three, the Bauer sisters, wanted to share a triple room so that meant that the next two, Richard Kramer and Michael Melon, were roommates. Friends? Gay? Don't know each other, but got put together because they were both single men? Singles who wanted to have their own rooms had to pay a single supplement. And what about Walter Everard and Elaine King? I asked Tessa about them.

"They're a couple. I suppose she just still uses her maiden name."

"That's done a lot these days," Lettie said.

"Not by me, I was glad to get rid of my maiden name," Victoria said.

"Why? What was it?"

"Crapper."

"I see what you mean."

I folded the list and tucked it in my purse, then scratched around for a bottle of aspirin for my stubborn headache. I guess it was the combination of thinking about my head and, at the same moment, seeing Amy slip her list into her own bag that made me remember the four words I had read on that little piece of paper before she snatched it away. It said "…crushed the baby's skull."

TWO

We had an hour to settle into our room before the pre-dinner welcome party. Beth Hines bounced in just as Lettie and I were making a momentous decision regarding who got which bed. Beth was a trim little elfin woman with dancing brown eyes. She and Lettie indulged in the requisite squeaks, squeals, and hand-holding, along with the usual, "Turn around; I want to see your hair!" I, myself, have never been able to do the squeak-squeal thing without feeling like an absolute fool, but it doesn't mean I'm not just as happy to see folks as anyone else is.

"Wait 'til you meet the group," said Beth, perching on the end of one bed. "A more…what's the word I want…eclectic? A weirder conglomeration of people you'll never meet."

"Weird, how?" I asked.

"Oh, I don't mean…well, it's just that you'd hardly think of such a…*diverse* bunch traveling together." Beth sounded like she was proud of herself for thinking of the diplomatic word "diverse."

Tessa had commandeered the Laguna Room, a small bar room near the hotel's restaurant, for a happy hour sponsored by our tour company. Before I could even get a drink, Beth introduced me to Meg. Never in my life have I taken such an instant dislike to anyone. A large, pinch-faced woman with a beaky nose and close-set eyes, she looked down her nose at me like an eagle watching a mouse. She offered me a limp hand, cold and wet from her gin-and-tonic, and muttered, "Dotsy Lamb? Oh, yes. You're the one whose h…"

She almost said it. She came within an inch of saying, "You're the one whose husband just left her for a younger woman." I got the distinct impression that it wasn't a slip of the tongue at all; that she meant to get right up to the word "husband" and then quickly change to the ridiculous, "...who's known Lettie since she was a child." I was not shocked that she knew about it. I assumed Lettie and Beth had discussed my troubles at length, and that Meg, who shared a house with Beth, would have heard about it. I certainly had bent poor Lettie's ear for untold hours over the past year. Dear thing, she never once picked up the phone and said, "You again?" although I'm sure she wanted to.

I snatched a glass of red wine from a waiter's tray with my shaking hands, oblivious of the peril it held for my white blouse. I leaned forward and sucked in enough wine to lower the level in the glass to a region of relative safety. Alone near the bar, a woman in a pristine white blouse sipped a white wine spritzer. She looked as though she could use some company, so I introduced myself, thus escaping further slashes from the talons of Meg Bauer. The spritzer woman turned out to be Shirley Hostetter, and the Crystal I had seen on the list was, as I had guessed, her daughter.

"Crystal is up in our room, brooding," she said. "She's fifteen, and since she's too young to drink, she didn't want to come down and 'hang around a bunch of old people,' as she put it." Shirley managed to dash out air quotes with her fingers while spilling not a single drop of her wine. I was impressed. "Crystal is going through a phase—you know what teens are like—do you have children?"

"Five," I said. I love that look I always get when I say that. "Four boys and one girl, but they're all grown now." People usually want my advice when they hear I've raised five kids. It seems to make me some kind of authority or something, but the fact is, teenagers confuse me as much as they do anyone else.

Over Shirley's shoulder, I noticed a man standing by the door with a professional-looking camera around his neck. *He's really playing the tourist role to the hilt,* I thought. A tall man with a coarse shock of salt-and-pepper hair pushed past him, head down, and out through a door into the hall. The man with the camera immediately jerked to attention and left by the same door. Somehow, I knew those two exits were not unrelated. There was something about the way the camera-toting man's face tightened. What was going on here?

"That was Paul Vogel," said Shirley. Apparently, she'd seen me watching him.

"Who was the other man who just left? The tall one with the hair?"

I almost said, "shaggy hair," but every time I say something like that, I get an answer like, "My fiancé."

Shirley looked around as if assessing who was absent. "Must have been Dick Kramer. He's head of some kind of company, and he's traveling with that rather handsome young man over by the window. His name is Michael."

So that, I deduced, must be Michael Melon, and "rather handsome" was an understatement.

"What sort of company?" I asked.

"Something to do with furniture, I think. Home décor—that sort of thing. I talked to him at breakfast this morning, and he was kind of vague, but I got the idea they import things and do renovations."

"Doesn't this seem like a strange way to go about importing things? I'd think they would just come over and visit manufacturers. Why waste time with a tour?"

"I don't know."

A little woman who looked like one of those Russian nesting dolls, but with bowl-cut black hair instead of a babushka, jostled Shirley aside and surged onto the bar. "Scotch and water," she ordered. "Easy on the water."

Shirley held her tongue until the woman had backed away with her fresh drink and then muttered, "Pellegrino Tours won't make any money on her; that's her fifth drink in…" She checked her watch. "In less than forty minutes."

"Who is she?"

"Lucille Vogel. She's a nightclub singer or something like that. Or used to be. I get the idea that her career is a thing of the past."

"Wife of Paul Vogel? The man with the camera?"

"Yes, or at least I assume they're husband and wife. But maybe not. Yesterday afternoon, shortly after most of us arrived, she was out in the hall yelling at Tessa because they had a room with a double bed, and she had specifically asked for twin beds."

"Yelling?"

"Oh, yes. Very unpleasant. I was embarrassed for her. Don't you just hate it when Americans go to another country and act like asses? It makes us all look bad."

"Do you travel a lot?"

"No, I didn't mean to give that impression at all. No. I had to save up for this trip. I ran into Meg Bauer—do you know her?" I nodded and Shirley went on. "I ran into Meg at her hospital in Baltimore this spring. I'm a nurse, too."

"Oh, Meg is a nurse?" I didn't recall Lettie ever telling me what Meg did. If she was a nurse, I'd like to nominate her for the Worst Bedside Manner award.

"Yes. Anyway, I'm head nurse in the neonatal unit of my hospital in Philadelphia, and we've just adopted a new scheduling system—new computer program to keep track of schedules—so I had to go to Baltimore for a few days because they were already using that program. I remembered Meg from when we had worked at the same hospital some, oh, I guess, fifteen years ago. Meg mentioned that she was going with her sisters to Italy in early summer, and I said to myself, 'That's just the thing for Crystal and me.'"

"Oh?" I slid my empty glass onto the bar and grabbed another red wine.

"Crystal is so hard for me to talk to now. It's like she's rebelling against everything that's important to me. The kids she hangs around with are just…" Shirley left that sentence unfinished. "Well, my husband was all for us taking this trip, although he couldn't take time off from work himself, so he couldn't come. But I thought it might be good for Crystal and me to have some time together, away from her friends."

"And you'll see new things together. New experiences." I glanced around the room. "Can you help me put any more names with faces? I just got here, you know, and so far I only know my friend Lettie, the three Bauer sisters, and the Reese-Burtons."

"You haven't met Tessa yet?"

"Oh, yes. She came to Milan and picked us up."

Shirley nodded toward a man standing at the window near the handsome Michael Melon. "That's Walter Everard. His wife, Elaine, is…well, she must have gone to the bathroom or something. She was here earlier."

"Our list said Elaine King."

"Right. See the couple over by the wall?" She nodded toward a sort of dull gray couple who sipped their drinks in solitary contemplation of their own napkins. They didn't appear to be mixing a lot. "They are the Kellys. Jim and…I forgot…oh, Wilma. They're from Canada. Somewhere near Toronto. Farmers."

"I see."

"And the man with his elbows on the bar is Achille—sounds like Achilles, the Greek hero, doesn't it?—our bus driver."

I tugged at Shirley's sleeve quickly to keep Lucille Vogel from flattening her. Lucille was back for another scotch-and-water-easy-on-the-water. The door to the hall swung open again, and a woman with tons of dark blonde hair pulled back in a scrunchy slipped in and quickly located Walter Everard with her eyes. "That would be Elaine?"

"Yes. And it looks like they're calling us in to dinner, now."

Behind the black-jacketed maître d' in the doorway, a halo of fluorescent pink radiated out from a clump of black leather. The magenta mass turned, and on the other side, a face burdened with several pounds of hardware poked painfully through holes in the brows, nose, lips, and ears, stared blankly at a display case full of Venetian glass. The eyes were heavily ringed with black pencil that exactly matched the lipstick and the nail polish. This was Crystal.

LETTIE WAVED ME INTO the dining room and to a table she had already selected. Meg, Beth and the Reese-Burtons were already there, and the table was set for six. I decided I was strong enough to have another go at making Meg's acquaintance, and the Reese-Burtons might help to soften the experience. I rather liked them. As I planted my purse beside Lettie's chair, Meg shouted across the table in a voice that could have been heard back in the kitchen, "We're having chicken tonight, Lettie. Careful you don't lose your teeth in it!" She followed this outrage with the sort of laugh I hadn't heard since I caught the neighborhood bully, Frankie Joe Norton, teasing my Brian about his stammer. I had taken care of Frankie Joe in a manner that I couldn't possibly use on Meg. I took a deep breath, edged shakily around to Meg's place, and bent over her shoulder.

"That was mean," I hissed through gritted teeth. "You need to apologize to Lettie, and I want to be there when you do it. Not now, though, there are too many people watching, no thanks to you. Don't even try to say you didn't mean to embarrass her, because you did! Before you go to bed tonight, I want to hear you apologize. You got that?" I don't think anyone heard what I said, but if they did, I didn't care. I reclaimed my seat with as much dignity as I could, as dozens of eyes cut sidelong glances toward our table.

Geoffrey Reese-Burton broke the awkward silence with, "Owd jufine yarum? Oll?"

"I'm sorry?"

"He said, 'How did you find your room? Is it all right?'" Victoria explained.

"Oh. Yes, it's just fine." I put my hand over my wine glass to keep the waiter from pouring any for me. "I've had two glasses already, and I'm diabetic, so I keep myself on a two drink limit."

I wondered how Meg would manage to throw that back in my face. There's nothing embarrassing about diabetes, but I felt certain Meg would find a way to use it.

Beth tossed out a question to the table in general: "What are you most looking forward to?"

I said I couldn't wait to see the museum of archaeology in Florence. Their collection of Etruscan artifacts is the best in the world. Of course, everyone but Lettie had to be told that I teach ancient and medieval history in a community college, so my interest in Etruscan civilization was not as strange as it might have seemed.

Geoffrey voiced a keen desire to see something that I didn't quite catch, and Beth said she couldn't wait to see Michelangelo's David. Victoria, shifting her cutlery to precisely align it with the edge of the table, chirped, "I plan to do a day trip to San Gimignano while we're in Florence. They have a medieval torture museum there, and medieval torture is sort of a hobby of mine."

Napkins rushed to mouths all around the table. I thought I must have heard her wrong, but if I had, apparently so had everyone else. Geoffrey spluttered, "Oh, nonono! Don't prack...read. Y'know." Or something like that.

Victoria smiled. "Oh, of course. I didn't mean I *practice* medieval torture. Oh dear, no. Poor Geoffrey! I'd never...no, what I mean is, I operate a book store at home, and I sort of specialize in medieval histories—early England, knights, Celtic stuff, Norman stuff, you know. I've always been fascinated by the horrid things they thought of to do to each other. Such short, painful lives they had."

Lettie cleared her throat rather self-consciously. "I'm looking forward to our gondola ride tomorrow night; something I've always wanted to do. So romantic! Too bad Ollie isn't here."

"Maybe you'll run into a sexy gondolier tomorrow," I said. "I won't tell Ollie." Everyone laughed—everyone except Meg. Meg just sniffed, pinching even further her already pinched-in nose. "Well I, for one, am going to register a complaint with Pellegrino Tours about this bait-and-switch job they've pulled. They're not going to get away with it."

"What do you mean, bait-and-switch?"

"I mean Venice. Is this Venice? The brochure promised two nights in Venice, and they've stuck us in this god-awful… whatever it's called. It's certainly not Venice. Do you see any gondolas? Canals? Where are the canals? Look out the window. Is that water or asphalt out there?"

"The brochure said our hotel would be in Mestre," Victoria said. "To get to Venice proper we have to take a boat. Tessa said we'd go over in the morning right after breakfast."

"She said hotels along the canals cost the earth. This is an economical alternative." Lettie dumped Parmesan onto her pasta.

"I wasn't aware we were taking a cut-rate tour," Meg sniffed. "For what we're paying, they should have put us on the Grand Canal."

THREE

"ALL GONDOLAS ARE black, and all gondoliers are men." Tessa, using a microphone at her little jump seat in the front of the bus, told us a little about the history of gondolas and the canals as Achille drove us down twilit streets to the dock where we would catch the vaporetto to St. Mark's Plaza and reassemble for our gondola ride. This would be our third vaporetto ride of the day. Our group had done a morning tour of St. Mark's Basilica and the Doge's Palace. The Byzantine domes and mosaics, reminiscent of old Constantinople, jammed in with Romanesque arches and Renaissance frescoes had overwhelmed me. I felt like I stood at the crossroads of civilization. Victoria Reese-Burton had to be dragged out of the dungeons and across the Bridge of Sighs, in the opposite direction from that forced upon the poor condemned prisoners who gave the bridge its name.

Lettie, Beth and I had shopped up and down the narrow alleys and passages all afternoon. I confess that I am not much of a shopper. Lettie and Beth seemed to have a lovely time examining hundreds of carnival masks and tons of glass. Whatever could you do with a carnival mask if you got one? I wondered. But I kept that thought to myself as Beth and Lettie were having so much fun. The glassware, in my opinion, came in two varieties: ugly and way too expensive. I bought a couple of paperweights for gifts and tagged along, soaking up the atmosphere of this unique, sinking city.

Tessa told us that the gondola business was strictly controlled as was the building of the boats themselves. They're built slightly asymmetrical so they will travel straight when steered from the right side only. "If you want to be a gondolier," she said, "you need to be the son of a gondolier. You can't just set up your own business."

She led us along the Grand Canal to the row of four gondolas we had hired. Meg, Beth, Amy, Lettie, and I climbed into the first one, which ended up being the last to leave the mooring. Amy stumbled toward a seat and fell across Meg in the process. Meg waved her hand as if fending off bad breath and muttered, "You're still hung over from last night. If you throw up, Amy, please do it over the side."

Amy tented her left hand over her right middle finger so only Lettie and I saw the gesture. Shifting several times to find a comfortable place to sit without unbalancing the boat, Amy called across to Tessa, "Can I go with you?" Tessa and our musicians, a singer and an accordionist (we had paid extra for them), had a gondola to themselves. Amy climbed out, giving our boat an unnecessarily vigorous push with her foot as she left.

The Vogels and the Hostetters had elected not to do the gondolas, but had ridden the vaporetto over with the rest of us. They left us and wandered off to "do their own thing." We pushed off the mooring to the strains of "Santa Lucia" and passed under the Bridge of Sighs to "Back to Sorrento." That song took me back to my childhood—to my grandmother's old Victrola and the 78-rpm record she had of that same song. I had sat on her living room floor and played it over and over. At seven, I had thought it the most romantic song in the world. It still was.

Oddly, many windows of regular homes were on eye level as our boat maneuvered through Venice's narrow passages. Windows and curtains, open to the night air, gave us an uncomfortably voyeuristic glimpse of their dinner hour. We glided past one window where a woman adjusted a table setting, and a man in a dinner jacket slipped up behind her and kissed her neck. The song at that moment was *The Godfather* theme, "Speak Softly, Love," or something like that. The pain of it hit me in the stomach as real as a fist. At that moment, I would have given anything for a kiss or just a snuggle from Chet. Damn him.

Down one dark passage, I heard a crash like a metal can falling over. Lettie and I both jumped. "Probably a rat in a trash can or something," I said. "I'll bet there are a lot of water rats and other…"

"If you don't mind, I prefer to believe it was a cat," Lettie said with finality. Subject closed.

Meg allowed as how it was probably Shirley Hostetter chasing Crystal through the alley, "And being her normal clumsy self. For a nurse, she's the most uncoordinated woman I ever met. It's a wonder she doesn't kill more patients than she does."

"Kill patients? You can't be serious!" Beth gulped.

"She generally manages to pump about a quart of air bubbles in 'em just changing an IV drip." That was not a specific accusation—it was more like a general bitchy comment, and we all ignored it.

As we rounded our last corner and swerved back into the Grand Canal, there was a flash and a scuffle from the sidewalk near Harry's Bar. Paparazzi? Why us?

Achille was waiting for us at the ramp to the vaporetto. I would have expected him to meet us at the bus on the other side, but I saw his face light up when he spotted Beth Hines. "Oh ho!" I nudged Lettie.

"Well, well," Lettie whispered. "A little summer romance might be just the thing." Lettie had talked to me at some length about poor Beth's marital nightmare. Harvey Hines had walked out on her a couple of years ago under circumstances not that different from my own recent ordeal—that is, out of the blue and because of another woman. But Harvey hadn't given any hint of trouble until he already had his things packed, the bank account cleaned out, and the woman waiting in the car. At least I had found out about Sweet Young Stephie in time to get a lawyer and a generous settlement. I glanced back in time to catch the glow on Beth's face. It looked to me like she was not surprised Achille was there.

"Does Achille speak English?" I asked Lettie.

"He has a thick accent, but his English is good."

Beth rushed up behind us, pushing me in the back. "I hope they have a restroom on this boat, I've been looking for one for two hours."

"What difference does it make if you find a bathroom or not? Isn't that what you wear a diaper for?" Meg's tone of voice was the same buzz-saw screech she had used on Lettie last night.

Achille turned away. Beth spun around and ran back down the ramp. Lettie ran after her. I started to follow, but then thought better of it. Lettie was the right one to offer the help Beth needed, and I'd have been in the way.

"I hate you, Meg. I really hate you!" Amy snapped as she raced past.

Meg sniffed and drew her sweater around her shoulders. "Incontinence is nothing to be ashamed of. I see it all the time. If you work in a hospital, you get used to it." She looked around as if for validation, but found only scowls.

As she plunged onto the deck, Amy grabbed my arm like she needed me to keep her from jumping Meg with fists and flying feet. "Let's find a seat as far away from her as possible," she pleaded. We grabbed a couple of vacant plastic chairs in the passenger cabin next to Tessa, who was thumbing through a *Bride* magazine. I noticed it was in English. "Talk to me," Amy said to Tessa. "Talk to me about your wedding and get my mind off that bitch."

EARLY THE NEXT MORNING we left Venice-Mestre and Achille drove us to Florence. The ride took us south through the beautiful regions of Emilia-Romana and Tuscany—past medieval walled towns with watchtowers on hilltops, broad fields of sunflowers and wheat, olive groves and tall feathery cypress trees. The warm sun flowed through the big window beside me, and I dozed off with my ear in the crack between the seats. The size of our group, happily, allowed us to sit either with someone or alone. There were plenty of extra seats. Behind me, Elaine and Walter chatted softly, and somehow, their words became a part of my dream. Like banners towed by advertising planes along the beach, I watched their words drift back and forth. Elaine's soft voice floated across from right to left, and Walter's mellow replies bounced back like a shuttlecock in a lazy game of badminton—in my half-dream I saw Elaine's words wave by, printed forward and Walter's return, printed backward. The motor hummed, and the tires whined.

"It was from Beth that I heard about this trip. She and her boss were talking about it when I was at their office for a meeting," Elaine said.

"What sort of business is it?" Walter's voice bounced back.

"He's an attorney. Beth is his secretary…girl Friday, sort of. I was there because of some litigation my office got mixed up in…a strip mall we wanted to demolish."

"Did you win?"

"It hasn't been completely settled yet. But anyway, Beth said Greg—that's the lawyer—had offered to pay for her to take this vacation."

"Nice boss. Do you suppose he's paying for Amy's and Meg's trips, too?" Walter asked.

"I doubt it. That would be a bit much, don't you think? Besides, Amy was the one who started the ball rolling when she ran into Tessa at some convention, so I imagine she just told Beth, and Beth probably mentioned it to her boss and…"

Walter raised his tone to a falsetto in a Beth imitation. "And I do so wish I could go to Italy with my sister, but I just can't afford…"

"Maybe something like that."

"I think there are several people in this group who'd be glad to send Meg home and give her a refund. Maybe we could take up a collection."

"What a piece of work she is."

The bus veered off the A1 motorway at the little Tuscan town of Scarperia. Tessa announced that we would have an hour and a half to "see the town, visit the fourteenth-century Vicar's

Palace, or shop. Scarperia has been known for its excellent knives since the fifteen hundreds, and it's been an important stopping place for travelers since Etruscan times."

My ears pricked up at the word "Etruscan," but I nearly missed it in the squeal of delight from Victoria following the word "knives." Lettie and Beth headed out toward a small row of shops, and I traipsed around to the Vicar's Palace. We reunited for a gelato break on a broad plaza near the Palace. Kicking off my shoes at a plaza-side table, I closed my eyes, tilted my face to the sun, and let the bright zippy gelato made with those huge lemons from the Amalfi coast trickle down my throat. "I'm having one of those moments, girls," I said. "Don't anybody say a word."

Beth decided to forego the gelato and head back to the bus. She left clutching a smallish bag, apparently a purchase, tightly to her chest.

"Did you enjoy having a seat to yourself this morning?" Lettie asked.

"Oh, yes. And I learned a few things, too."

"Like what?" Lettie used her tongue to trap a down-cone stream of melting gelato.

"Like Walter and Elaine aren't married."

"How did you discover that?"

"I heard them talking. They were saying things like, 'I first heard about this trip from Beth.' Now, if they were married, wouldn't they both already know how they heard about the trip? And Elaine said something about some legal problem—a lawsuit she was involved in at work—something a husband would already know about."

"Huh." Lettie snorted. "That sounds like they don't even know each other that well."

We all converged on the bus at the same time and jammed ourselves up at the door like kindergarteners in a bathroom line. Lettie accidentally swiped Meg's purse with her gelato cone while rummaging through her own purse. Since she already had a paper napkin in her other hand, Lettie tried to wipe her mistake off the purse strap, but Meg wasn't having it. She twisted abruptly, tearing the purse from Lettie's grip with a curt, "I'll clean it myself," then pushed me aside in her haste to board.

Beth's purchase kept us from leaving immediately. All of us, including Achille, had to admire and pass around the knife—the "Coltello d'Amore." It had a carbon steel blade about eight inches long that was engraved with hearts and scrolls. The polished black buffalo horn handle, with inlaid silver and ivory, curved gracefully to fit the hand. If a knife can ever be said to be beautiful, that one surely was. The workmanship was splendid.

"I hate to tell you how much I paid for this," Beth said in a tone that hinted she really wanted us to ask. "But I've been stressing for a month about what to get my boss and his fiancée for a wedding present. Talk about a guy who has everything. And she has everything, too."

"She paid five hundred Euros for it!" Lettie, subtle as always, broke the suspense.

"The knife of love is an old tradition." Beth patted her hair and wiggled primly in her seat as the knife made its rounds. "A man may give it to his bride to symbolize how he will always protect her," she informed us as she cast a wary eye on Victoria, who drew her thumb across the sharp edge of the blade and hefted it several times from one hand to the other. "And the woman gives one to her new husband, to symbolize…oh, I don't know…something or other. Sometimes they would put the two knives, crossed, over their bed."

"Don't get any ideas, Wilma. It's bad enough you leaving all those whips and chains behind our bed. Knives are out of the question." Jim Kelly got a laugh all around for that remark, and Wilma swatted him.

"How do you think you'll get that thing home? On the plane?" Paul Vogel asked.

"Don't put it in your carry-on," muttered Lettie. "Not unless you want to model your underwear for the whole Italian army."

"Huh?" Meg's ears perked up.

I scowled at Lettie lest she explain and give Meg more ammunition for her dignity-smashing artillery. I could just hear what Meg might do with the story of Lettie and the strip search.

"I'll have it shipped home when I get to Florence. I just took it with me today so I could show it off a bit first." Beth retrieved her knife and nestled it in its gift box.

As we shuffled back to our seats, Michael Melon whispered over my shoulder, "If I had to share a room with that harridan, Meg, I wouldn't trust myself with a knife."

THE NEXT MORNING, a Friday, dawned bright and hot in Florence. Fortunately, our hotel was air-conditioned and centrally located because I could already predict I'd want to nip back to our room periodically for breaks. Lettie, Beth and I started with a short trek to the Duomo, actually the Cathedral of Santa Maria del Fiore, topped by Brunelleschi's famous dome. When we rounded a corner and got our first sight of its glorious façade of pink, green and white marble, a gasp rose from all three of us.

"Unbelievable!"

"Oh, my God."

"Almost too much, isn't it?"

From there, we wandered down a side street called the Via della Studio and stopped at a Gypsy sidewalk vendor's display of paper Disney character puppets. Minnies and Mickies with string legs and weighted feet danced on a board, their string arms bouncing, powered by the vibrations from the Gypsy's boom box. Lettie had to have one, and Beth was mesmerized. I warned them that they'd probably never get a jiggle out of them once they got home, but they paid no attention to me.

We were back at the hotel before Beth discovered that her cash, a credit card and the card that opened the door to her room were no longer in her fanny pack. It wasn't too hard to figure out where they were, since she had last opened it to pay for a Minnie Mouse puppet. We dashed back to the Via della Studio, but the Gypsy had apparently folded up shop and gone out of business.

It's Friday the thirteenth, I thought. It was Friday, but I had lost track of what day of the month it was somewhere over the Atlantic Ocean. Then it popped into my head: *Bad things come in threes.*

FOUR

I KNEW IT WAS Lettie as soon as I swung through the big lobby door. Perched in a wing chair facing the elevator and with her back to me, her wispy red hair stuck out above the bargello upholstery like reeds in a needlepoint swamp. One foot dangled, not quite touching the floor, the other probably crossed over and swinging to the rhythm of whatever tune was making her fingers tap on the chair's arm.

"I'm doing elevator duty." Lettie turned and saw me at the same moment the elevator opened and Wilma Kelley popped out. Lettie caught her eye. "We're not leaving 'til six. Tessa told me to tell everybody."

"I know. I stopped by Beth and Meg's room. Meg told me." Wilma looked past me toward the lobby door. "Why the change?"

"She had some sort of emergency…had to run downtown for a few minutes, she said."

"I just came from the parking lot. Achille told me," I said. I had cut my time pretty close. After lunch, I had walked to the Museo Archeologico by myself and lost track of time. At five o'clock, Achille was supposed to drive us to the Piazzale Michelangelo, the hilltop that offers the view of Florence seen on thousands of postcards, and I had dashed straight to the hotel parking lot only to learn that we weren't leaving for another hour. Actually, I was glad for the chance to run back to my room for a new supply of Wet Ones. It was a hot afternoon, and I'd been using them like napkins at a toddler's birthday party.

Lettie had found a pleasant little nook across from the

elevator. It had two armchairs and a table with a house phone on it, centered on a pleasantly worn oriental-type carpet. I took the empty chair.

"Tessa asked me to wait here for a few minutes so I could tell whoever gets off the elevator that we're not leaving 'til six—save them a trip out to the parking lot." Lettie tapped her fingers lightly on the arm of her chair.

Now that I had settled down, I could hear "Funiculi, Funicula" wafting through from the restaurant behind us.

"It's fun to watch people get on and off the elevator," Lettie continued. "So colorful. It's almost like a parade."

"What do you mean, colorful?" I asked. As if to answer my question, the elevator doors opened, and two men in bright swirling dashikis got off. A family, all wearing green Tyrolean hats, got on. "I see. How did Wilma know already about the change in time?"

"Didn't she say she'd just dropped by Beth and Meg's room? I talked to Meg on the house phone a few minutes ago. Tessa asked me to call them as she was running out…said she wanted them to bring her sunglasses when they came down later. She left her glasses in their room last night."

The elevator opened again, and a tear-stained Crystal Hostetter raced out. Her black eye liner ran down from the inner corners of both eyes; she resembled an ocelot. She stumbled out the lobby door, colliding blindly with the Reese-Burtons who were coming in. I popped up and held the elevator door open for them. Geoffrey mopped his brow and muttered, "Muddoes in glitchmun." Victoria smiled and thanked me as the door closed on them.

"'Mad dogs and Englishmen,' maybe?" I guessed. "Good Lord, I think I'm starting to understand him."

The next opening of the doors revealed a harried-looking Shirley Hostetter. "Have you seen my daughter?" she asked.

"She went that-a-way," Lettie said, jerking her thumb toward the lobby door. "Did you know we're not leaving until six?"

"I'll be with you if I can. That is, if I can find Crystal before then." Shirley dashed out in hot pursuit of her daughter.

I was so glad of the nice cool spot Lettie had found, I was reluctant to leave. Lettie was right. It was fun to just sit here and watch the human parade. A couple in matching plaid shorts and clashing T-shirts breezed by in a swirl of English Lavender.

"Americans," I said. "What did Meg say about Beth getting her money stolen?"

Lettie threw up both hands. "It was not a pretty sight. Let's see…Beth is worse than a six-year-old…she deserves to go for the rest of the trip with no money…only a fool would put her money in a fanny pack…" She ticked these items off on her fingers. "I don't know how she stands it. Meg treats her like a kid."

"And they live together?"

"I told her the other night. I said, 'Beth, honey, you need to get out of Meg's house.' I know it's been hard on her, though, with Harvey leaving her with nothing but an empty back account. It's taken her all this time to get her finances in order…but you asked about the theft. She's already called the credit card people and the traveler's check people…"

I stopped her with a touch on the arm as the subject of our conversation tramped up behind us. Beth's face, red and set in a tight-lipped scowl, was wet with sweat, her hairline dripping. She swung a pot of paper-white narcissus recklessly, holding it by the rim with one hand; the entire contents threatened to plop out on the floor. "I don't want to talk about it!" she growled over her shoulder to us, as she headed for the elevator.

Lettie and I had enough sense to stay quiet. We watched the door close and the red lights blink in succession until it paused on the third floor.

"What was that about?" Lettie asked.

"Apparently somebody 'said it with flowers,' and Beth doesn't like what they said."

"Who would send her flowers here?" Lettie turned to me, eyebrows lowered.

"Achille? But why would that make her mad?"

An eruption of shuffling and confusion from the general area of the reception desk made Lettie jump. I hopped out of my chair to peek around the corner. A manager in a black tie dashed through the half-door beside the desk, a walkie-talkie against his mouth, and the man I had seen asleep near the front door a few minutes ago blossomed instantly into a security guard and ran to the elevator door. By the time the elevator reached the ground floor, four employees, including the woman from the concierge desk, had gathered to scowl at the row of red lights, as if scowling would speed it up. They hissed softly at each other in Italian.

When the wall had gobbled them up, Lettie and I stared at each other and then at the row of red lights. The elevator inched up to the third floor and stopped.

Lucille Vogel came out of nowhere, smiled serenely, and punched the up button. "Hi, ladies. I guess you're not going on the bus trip either."

Strange. Not only did the comment seem inappropriately casual—we knew something was dreadfully wrong, although there was no reason Lucille should have known it—but it was the first time I had seen Lucille smile. Or say anything remotely pleasant. She had, up to that point, been a little black cloud over our group, but now she seemed, well, sweet.

I found my voice before Lettie did. "We're not leaving until six. Tessa had something come up."

"It's almost six, now," Lucille said.

I checked my watch. It was a quarter to six. Lucille pushed the up button again and waited. The elevator light didn't budge.

"It's stuck," Lettie said, after a suitable length of time. "Let's take the stairs. Are you ready to go up, Dotsy?"

I was ready to find out what was going on, but I didn't want to do it with Lucille Vogel. Our room was on the first floor, which in Europe is the one above the ground floor, so Lettie and I slipped through the first set of swinging doors off the stairwell, leaving Lucille to climb another flight by herself. I nipped into a cubbyhole out of the line of sight from the small windows in the stairwell doors and waved Lettie over. "Let's wait until she's out of the stairwell and go on up to the third floor. I want to find out what's up."

"Is your antenna beeping?" Lettie has the nicest ways of calling me a snoop.

"My antenna is about to short out."

The stairwell doors on the third floor landing were locked. I peeked through the little window on the right hand door, while Lettie took the one on the left. I'm sure that, from the other side, we looked like a pair of those big-nosed "Kilroy was here" cartoons. The fifth door down on the left was open, and the hallway was empty except for the man with the walkie-talkie and the black tie. He stood at the open door, gulping air. He stumbled as if he was about to pass out. The woman from the concierge desk, a brisk, efficient-looking woman, crossed the threshold, pushed the man aside, and vomited against the right-hand wall.

"Ooohh!" was all Lettie could say.

"Who's in the fifth room down, I wonder? Someone's been killed in that room, I just know it."

"Don't say that, Dotsy. You don't know anything of the kind."

"You're right. I don't. But something terrible has happened."

"That's Beth and Meg's room," Lettie whispered. She choked a little on her words.

I turned to her; she was almost green. "How do you know?"

"I was in their room last night. They sent me out for a Coke, and I got it from this machine right here." Lettie pointed left, her finger against the window. From my window, I could just see the glow of the cold drink machine. "I counted as I went down the hall; there were five doors from their room to the machine—including their door."

"You counted?" From anybody but Lettie, that might have been a sign of incipient senility, but from Lettie, it was normal. She'd always been like that. Sometimes she misses the whole forest, but she counts the trees. I counted again to make sure. The open door was, indeed, the fifth one down.

The security guard emerged and jerked his head to the right. He saw us. Tromping heavily the length of the passage, he pulled a big ring of keys from his belt and opened our doors. He shooed us with the back of his hand, and blustered, *"Mi scusi! Per favore, no, no, va via, grazie…"* in a flood of Italian that obviously meant, "Go away."

"Back to our room?" Lettie asked when he had relocked the doors.

I didn't want to do that, because we'd just sit there and stare at each other. "We're supposed to be at the bus. Let's go through the lobby."

We could have gone straight out the side door from the stairwell to the parking lot, but I wanted to go to the lobby. Something might be happening there.

Something was. Two uniformed officers flanked the man who was obviously in charge. His gaze swept the lobby as he conferred with a young woman wearing a hotel badge. There are a few people who radiate power, I've noticed. I don't know what it is, but they seem to fill the space around them, and simply allow others to move about within their sphere. This was one of those people. He had a short, neatly trimmed beard and warm brown eyes. His gaze darted left and right. I guessed his age at about fifty-something; his hair and beard were about an equal mixture of black and white. I wondered if he was older or younger than I. The years pass so quickly now that I can't keep my mental image of myself up to date.

Lettie charged toward the center of the lobby, but I caught her arm. I didn't want to intrude on the conference. Tessa and Amy burst through the lobby doors just then, laughing. Amy waved her arms in front of her, to augment some story that tickled Tessa. Their faces sobered quickly when the grim-faced woman with the badge motioned Tessa over.

"Come on, Lettie. Let's go out the side door."

We turned on our heels and retraced our steps. The side door was locked; a crudely printed sign with an arrow pointing toward the lobby was taped at eye level, and a uniformed sentry stood just outside so we had to walk through the lobby after all. The detective—I assumed he was a detective; plain-clothes policeman at least—had his back to us as we passed. I caught the looks on Tessa and Amy's faces as I passed. Shock. They both appeared to have been drained of all blood. The detective spoke in a soft, measured tone to Tessa, who nodded ever so slightly in response.

A doorman stopped us. He said, *"Inglese?"*

"Yes."

"Are you with a group?"

"Yes, we're with the Pellegrino Tour group," I said.

The doorman flushed brightly around the neck, but his tone of voice didn't waver. "I need to write down your names and ask you not to leave the area for a little while."

Lettie and I spelled our names slowly for him. I saw him glance once or twice toward the summit conference in the center of the lobby as he wrote.

"We were just going out to the parking lot," I said. "Our bus is supposed to be out there."

"Yes, yes. That is fine. Your bus driver should be out there. He will explain to you."

But Achille wasn't there. When we reached the bus, we found the Reese-Burtons, Lucille Vogel, and the Kellys standing beside it. On the far side of the parking lot, Crystal and Shirley Hostetter approached, looking grim.

"Wullapar…" Geoffrey began.

"I'll tell them." Victoria took over. "We got here just as Achille was dashing off in a dreadful rush over in that direction." She pointed toward a street that ran eastward away from our hotel. "All he said was, 'Miss Meg Bauer is dead. She's been killed. You must stay here.' And then he ran off."

"Onotelprop," Geoffrey said.

"That's right. He said, 'On hotel property.' He didn't mean we have to stay right here in this spot."

"Dead?" Lettie's face screwed up like a punctured balloon.

"Killed?" Shirley had arrived in time to hear Victoria's announcement.

Lettie sank onto the steps inside the open bus door. "Meg! I can't believe it." She lowered her head to her knees.

I knelt down to see if she looked like she was about to faint. To avoid staying bent like that any longer than necessary, I nudged her over and sat beside her. Meg, of all people. I wondered if we were going to indulge in a phony charade now. I was afraid we'd all feel obliged to pretend that we adored her, admired her, missed her. What would I say when I had to come up with something nice to say about her? She had good posture; that was about it. The worst of all possible scenarios, I thought, would be if we all found ourselves indulging in such disingenuousness to avoid being seen as a suspect.

Lettie raised her head. "That must mean it was Beth who found…who found her. It must have been Beth who called the front desk. Oh, poor Beth!"

Through the heat waves dancing across the asphalt parking lot, I saw Tessa coming toward us. At the same time, Michael, Dick, Walter and Elaine appeared, having come apparently from the downtown area to the south. I was beginning to think of them as the "curious quartet" since they seemed to always be together, but somehow not to know each other very well.

Tessa waited until we were all gathered. "Have you heard? Meg is dead." She glanced around quickly, stopping at Lettie's face. "The police have their hands full right now, but they'll have to talk to each one of you individually. This was not an accident. It was murder."

The word sounded so cold coming from Tessa's sweet young face. From where I stood, I only caught the immediate reactions of Crystal and Shirley. Crystal's mouth quivered in what looked like a barely suppressed smile. Shirley caught her breath and glanced toward her daughter as if she would have preferred the child not hear the dreadful word, "murder."

"How?" Shirley swallowed. "How was she...?"

"I think I'd better let the police tell you. And, oh yes. It's not the police handling this. It's the carabinieri. In Italy, as you may already know, there is a police force, and there's the carabinieri—kind of like military police, but not really—it's hard to explain. Their duties overlap a lot. Anyway, it was the carabinieri that were called, so they're the ones handling it. They've asked me to act as interpreter although Captain Quattrocchi, he's the one in charge at least for right now, speaks English... somewhat."

"When do they want to talk to us?" Lucille asked.

"Well, that's what I have to explain. It'll take some time. They're setting up an interview place now. They prefer to get information straight from each one of you individually. That is, to find out what each of you can remember personally, not what someone else told you. In court they call that hearsay, don't they? Anyway, Captain Quattrocchi says he'll get better information if you don't influence each other with, you know, he said/she said stuff.

"So, here's the deal. He wants everybody to go to their rooms for now and wait to be called downstairs to talk to him. It'll be dinnertime soon, so the kitchen will deliver your meals. Hey, free room service. Don't knock it. So when you get to your rooms, you can call room service and make your dinner selections. They'll tell you what your choices are."

"Can I still get my vegetarian menu?" Wilma asked.

"Sure."

We all trudged back to the front entrance as a group. As Michael held the door open for everyone, Shirley glanced over her shoulder. "She's gone again! Sorry, Tessa, I promise I'll come back, but I have to find my child first."

FIVE

OUR ROOM IN THE Hotel Fontana had a tiny balcony with French doors that overlooked the heart of Florence. We could see the top of the Duomo behind the rooftops to the south and beyond that was the River Arno. If I looked straight down from our balcony rail, I could see the street in front of our hotel. I could watch people as they approached the main entrance. The hotel and its parking lot occupied the entire block. Ideally located between the railway station and the Piazza del Duomo, it was almost fully booked now, late June, as the tourist season got into high gear.

We were, for the moment, its prisoners. I checked my blood sugar, and it was quite low. "Let's order now, Lettie. I've just burned up my last biscuit." That's a phrase I've used ever since my son, Scott, said it when he was about six. One day he sprawled out on the lawn, unable to run another step, and groaned pathetically until I rushed out with a cookie to refuel his little engine. He looked up at me and said, "Thanks, Mom, I just burned up my last biscuit." He was so cute.

I called room service, relaying the choices to Lettie and getting her the detailed description she required of just what *fagiolini alla Fiorentina* was. They assured us it was green beans in olive oil, not Great Northerns, if they even have such a bean in Italy.

"Before we forget, Lettie, let's make a list of everybody and where they were when…when we were sitting by the elevator."

"Why?" Lettie kicked off her shoes and curled up on her bed in a semi-fetal position. She stared blankly at the wall.

"Because we'll forget if we don't do it now."

"Why do we need to do it at all?"

"Because I have a feeling we'll be glad we did." That was no reason at all, but it was good enough to satisfy Lettie. She clasped her hands between her knees and sighed.

"I feel worse about this for Beth than I do for Meg," she said. "I guess that sounds awful, but…"

"Not at all. It's Beth that you're close to."

"And she's had so much trouble the last few years."

"Someone in our group did it."

"What? Oh no, Dotsy, how can you even think that?"

"Have you ever heard of a tourist being murdered by a stranger in his or her hotel room?"

"It could be a case of mistaken identity." Lettie sat up. "Maybe a robber who thought the room was empty, and then Meg surprised him."

"Of course, that's possible. It could have been a thief… startled…panicked." It seemed as if that might actually be the most likely scenario, now that Lettie mentioned it, but I still wanted to make my list.

I wrote the names on a sheet of hotel stationery and filled in the whereabouts as we rehashed the last couple of hours:

Meg—in her room, as far as we know. (At least she was there when Lettie called, at about 4:45 p.m.)

Beth—out, picking up potted plant, returned to hotel.

Amy—out somewhere, came in with Tessa.

Tessa—out somewhere, came in with Amy.

Victoria and Geoffrey Reese-Burton—out somewhere, came in as Crystal was leaving.

Crystal—in her room (or at least in the hotel) until shortly after 5:00 p.m., when she got off the elevator and left.

Shirley—ditto, but left a few minutes after Crystal. Both she and Crystal came to parking lot at about 6:00 p.m.

Dick, Michael, Walter, and Elaine (the curious quartet)—

out somewhere together until they came to the parking
lot a little after 6:00 p.m.

Paul Vogel—?

Lucille Vogel—out somewhere, returned late and walked
upstairs with us.

Wilma Kelly—went to the Bauer's room and talked to
Meg sometime after Lettie talked to Meg on the phone,
then left the building.

Jim Kelly—? Whereabouts unknown, until we all met in
the parking lot.

Achille—in the parking lot by the bus (at least he was there
when I stopped by, around 5:00 p.m.)

"So we can't account for two people at all," I said. "Jim Kelly
and Paul Vogel."

Lettie folded her hands across her breast and stared at the
ceiling. "Paul never did show up, did he? Even when we were
all in the parking lot."

The phone rang and a voice said, "Mrs. Lamb, would you
please come to the front desk?"

I told Lettie to go ahead and eat when the food arrived and
jabbed a straw into a little carton of orange juice on my way out.
I kept a six-pack of individual cartons for just such times as this.
The orange juice sent a marvelous burst of energy to my whole
body as I punched the elevator down button.

Captain Quattrocchi touched my elbow as he seated me in the
little room that was obviously a manager's office in normal
times. Tessa sat beside the desk, and Quattrocchi rolled out the
chair behind it for himself. "Mrs. Dorothy Lamb?"

I nodded. He had a printout, presumably of our tour group
members, and a yellow legal pad on the desk in front of him.
"You know Miss D'Angelo, of course," he said in a thickly
accented voice. I nodded again. Captain Quattrocchi nodded to
Tessa and gestured to her with his hand in a you-take-it-from-
here sort of way.

"As you can tell," Tessa began, "Captain Quattrocchi speaks some English, but it's important for us to communicate clearly. So he'll ask you questions in Italian and I'll translate to you. I'll also translate your answers to him, so try to pause every so often. I can't remember all that much. We are also recording this, but don't let that make you nervous. It's for clarity."

Quattrocchi began. *"Dove lei era tra i quattro-trenta e...?"*

Tessa translated, "Where were you between four-thirty and six o'clock today?"

I told him about my solo trip to the Museo Archeologico and that I had returned to the hotel and spoken to Achille in the parking lot a little before five—five or six minutes to five, trying to be as precise as I could. Quattrocchi's warm brown eyes made it hard to concentrate. I was glad Tessa could repeat my responses to him in a firmer voice than I was able to squeeze out at the moment, but I imagine he caught the quiver anyway. He glanced at my left hand—at my naked ring finger, I thought. My stomach did a little jump. Both his hands were devoid of jewelry.

"...di venti cinque dopo sei." Tessa relayed my words and waited for his next question.

"Did you actually see Mrs. Wilma Kelly get off the elevator, Mrs. Lamb?"

"Yes. She said she already knew we weren't leaving until later, because Meg had told her."

"Sì, ha detto che..."

We soon settled into a rhythm of question-translate-answer-translate. Quattrocchi paused now and again to jot notes on his yellow pad. He had large, strong-looking hands. I wondered if he wore contacts, so I shifted in my chair far enough to see his eyes from an oblique angle. He glanced up just then and grinned. Could he possibly have known what I was doing? The yellow jumper I wore had a slit up both sides that went a little too high. It didn't bother me walking or sitting at a table with my knees under a tablecloth, but in this chair, my left thigh was exposed about halfway up unless I kept my left hand over it. I shifted again, moving enough yellow denim across my knees to tuck some under my leg.

Tessa showed me out and asked the desk clerk to call Lettie. My interview had only taken about ten minutes, so I decided to browse the glass-fronted gift shop until Quattrocchi and Tessa finished with Lettie. From that vantage point across the lobby, I could watch the office door. After twenty minutes, it occurred to me that they'd probably take a lot longer with Lettie, since she had been in a critical spot throughout the whole relevant time period. From the time when Meg was certifiably alive—both Lettie and Wilma had talked to her—until she was certifiably dead, Lettie had sat just outside the elevator, where she observed the comings and goings. In all the world, there was no better person than Lettie to have been sitting there. My little round friend sometimes missed nuances and deeper meanings, in fact she often did, but when it came to the minutiae of life, Lettie's brain functioned like a thousand-gigabyte data bank.

I found some lovely stationery in a swirly Florentine pattern and was in the process of paying for it when I heard scuffling noises and Crystal Hostetter's irritated voice, "Stop! You're gonna make me drop it!"

I poked my head out the gift shop door. Shirley had Crystal by the elbow. Crystal held a clear plastic bag, similar to the ones we use in the states for newspaper sleeves, in front of her like a hand grenade missing a pin. In the bag was a knife—unquestionably the "Coltello d'Amore." How many buffalo horn-handle knives, engraved and inlaid with silver and ivory, does one see lying around in the street? I wasn't close enough to tell if it was real silver, ivory, or buffalo horn, but I had no doubt it was the same knife Beth bought in Scarperia. I had never seen another even remotely similar to it.

Shirley and Crystal both babbled, interrupting each other, until the desk clerk picked up the phone. "He'll be right out," the clerk said. Quattrocchi strode out and strode straight to the desk. He motioned to a uniformed officer who, until that moment, had been part of the wallpaper. The four of them hurried into the interview room, and a few seconds later, Lettie popped out.

"Well, something more important than me came up. Did you see that knife?" Lettie glanced back over her shoulder, but the door had already closed behind her. "You should have seen Tessa's face when they came in! That's the knife Beth bought yesterday, Dotsy."

"I know. Did you hear Crystal or Shirley say anything?" We stood at the elevator, apparently on our way up to our room without having consciously decided to go there, and I remembered the stationery I hadn't finished purchasing. I had left the gift shop attendant with both the stationery and ten Euros. It only cost five something.

"Crystal said she found it in a fountain. That's all I heard." Lettie walked with me back to the shop. The clerk had my purchase and my change in a bag behind her counter.

Seconds later, another commotion. Two officers barreled in, past the sentry at the side door, with a scruffy man between them. Each had one of the scruffy man's arms by the biceps, just under his armpits, so he was propelled along with his feet barely touching the polished marble floor. Close behind them was Achille, our bus driver. His face fairly glowed with what looked like self-satisfaction or maybe even pride. They turned the corner, headed for the reception desk, and spun off a breeze thick with the odor of unwashed hair and perspiration as they passed. The former aroma obviously came from the captive man in the middle, whose hair didn't look like it had ever been washed, but the sweat could have come from all four of them.

The scruffy man wore a dark red shirt with sleeves rolled up, an embroidered vest, and black pants that probably had been chinos at one time. Around his left wrist, a tattooed serpent—green with blood-red eyes, coiled, its fangs in strike position over his pulse. He stumbled along in his dilapidated cross-trainers, saying nothing as the policemen—or more accurately, the carabinieri—growled and hissed at him in bursts of Italian.

"Dotsy! That's the same man who sold us the little Disney puppets this morning." Lettie threw both hands over her mouth.

"It sure is." I would have known that even if my friend with the photographic memory hadn't pointed it out. I had noticed that snake around his wrist when he was making change for Beth. I wondered if the snake wasn't a deliberate distraction. While his left wrist flashed around in front of a customer, his right hand could be exploring a purse, pocket or fanny pack. That's how pickpockets worked, I had heard. Like a magician, they divert your attention away from the real action. "And I'd say he's almost certainly the one who took Beth's money and cards."

"Oh. You might be right."

"Of course I'm right." I hadn't meant for that to come out sounding quite so arrogant, but I didn't think it was worth amending.

The desk clerk picked up a phone and, within a few seconds, Captain Quattrocchi strode across the lobby. He glanced all around, as if searching for another door to stuff these new guys behind. Achille saw us and sent us a little wave with the fingers of one hand.

The elevator door opened and closed, but Lettie and I stayed where we were. I couldn't leave right now. Quattrocchi dashed back to the interview room, leaving the four men at the desk. The scruffy man—the Gypsy/puppet vendor—stood stiffly, eyes darting from left to right as if he was looking for a chance to make a run for it. Then Crystal and Shirley emerged, minus the plastic bag, and Quattrocchi waved the four men in.

I called the elevator back and held the door open for Crystal and Shirley.

Crystal looked uncertainly at her mother. "Do you think it's okay for us to go to our room? He said he needed to talk to us some more."

Her words were polite enough, but her tone held that contemptuous insolence only a teenage girl could convey. She might as well have said, "Only an idiot would make me go to my room."

"Crystal found the knife in a fountain in front of that church by the train station when she…when she left a little while ago." I imagined that Shirley had started to say "ran away" and changed it to "left." The church she referred to had to be Santa Maria Novella, which I knew was close to the northwest corner of our hotel. "She said it was just lying there…"

"It was just there! All shiny, and like, you couldn't miss it. Like, I knew immediately it was the knife we had on the bus yesterday, and I thought to myself, 'I guess I should just leave it there and call the police.' But then I thought, 'what are the chances it'll still be here when I come back with the police?' Zero, right?" Crystal nodded and looked around as if for confirmation that the knife would have been taken if she had left it there. She had a good point.

"So I found this plastic bag, and I had to step in the fountain with one foot to reach the knife." She kicked up one wet boot that looked as if it was made of some material that wouldn't be affected by battery acid, let alone water. Above the boot was a soggy black-and-white striped stocking that sagged below her knee. "You shoulda seen that man, the Captain, when I walked in carrying that knife! His eyes 'bout popped outta his head!"

"Crystal, fortunately, has learned to speak quite good Italian. We had an exchange student…"

The elevator stopped at our floor. Crystal and Shirley had one more floor to go, so we said goodbye and left them.

As the door closed again, I heard Crystal whine, "Mom…" She dragged it out to three syllables that sounded like the first three notes of "Over There."

SIX

OUR DINNER WAS COLD. As twilight crept over the city, lights came on and the huge Duomo, to the east of the Hotel Fontana, lit up. We could see the top of it beyond the rooftops from our French doors. I opened them up to the evening air.

"So they must think that Gypsy did it," Lettie said, stacking the stainless steel plate covers on the desk.

"It would appear so."

"Do you think he did?"

"Now, Lettie, how should I know? I don't know any more about it than you do." I dragged a chair to the table and seated myself in front of the chicken cacciatore. Lettie had arranged everything nicely. "But it is odd, you know. I hate to sound like I'm stereotyping, but this guy is a Gypsy, and they're infamous thieves." I paused, not really sure what I did think, quite yet. "If you are a thief, you get used to breaking and entering, taking stuff, getting away without getting caught...don't you?"

"Right."

"So if you break into someone's hotel room, you'd have a standard little song and dance you go through if that room turns out to be inhabited, wouldn't you?"

"I guess so."

"You know what? He could have used Beth's own room card to get in! Didn't he take her room card along with her money?"

"Yes, but how would he have known what room or what hotel it was for?"

I grabbed my bag off the floor and scrambled through it for my room card. "It's just a blank card. It doesn't have the room number on it. But it does say 'Hotel Fontana.' Wait. They gave us the cards yesterday in a little paper sleeve that did have the room number on it, didn't they?"

"Yes, my card is still in the paper sleeve."

"You really should toss that, or leave it here in the room, Lettie. They do it that way so in case it gets taken, the thief won't have your room number."

"But if Beth left hers in the sleeve…"

"Which is possible, after all, you did."

"I'll take it out right now." Lettie retrieved her bag from the dresser, slipped her card out of its paper sleeve, and put the sleeve in the top dresser drawer. "There."

"So it's likely he did go to Meg and Beth's room, or at least came here with the intention of doing so, and then what? See, that's the part that makes no sense."

"I don't see."

"Say he goes into their room using Beth's card and finds Meg there. He what, kills her? Just happens to find a lovely collector's item knife—extra-sharp—lying there, so he grabs it and kills the woman?"

"We don't yet know if she was killed with the knife."

"Pretty good odds, wouldn't you say? The knife sure didn't belong in that fountain. But whatever she was killed with, it's the same problem: a career thief, a pickpocket, an artful dodger has ways of getting out of embarrassing situations like that. He's been through it before."

"Well, I don't know…" Lettie wiped a wine spill off the table with her napkin.

"If murder was how he dealt with getting caught, there'd be a trail of dead bodies, wouldn't there?"

"Maybe he's not in the habit of breaking into hotel rooms. This was a fluke, you know. It wouldn't be every day he'd get a free pass into a tourist's hotel room."

I put the tray of dirty dishes outside our door and suggested we take in the night air on the hotel roof. I had heard it had a lovely view, and I had already noticed the elevator had a button for *tetto,* which I figured, must mean roof.

Just before we closed the door, the phone rang, and Lettie ran back to get it. "They want me back downstairs. I guess I'll have to take a rain check on that trip to the roof."

"If I'm not here when you get back, that's where I'll be." I didn't feel like staying in the room by myself. I'd already checked out the TV; game shows in a language you don't know are the ultimate bore.

"Lettie, oh good, you are here." Beth stood in the doorway. She looked so tiny; as if her sister's death had diminished her. She still wore the same flowered blouse and navy slacks I had last seen her in when she had stood at the elevator, sweating, muttering and swinging that pot of flowers by its rim. Lettie held out her arms and Beth moved into them, letting the tears fall on Lettie's shoulder. I considered leaving the room because Beth, after all, was just a new acquaintance of mine, and I felt like an intruder on a private moment. But to announce that I was leaving would be an interruption, and to walk out without saying anything would be rude. So I stepped out onto the balcony. From the street below, lights were popping on in all shades, from the amber glow of the sidewalk lamps to the blue-white beam of a Vespa's halogen headlight. But no neon. I wondered if they had a local ordinance that forbade neon lights, and my common sense said, "Of course they do." In fact, it probably would be so unthinkable in this city that survives on its medieval heritage that they don't even have to make it a law. Instant death for possession of a neon device.

"I'm so sorry I have to rush off, but they called me down to the lobby right when you walked in," I heard Lettie say. "Can we talk when they finish with me? I don't think it'll take too long." She dashed out, leaving Beth standing there.

I said, "I'm going up to the roof, Beth. Would you like to go with me? A little night air…"

"Oh. Oh, yes, I'd like that. I didn't know we had a roof that you could go out on."

Beth followed me onto the elevator, and I pushed the top button. I had decisions to make and make quickly. Should I mention Crystal finding the knife, and should I mention seeing our Gypsy friend in the lobby? In an official investigation of this sort, I knew it was crucial that witnesses not taint each other's recollections. Things can get hopelessly bogged down if people start "recollecting" what somebody else tells them. That was obviously why they'd insisted on us all going to our own rooms earlier. But it was Beth's knife, after all, and it had been found. Did Beth even know her knife was missing? And the man who almost certainly swiped her money and her cards—the man we had tried unsuccessfully to hunt down earlier—was downstairs, or at least had been downstairs a little while ago. Wouldn't I be remiss if I *didn't* tell her? I decided to err on the side of caution and not mention it. The knife and Beth's other belongings would certainly be returned to her, anyway.

The elevator opened onto a wonderful little patio, but I barely noticed it. For the moment, my breath had been taken away. The Duomo, floodlit from all sides, glowed like a huge Fabergé egg nestled in the carnelian tile rooftops of the city. Rooftops that by day were orange-red had deepened to a rich, dark wine. It was a sight I'll never forget.

Beth gasped. "Oh my."

We ventured over to the iron rail at the edge of the roof. Its bars slanted inward at about waist level, so it would be hard to fall off accidentally, and I imagined it was sufficient to thwart the gymnastic efforts of toddlers. At the back of the patio, near the elevator door, was a wet bar, closed down and padlocked. Several metal tables and chairs were scattered around; tables that had a hole in the center for the insertion of an umbrella. The umbrellas, apparently, were stashed away.

"I'm still in shock," Beth said. She curled her fingers around the protecting bars.

"I'm sure you are. It was you who found her, wasn't it?"

She paused a moment before she answered. "Yes. It was awful. I just can't describe…"

I stayed quiet.

"She was lying there, blood all over the wall, all over the floor…everywhere. Her throat was cut. It looked as if someone had tried to take her head off."

I shuddered and glanced toward Beth. Her eyes glistened in the reflected light of the Duomo. She quickly turned her head, and still I said nothing; I wanted her to go on without any interference from me.

"She was at the entrance to the bathroom." Beth sucked a deep breath and went on. "Across the threshold. Her legs were on the tiles, and her…the upper part of her was on the carpet. She wasn't wearing anything but her bra and panties…and socks…black socks. Like she had been in the bathroom, and… Well, Meg usually puts on her makeup at the bathroom sink before she gets all the way dressed. So it looked to me like someone had surprised her, like she heard something and came out of the bathroom to see, and…"

"I'm so sorry," I said. "So sorry it happened, and so sorry it had to be you who found her."

"I haven't got my head around it yet." She stood silent for another long minute, staring out toward the Duomo as if its womb-like bulk might offer her safe harbor. "Meg was my sister, but she was a hard woman to like."

"I gathered as much, but Lettie told me you and Meg have shared a house for some time. You must have found a way to coexist peacefully."

"Oh, well. I didn't have much choice, did I? My husband—ex-husband—Harvey left me quite suddenly and unexpectedly two years ago. Same old story, another woman."

"Did Lettie tell you my husband left me last year?" I asked. "Left me for another woman, so I know how you felt."

Beth nodded and glanced toward me. "I knew absolutely nothing until one day he came home, walked in the house, dropped a note on the hall table, and walked out. I ran to the window in time to see his car pull out, loaded to the gills with all his stuff, and a woman in the passenger seat."

Hugging herself as if a cold wind had swirled out of her past, she went on. "He had cleaned out our bank account, our 401k and our savings account. He had cancelled the life insurance, taken the Mercedes, and left me with the Toyota—which, by the way, was uninsured because he cancelled that policy, too."

"Oh dear. At least I was able to get a decent settlement. And I had my own bank account."

"Right." Beth looked down toward her feet.

I hoped she didn't think I was implying that she was stupid not to have had her own account. I simply wanted to say that she'd had it tougher than I had. "You probably didn't even have enough to pay your household bills."

Beth nodded. "I had no choice but to move in with Meg. I had to sell the house because I needed the equity. I had a job, with this lawyer, same one I work for now, but it was just part time, and I didn't make much." She leaned back and, holding on to the rail like a child, swayed left and right. "My boss is just wonderful. He doubled my salary and put me to work as his personal secretary. Before, I was a receptionist. So I've been struggling to get myself in shape financially…and now this."

"From the little I've heard from Lettie, it seems you got along with Meg better than anybody else did."

"I did the best I could, but sometimes…in fact, just today, when I went up to the room…" Beth stopped, as if she had started a sentence she couldn't finish.

"You were angry, weren't you? Was it because of those flowers you had?"

"The flowers. Oh!" She hesitated. "The narcissus? What happened was, I got a phone call from the front desk this after-noon. The woman, she had a really thick accent…hard to under-stand. But she said there was an urgent message for me in my mail slot at the front desk. So I rushed down, but it wasn't urgent at all. It just said, in English, 'There's a gift for you at' this certain florist shop—I forget the name. It said, 'We tried to deliver it and couldn't, so would you please pick it up ASAP?'"

"That's odd. I wonder why they couldn't deliver it?" As I said it, I remembered seeing a delivery boy with a vase of yellow roses in the lobby earlier today. *What kind of gift is it, if you have to go pick it up yourself?*

"I don't know why they couldn't deliver, but I ran into Tessa, and she said the florist was just down the via Nazionale, so I decided to walk. It turned out to be a hell of a long way, so by the time I got back, I was fuming."

"At Tessa or at the florist?"

"At the whole thing. I wouldn't have walked over there at all, but I sort of thought they might…might have been from…"

"From Achille?"

"Yes," she said, her gaze darting toward me, "because we had been talking, just last night, about how much I love flowers. Or I thought they could be from Greg, my boss. You can send flowers internationally, you know, with a credit card, and Greg is sweet like that. Or they might have even been from this man I've gone out with a few times back home. Anyway, there was no name on the card, but I think they were from Meg. You know what the card said? It said 'Vanity, vanity.'"

"I don't understand."

"The other night when we were in Venice, we were coming back from our gondola ride and…" Beth took a deep breath.

I thought I'd save her the embarrassment. "I remember. I was behind you when we walked down the ramp. I heard what she said when you said you had to find a bathroom."

"About the diaper?"

"Yes."

"I was furious over that because I saw Achille standing right there. He had very nicely asked me to go to a little bar where the locals hang out when we got back to Mestre—to our hotel. Meg deliberately said that because she saw him waiting for me. She timed it so it came out when she was right in front of him."

"You're sure it was intentional?"

"Certainly. Meg was like that. She liked to hurt. So when I picked up those flowers today and read that card, well."

I shivered. "How cruel."

"If you know anything about the language of flowers—it's sort of a Victorian thing—white narcissus is the symbol for vanity."

"Oh, of course. Like Narcissus in the Greek myth."

"I hate to think about it now, but if Meg hadn't been lying there dead, I would have given her a piece of my mind. I guess I have to live with that."

"Live with what? You didn't say anything."

Beth turned her face away from me. She retreated to the opposite side of the roof, and I followed her. From here, the train station dominated the view. On this side of the station was the beautiful church of Santa Maria Novella, and in front of the church, a broad piazza and a fountain. Lit now from underneath, it seemed much closer than it had earlier today when I had passed it on my way downtown. Was that the fountain Crystal found the knife in? I almost asked that out loud but caught myself.

"Beth, when you reached your room, was the door locked or unlocked?"

"That's the first thing that policeman asked me. It was open. That was odd, but, of course, I didn't think about it then, because I didn't have time to. As soon as I pushed the door and walked in, I saw Meg. I think I screamed. I know I dropped the flowers."

"Then you called the desk."

I looked down at the fountain again. Would it have been possible for someone to throw the knife from the hotel to the fountain? I couldn't tell. Which part of the hotel would it have come from? From what window? I could feel an experiment coming on.

"There you are." Lettie sneaked up on us from the right.

"Where did you come from?" I was confused. The square brick box that housed the elevator shaft was just behind us. If

Lettie had ridden up in the elevator, she should have come from there.

"Stairway. How did you get here?"

"Elevator," Beth said. "We didn't know about the stairs."

"They're finished with me for now," Lettie said. "Captain Quattrocchi says if we need to talk to him after tonight, he'll be in his casar… I forget what he called it. He'll be in his office downtown somewhere." She turned, caught her first sight of the Duomo at night, and paused for a suitable length of time, in awe. "Beth, where are you staying tonight? Surely, they won't make you stay in your room."

I hadn't even thought of that. Meg and Beth's room was now a crime scene. Of course, Beth couldn't stay there, but all her things would still be in the room.

"They've moved me to another room. This one's on the second floor. They said they'd transfer my things. I can't possibly go back in that room."

"Of course not. And what about Amy?"

"She was in the room next door to Meg and me. They didn't have a triple room for us, like they did in Venice. Amy said that was just as well, because she was kind of…miffed." Beth caught herself, as if she didn't think she should have mentioned that. "Anyway, Tessa said she'd like to spend a night or two in Amy's room while we're here, to talk over old times, you know. Tessa has an apartment here in Florence. An apartment with a roommate, I believe. But she said she might get Pellegrino Tours to split the cost of the room with Amy if she could think up some logical reason for them to do so. Then Amy wouldn't have to pay extra for the single supplement."

I leaned over the rail and peered down the side of the building. Unless I was all turned around, this was the side Meg and Beth's room—and Amy's room—would be on. It wasn't far from the fountain. Lettie and Beth headed for the stairs, but tugged on the door and discovered it couldn't be opened from the outside.

"I guess that's a safety feature," I said.

and saw him standing there. He might panic. And if the knife was there, say, on the dresser beside the door...

I couldn't convince myself it could have been like that. They must have the wrong man. Strange coincidences, of course—that he happened to have the room card, that Achille happened to notice him, that the police caught up with him—but coincidences happen every day.

So, if Ivo didn't kill Meg, who did? The most obvious second choice would be Beth. She called the front desk, it was her knife, and she was already mad at Meg. But that pot of flowers, no matter how insulting, would hardly be a motive for murder. Beth had had years of practice putting up with Meg. Sometimes, though, a person takes it and takes it for years, and then something happens. They snap. Or do they, really? I know children and teenagers do. They "go postal," as the kids say. But adults have better-developed pressure gauges, don't they? I tend to be skeptical of those defendants who claim they don't know what happened—a gun just came into their hand and went off. I don't believe people black out and weapons take that opportunity to animate themselves.

At any rate, I decided I would not voice any of these thoughts to Lettie. Not yet. I needed to look again at the list I had made before dinner. I had the seeds of a couple of ideas—things I wanted to look into. The historian in me loves to uncover things, and the mother in me hates to be lied to, or maybe it's the "ex-wife of Chet Lamb" in me that refuses to be lied to again.

I pushed my face into the pillow and tried to relax. The big problem was the fact that this was a fourteen-day trip; that's all we had paid for, and it's all the time most of us had taken off from work. We had already used up four days. In ten days we would leave Italy with the murderer still in our midst and an innocent Ivo facing a trial that might well be stacked against him.

Alternatively, the carabinieri might come to their senses and realize they had the wrong person. Then what? Once we left the country, the investigation would grind to a halt. It would be nearly impossible to follow thin threads of evidence across the ocean, and it would undoubtedly raise huge problems about jurisdiction, extradition—it made my head hurt to think about it.

So, they might rush to judgment and grab the second most obvious suspect, Beth. Lettie had already told me, in no uncertain terms, that Beth could not possibly have killed her sister—that was unthinkable. But I, having only met Beth three days ago, could not be so sure. If Beth was guilty, she deserved whatever she got because even though she had had ample reason to loathe Meg, she was an adult, and she knew she had other options. She hadn't had to live under Meg's thumb. But if she was innocent, would we, ten days hence, leave her at the mercy of the Italian authorities? I'd heard stories about foreign jails. Neither Lettie nor I could possibly let that happen, and yet what could we do about it?

I couldn't allow an innocent man to go to prison, probably for life, and I couldn't allow a guilty Beth to go home on the same plane with me. I couldn't allow an innocent Beth to be thrown to the vagaries of a court system whose language she didn't even understand, and go home on the plane with the real killer. Lettie loved Beth like a sister, and Lettie was like a sister to me, so I reluctantly accepted the only course left. I wouldn't leave Italy until I knew who really killed Meg Bauer.

EIGHT

"DID YOU HEAR? Crystal's missing."

Wilma Kelly went out of her way to walk past our breakfast table and bring us the news. The Hotel Fontana had a delightful little terraced area under a vine-draped arbor just outside the main dining room. Dappled sunlight on white linen and fresh flowers on every table. The only problem was that it was separated from the busy street by a thin hedge so the street noises, banging trash cans and motorcycles revving up at the corner stoplight, made conversation a little difficult.

"Missing? What do you mean?" Lettie buttered her second croissant and licked her fingers.

"Shirley said Crystal went out last night, supposedly for a few minutes, and didn't come back. She's absolutely beside herself. She was at the police station most of the night."

"Why did Crystal go out by herself? She did that a couple of times yesterday, too," I said.

"Well." Wilma leaned over our table. "Crystal has been popping out every so often for a cigarette. Shirley is horrified that her daughter is smoking, so they've had several bouts over that the last few days. At home, Crystal can probably go out with her friends and smoke without her mother knowing about it. If she smells smoke on her, Crystal can always just say, 'I was in a smoky room,' but here, she goes out by herself and comes back fifteen minutes later smelling like smoke…well. Shirley may be dumb, but she's not that dumb."

"Maybe it's more like, at home she can pretend not to know, but here it's too obvious to keep up the pretense," I said.

"I suspect that's it." Wilma started to leave, but turned back. "Did you hear about the meeting? Tessa wants us all to meet in the conference room beside the front desk at nine. Hopefully, we'll hear more about Crystal."

I thanked her and checked my watch. We had twenty minutes. No sense going back to the room now, so I'd just have another cappuccino...and another croissant.

"I'm so glad I'm finished raising my teenagers, aren't you?" Lettie's two, a boy and a girl, were grown now and out on their own.

"Very, very glad," I answered with feeling. "Especially the teenaged girl. Give me boys, any day." My mind flitted quickly past my own daughter, Anne, who at that moment was sailing in the Caribbean under circumstances I refused to ruin my vacation thinking about. My four boys—I was so proud of them. My daughter—well, I still had my fingers crossed.

Lettie asked, "Speaking of Anne, how is she?"

Paul Vogel interrupted before I could answer.

"Morning, ladies, morning! Mind if I join you?" He yanked a chair from a nearby table and seated himself. His ubiquitous camera with the macho lens swung from his neck as he flashed us a yellow-toothed smile.

"Croissant?" I held out the basket to him.

"No, thanks. I guess you ladies have a big day planned?"

Paul Vogel's sudden joviality seemed as contrived as a hair compliment from a used car salesman. "Just sightseeing," I said.

"Yeah, me, too...me, too." He fiddled with his camera. "Lettie—you don't mind if I call you Lettie, do you? I understand you were in the cat-bird seat yesterday."

Lettie looked confused. It surprised me that Paul knew her name; this was the first time he had spoken to either of us directly.

Her brow furrowed. "What do you mean, cat-bird seat?"

"Weren't you sitting at the elevator when all the...you know...stuff hit the fan?"

"Oh, right. Yes. Lucille must have told you. She popped in just when...well, as a matter of fact, we all, Dotsy and your wife and I...we all had to walk up the stairs because they stopped the elevator."

"My wife? I'm not married."

He said it so simply, I wondered if I had got the last names wrong. *Please don't tell me you and Lucille are having an affair.* They might be brother and sister, of course. I found it mind-boggling enough to imagine either of them in the bonds of matrimony. But a passionate affair? Fly off to Europe to melt in each other's arms? My imagination simply would not leap that far.

"Oh, no," Paul continued. "Lucille is my sister."

Now that, I could imagine. I remembered Shirley telling me Lucille had pitched a fit in Venice because they wanted twin beds and had been given a double. It all made sense now.

"How nice that you travel together," I said.

"We don't usually, but she was keen to go on this trip and didn't want to go alone."

"What do you do back home?" I asked.

"Security." Paul coughed and tapped his lens cover a couple of times. "Security service. Electronic sweeps. Photography. Location and recovery."

"That explains the state-of-the-art camera," I said.

I hate it when people tell you what they do in such nebulous terms you still have no idea what they do even after they've told you. That happens to me all the time whenever I talk to someone who has a government job or something to do with computers. Paul's answer sounded to me just like, "You wouldn't understand if I told you, and if I told you, I'd have to kill you."

"This camera is not state-of-the-art anymore, I'm afraid. Nope. I need to go digital, but I've been putting it off because it means taking courses to learn what the hell it's all about and I just haven't had the time."

"I see," said Lettie. "Is your sister enjoying Italy as much as she thought she would?"

"Oh, I think so. Of course, we've not exactly had just a happy little tour so far, have we? I mean, this whole thing is extraordinary. At the elevator yesterday, did you see Jim Kelly at any time?"

"No, but I saw Wilma," Lettie replied.

What a strange question. It had nothing to do with what we had been talking about. It made me feel uncomfortable, so I cleared my throat and changed the subject. "You and Lucille didn't do your sightseeing together yesterday, did you? Lucille came into the lobby by herself."

"No. I spent my day at the Ponte Vecchio and the Boboli Gardens…taking pictures, you know. Lucille went to the Uffizi Gallery." Paul sipped my water, apparently not noticing that he had done so without asking me first.

"So Lucille is the art aficionado in the family?"

"She's an artist, all right, but not the visual kind," he said, tapping his right ear. "The auditory kind." He leaned forward, one hand on his knee and looked into my eyes in a confidential, almost uncomfortably intimate, way. "Lucille has had a tough time. She was a singer—a classical singer. Voice like an angel. But you know how it is, show business. Tough life."

"I'm sure it is."

"She always thought that by the time she reached this point in her life—mid-forties—she'd be an established artist, maybe even famous. But she kind of slipped downhill instead of rising up. She went from concert halls to smaller venues to night clubs to…well." Paul glanced over his shoulder and checked his watch.

"You said you didn't see Jim Kelly yesterday." He looked straight at Lettie. "Did you see that Brit? What's-his-name, Reese-Burton?"

Lettie's eyelids fluttered. Since she is not quick to pick up on subtleties like a cough or a throat clearing, I resorted to the old kick under the table. With Lettie, though, you run the risk she'll yell "Ow! Whadja do that for?" Paul was fishing for information. Why, I couldn't guess, but I felt strongly that it was time for us to clam up. Captain Quattrocchi we would talk to, but Paul Vogel? This was beginning to feel like high-stakes poker, and I knew enough to keep my cards close to my chest. Who was Paul, anyway, and why was he pumping us for details on what Lettie may have seen or not seen yesterday?

The kick to the shin worked. Lettie grabbed my arm from across the table, looked at my watch, and said, "Oh dear, we're late for the meeting."

We were the last to take our seats in the small conference room. A quick glance around told me that everyone was there except Crystal. And Meg, of course. Beth and Amy sat beside Tessa, Amy holding Beth's hand. Tessa explained that we were going to play it by ear for the next few days. We were scheduled to stay four nights in Florence, then go to Pisa on the West Coast, but things being like they were, we might stay on here a bit longer. "This hotel has room for us if we need to stay. In fact, you'll probably be able to stay in your current rooms, if you want to. We can go to Pisa as scheduled, but we might just make it a day trip and return here for the night.

"We didn't get to do our excursion to the Piazzale Michelangelo yesterday, of course, but we can still do that. We just don't know exactly when, yet." Tessa paused and looked around. "Is this okay with everybody?"

Lucille Vogel boomed, "Will we get a refund on whatever we don't get to do, because of circumstances beyond our control?" and silence dropped like an anvil.

It was an outrageously inappropriate question, but Tessa had to say something. "Pellegrino Tours always goes out of its way to be fair to its guests. I'm sure they will be this time, too, but you must understand that we haven't been able to discuss any specifics yet. Today was scheduled to be a free day, anyway. So that won't change, but Captain Quattrocchi has asked that you keep the front desk here informed about where you are. Not in any great detail, of course, but if you're, say, taking a bus trip to

San Gimignano, you should let the hotel know. In the event that Captain Quattrocchi needs to speak with you again, he will probably want you to come to the caserma—that's what we call carabinieri headquarters. It's located down near the river on the Borgo Ognissanti, easy walking distance from here. Now, Amy wants to tell you a couple of things."

Amy Bauer released her sister's hand and stood up. "Beth and I want to thank you for all the help you're giving us. This is a hard time for us, but everyone has been so kind." She cleared her throat and lowered her head. "It was Meg's desire to be cremated. We've decided to have that done here, and then we will take her ashes back to the States. Our brother Joe is planning a service for her at home, but the date will have to be left open until we know how long everything here will take. We understand a cremation may take some time. At any rate, until then, Beth and I will continue on with the group, and like I said, we appreciate your help."

Tessa smiled at Amy and stepped forward again. "One more thing. Since it's Saturday, restaurants all over town will be jammed tonight. I thought some of you might like to have an authentic Tuscan country dinner, so I've contacted a charming little place I've been to many times. It's about ten miles out of town. Achille can drive us. If you want to go, tell me soon so I can call in a reservation. We'll leave here about seven."

Paul Vogel stood up. "I heard they've arrested some local guy for the murder. Is that true?"

"Captain Quattrocchi has asked me not to discuss specifics of the case with anyone, and to tell you the truth, I don't know much about it, since I only sat in as translator when he was talking to each of you." She hesitated a moment. "But, yes. I think it's okay to tell you that they did arrest a man yesterday. That's all I really know."

I had a strong feeling that Tessa knew a great deal more, but, of course, she really couldn't talk about it. People began to stir, and it looked as if the meeting was over.

Shirley Hostetter barred the doorway with her body before anyone could get out. "May I have your attention for a minute?"

"Oh dear, Shirley, I forgot to call on you," Tessa said, her voice apologetic.

"As you may have heard, Crystal is missing." Shirley's whole face betrayed the fact that she hadn't been to bed at all last night. Her hair was a mess and her makeup was gone. "She was last seen by some of the hotel staff outside on the street at about nine o'clock. They saw a young man—black hair, about five feet eight, wearing a blue denim shirt and jeans—talking to her, but nobody actually saw them leave. We don't know if she left willingly or not. We don't know if she left with that young man or not. Those who saw him say he looked like a Roma—that's what they call Gypsies. They said he dressed like a lot of the Roma teenage boys do. They guessed his age at about fourteen to sixteen.

"Anyway, if you were out last night at about that time, would you please, please, search your mind for anything you might remember seeing? Anything at all. Tell me, or tell the police, or the carabinieri. And while you're out and about today, please keep your eyes open. Okay?"

Her voice broke on those last few words. My heart bled for her.

In the lobby, two young men—cool, debonair, like fugitives from a Milan designer's summer collection—waited. Their eyes lit up when Tessa and Amy emerged from the conference room.

"The fiancé and the new boyfriend, I presume," I whispered to Lettie.

As we watched them, I filled Lettie in on my plan. "I worked something out in my head as I tossed and turned last night," I told her. "I want to know if it was possible that Beth's knife was thrown into that fountain where Crystal found it, or if it had to have been carried there."

Lettie said nothing, but her eyes danced like she smelled an adventure.

"So, if we're lucky, either Tessa or Amy, but not both of

them, will go up to their room now," I said. "We need to station ourselves at the end of the hall on the third floor so we can see who's going in. Let's get the elevator."

"Isn't Amy staying with Beth now, in a room on the second floor?"

"But she and Tessa still have their things in Amy's original room. We need to drop by when only one is there. Which one doesn't really matter."

"Why?"

"Because it will be easier for you to keep one person distracted while I do what I've got to do," I said.

"Which is?"

We dashed to catch the elevator and rode to the third floor. I shoved Lettie down toward the end of the hall just in time. Through the little windows in the stairwell doors, we watched Tessa insert her room card and open the door. Yellow crime scene tape still crisscrossed the door on her immediate right.

"Perfect," I said. "You let me handle everything, and I'll explain it all later. I hope this works. Your job is to distract Tessa for about one minute while I poke my head out the window."

"You mean balcony door."

"No, I mean window. The rooms on this side don't have balconies."

"Aren't we special."

"Contain yourself, Lettie. Now think. How can you keep Tessa distracted?"

"Well, I could ask to see her clothes…no…wait! Isn't Tessa planning a wedding?"

"Good! I've noticed she reads bride magazines every chance she gets. Brides can go on for hours about weddings."

Lettie and I traipsed down the hall and rapped on Tessa's door. She held her unbuttoned blouse around her as she let us in.

"I'm so sorry, but I dropped a scarf off the roof last night," I said. "And I couldn't, for the life of me, find where it fell. I need to peek out your window, if you don't mind."

Lettie lit into a perfect song-and-dance. Really, I'm afraid I underestimate her sometimes. I had to bang on the window, the paint on the frame having been melded by the summer sun into something like glue.

"Oh, that green blouse, Tessa," Lettie gushed. "Green is your color! Tell me, have you picked out the colors for your wedding yet?"

Good going, Lettie, I thought. After the third pop, the window shuddered up. I stuck my head and both arms out and pulled the silk scarf out of my left sleeve with my right hand. I peeked around my shoulder to make sure Tessa was not watching me— she wasn't; she and Lettie were examining a pair of green shoes—then reached into my pocket for the knife I had stolen from the restaurant. I threw it as hard as I could in the general direction of the fountain, drew my head back in, and flourished the scarf. "Ta da! Got it. It was stuck on the rough stone outside this window."

Absorbed in the fabulous green shoes she had bought for her bridesmaids, Tessa evinced no more than a passing interest in my scarf.

NINE

It took a while, tramping back and forth from the northwest side of the hotel to the fountain, but we found the knife under a bush about twenty feet from the edge of the fountain. I looked up and, by counting, pinpointed the correct third-floor window. "So, it could have been done," I told Lettie. "I'm not very strong, so any number of people could have flung it farther than I did. As far as the fountain. I think I could have done it myself, if I could have wound up and given it all I had. As it was, I had to do it with my elbow and wrist."

"But the killer would not have been at that window. He—or she—would have been at the next one on the left." Lettie's gaze darted left, then right. "But from here, there doesn't seem to be much difference."

"That's what I think, too." I tucked the knife into my bag. "Are you ready for our next investigation?" Lettie knew she didn't have much choice. "I want to visit the shop where Beth picked up those narcissuses—or should that be narcissi? What street did she say it was on?"

"Via Nazionale," my little data bank answered.

I opened my city map. The via Nazionale started on the opposite side of the church we were facing and ran off to the northeast. "It's right there," I said, pointing to the right of the church, "but Beth said it was a long walk, and we might find there are dozens of florists. I don't feel like checking out a bunch of wrong stores."

We returned to the hotel and found Beth in her new room on the second floor. She didn't remember the name of the florist and had dropped the offending card, along with the entire pot, on the floor when she saw her sister's body. It seemed a lost cause until I remembered the note. "I suppose you wouldn't have saved the note you picked up at the front desk."

"I think I did, in fact. Let's see, it might still be in my purse." Beth rooted through her purse. "Not here," she muttered as my hopes sank. She unzipped a side pocket and ran her hand around inside. "Oh, here it is." She handed me a printed note that directed her to pick up an order at Fioretoscana, a florist on via Nazionale. "But why do you need to know the name of the florist, Dotsy?"

"I want the name of any good florist, and the flowers you carried looked nice and fresh."

Beth raised one eyebrow, as if she'd rather not think about those flowers at all.

It was a long hot trek to Fioretoscana. I could understand why Beth's nose had been out of joint yesterday. But the long walk gave Lettie and me time to rehearse my plan for finding out who sent those flowers. "It's a little too handy, don't you think? It's as if the flowers were someone's way of getting Beth out of the hotel."

"As if *who* was getting Beth out of the hotel?" Lettie asked.

"That's what we want to find out."

"You mean you think that Gypsy ordered the flowers?"

"Possible, but it doesn't seem likely, does it?"

"No. I've never had a Gypsy send me any flowers."

Sometimes I can't tell if Lettie is joking or not. I think of her as living in a simple, concrete world where everything is just what it seems to be, but when she comes out with something like that last statement, I suspect she's putting me on. I laughed and glanced quickly toward her in time to catch an almost-successfully suppressed grin. "I guess it's possible," I said. "After all, he had her credit card. If we find the flowers were ordered by Beth Bauer Hines, we'll have our answer." I dodged around a workman who was jackhammering the sidewalk. "Lettie, if you saw a long row of numbers, how many do you think you could learn in, say, fifteen seconds?"

"I don't know. Maybe seven or eight?"

My plan was to get the florist to show us the sales ticket for Beth's flowers. If they had been ordered by phone or online, there'd be a credit card number. But if they had been ordered in person, they might have been paid for by check, cash, or credit card, and we might not find out anything unless the person who waited on us could give us a description of the purchaser. If they were ordered by anyone in our party, since we were all foreigners, they could not have been paid for by check. I said, "A credit card number usually has sixteen digits. You take the first eight, and I'll take the last eight."

"Do they all have sixteen?"

Lettie and I stopped and counted the numbers on the cards we had with us. All of them had sixteen except one, which had fifteen. "You have a better memory than me. So I want you to count the digits *and* remember the first eight. If it's only fifteen, your last number and my first will be the same."

We had come to the end of a block. I threw out my arm to keep Lettie from walking out in traffic, and she rolled her eyes like my kids used to do. Heat radiated off the pavement as we crossed the street.

"Slow down a minute," I said. "I need to look up some words in case they don't speak English in this place."

Lettie guided me around a couple of oncoming pedestrians as I flipped through my little English-Italian pocket dictionary.

"I want to buy…*vorrei comprare*…*vorrei comprare*." I practiced it a few times. "Pot…*pianta*…my friend…*mi amica*."

"There it is." Lettie spotted the sign.

Fioretoscana might as well have been any florist back home in Staunton. The carnation-funeral smell hit my nose as we burst through the door into the blessed coolness. Condensation water ran down the glass doors of their refrigerated display cases. Behind the wet glass, gladioli, roses, birds of paradise, baby's breath and carnations in a dozen unnatural colors leaned in their containers on slatted wooden shelves. Tortured arrangements in dish gardens, ceramic bunnies, and turtles nestled in moss or perched on fake driftwood. I felt as if I was back in Virginia. A young girl behind the counter, painting her toenails, jerked her left foot off the counter when she saw us.

I said, *"Per favore, vorrei comprare un* pot...*pianta di narcissus*...white...*bianco."*

The girl hobbled to the back room on one shod foot and one bare heel. She reappeared with a pot quite similar to the one Beth had yesterday. *"Piace questo?"* she asked, but I frowned and shook my head.

After several more tries and disappointed shakes of the head, although I was pretty sure everything I had seen had come off the same truck, I took out a piece of paper and wrote "Beth Hines" on it. *"Mi amico...amica...*yesterday...*ieri,"* I said. I considered pressing my fingers together and thrusting the back of my hand at the girl, thinking that perhaps Italian gestures would make it clearer. *"Vorrei vedere* the ticket...*vendita.* Beth Hines *vendita. Per favore?"*

The girl looked confused, but I assumed my most desperate expression and, eventually, she began thumbing through a stack of tickets on the work counter behind her. She pulled one out and placed it on the counter in front of Lettie and me. I flashed a look that I hoped conveyed absolute rapture and—holding one corner of the ticket in a vice-like grip, so that if the girl tried to take it away she would have to rip it—quickly committed the last eight digits to memory and prayed that Lettie could see the first eight. When I had burned them into my brain, I let my eyes wander up the page a little and discovered that the entire exercise had been unnecessary, because the ticket also listed the card's expiration date and the name of the cardholder...Margaret Bauer.

Having made so much fuss, I felt obligated to actually buy. Lettie and I both smiled as we left with a pot of narcissus identical to any of the half-dozen pots I had just rejected. As I opened the door onto a blast of city heat, I turned and caught the salesgirl's gesture to somebody in the back; forefinger pointed at temple and rotated clockwise. I imagine that means the same thing in Italian as it does in English.

"So Beth was right. Meg did send those flowers. What a great sister!" Lettie said sarcastically. "Sorry, I know it's wrong to speak ill of the dead, but…"

"Is it possible that Beth was carrying Meg's credit card in her fanny pack? That the Gypsy got hold of Meg's card?" I asked.

"No chance. Meg wouldn't have let anyone else have her card. She was as tight-fisted as an old Scrooge."

Lettie and I walked back to the hotel the same way we had come—a route that took us past the Church of Santa Maria Novella and the fountain I now thought of the as the Fountain of the Bloody Knife. We passed a building with a glass-fronted bakery and a stairwell on one side, which I gathered led to an upstairs apartment—a deduction I based on the line of laundry that stretched from an upstairs window to the building next door. "Just a minute, Lettie." I stopped and used my pocket phrasebook to jot *"un ammiratore segreto"* on the little card the girl had stuck in the potting soil. "That says, 'from a secret admirer.' Might brighten someone's day, huh?" I ducked into the stairwell and left the flowers on the bottom step.

Lettie turned sideways, looked back toward the stairwell, and stepped on a cat. "Or it might start a big fight."

Shirley Hostetter rounded the corner of our hotel as we strolled past the fountain. She glanced toward us but didn't stop or speak. Shirley looked like she was in a parallel universe. Her face had assumed a vaguely haunted expression, as if she were about to embark on a voyage into the unknown, as if she had psyched herself into a state where she could walk on hot coals barefoot. She wore a beautiful green silk blouse and multi-colored skirt with a gold rope belt.

Lettie said, "Not your typical Shirley outfit, is it?"

"Not at all," I replied. "It's the first thing I've seen her in that isn't ultra-conservative."

"Not her usual tan and navy."

"Very nice, though...obviously expensive," I said. "The way that skirt moves, it's not from a discount store. You know what? It looks like a skirt she'd normally wear with a simple shell top. And a blouse she would wear with tan or white slacks. It's as if she decided to throw on all her bright stuff at the same time."

"Maybe she needs it to keep up her spirits," Lettie said. "This has got to be pure hell for her. Do you suppose she's called her husband?"

"I imagine she has, but what can he do? Do you suppose he's on his way here?"

"What good would that do?"

"None, probably, but if it were me, I'd want to be on the scene," I said. "Come on. She's headed toward the train station. Let's follow her."

"Your antenna's beeping again?" Lettie stopped and looked at her watch. "I promised Beth I'd meet her at the hotel at eleven. Oh, well, I guess I have enough time. Let's go."

We lost sight of Shirley in the crowd outside the station. The majority of people seemed to be milling aimlessly about and a lot of them were young—teens in groups of three or four. I watched two teens, a boy and a girl, walk unobtrusively toward a man in an orange and blue T-shirt that said MIAMI DOLPHINS. The boy draped a newspaper over his own right arm. The girl moved directly in front of the man, talking rapidly and pointing to her wrist as if she needed to know the time. The Miami fan moved back slightly and looked at his watch as the boy asked something and gesticulated with his empty left hand. Apparently aware that something was wrong, the Miami fan dodged sideways but was blocked by the girl. Beneath the newspaper, the boy's right hand darted into the man's hip pocket, but the man jumped back, chopped downward with both hands and yelled, *"Va via!"* The wallet skidded across the sidewalk, and the Miami Dolphins fan pounced on it a microsecond before several other hands closed in.

Lettie, wide-eyed and incredulous, said, "It's like a shark feeding frenzy! It's absolutely awful. I never…"

"Are you up for going inside? Looks like we can't get in the door without running the gauntlet. See? Over there are some more of them—" I pointed "—and over there." Approaching the main entrance, I felt like Tippi Hedren driving through the flock of devil-possessed seagulls in *The Birds*—one false move and I'd be pecked to death.

"Let's stick together," Lettie said, "and shoot through the middle."

"Remember what that man said? *'Va via.'* I guess that means 'Go away.' I'll try to remember that." I checked to make sure the clasp on my shoulder bag was next to my body, locked my hand around the strap and forged ahead.

"I don't think it matters what you yell, as long as you yell something," Lettie said. "Just draw attention to yourself any way you can."

Once inside, we found a relatively empty space near a rack of timetable booklets where I felt safe enough to stop and look around. We watched the bustle of comings and goings for a few minutes, but I didn't see Shirley. There were quite a lot of people who didn't seem to be going anywhere—loiterers, many of them teens who didn't look much different from those in the U.S. "You know, Lettie, it occurs to me that Crystal would stand out even among these kids as the weird one."

"Do you really expect to find her here? I mean, what are the odds?"

"Very slim, I know, but at least we're looking," The station smelled of axle grease and diesel fumes. Brakes squealed against the background drone of a hollow female voice chanting arrivals and departures. I got knocked and bounced into a spot between two opposing streams of foot traffic.

Down near the tracks, a middle-aged woman in jeans yelled out something that sounded like "Don't want your baby!" A rail-thin Roma woman in a shawl had handed her a blanket-wrapped bundle and was groping for the other woman's waist pack. Several men jumped to the rescue and wrestled a pilfered coin purse away from the Roma woman. The almost-victimized woman stood with her mouth open. The infant she held was, for some strange reason, not crying.

"This place is a zoo, Dotsy. I can't believe…why don't the police do something?"

"Let's check a bathroom or two just in case."

We trekked around the cavernous station, checking ladies' rooms, and trying to stay well away from the tightest knots of people.

"Look, Lettie! Over there."

In a corner beside the porters' station stood a short, round woman with salt-and-pepper hair cut in a blunt, Dutch-boy style. She exchanged something—a small package, folding money— with a very scruffy man I might have thought was Ivo, had Ivo not been in jail. I think I knew, even before she turned her face toward us, that the woman was Lucille Vogel.

"Do you think it's a drug deal, Dotsy?"

"It would appear so. That would explain her mood swings, you know, if she's an addict she might have been suffering withdrawal symptoms in our first couple of days here. She would have been irritable."

"And yesterday, she might have finally got hold of…well, got a fix or whatever they call it. That would explain why she was nice when she came up to the elevator. You remember?"

"Right. Now if we could just find out what's happened to Crystal and who killed Meg as easily as we found out why Lucille Vogel has mood swings."

"Wonder how she found out where to get drugs?" Lettie turned away from the porter's station.

Lucille walked toward us, her head lowered, her eyes down. She zipped her bag, glanced around quickly, and headed for an exit.

"These people, drug dealers and addicts, they have ways of

finding each other," I said. "A sort of underground network, so I've heard."

I suggested we take one more look around the station. Too bad I didn't know enough Italian to strike up a conversation with some of the kids. I'd be willing to bet some of them knew something. The police weren't knocking themselves out to find Crystal. If it worked the same way as it did in the U.S., she wouldn't even be considered a missing person until she'd been missing twenty-four hours.

"What do you think, Dotsy? Has Crystal been kidnapped, or has she run away?"

"Ordinarily I'd guess she had run away, but with this man, Ivo, in jail, it's possible she's been taken. Maybe somebody wants to offer her in exchange for the prisoner."

Lettie shivered. "If that's the case, they'll contact the police, won't they?"

"Yes. In fact, I'd think they would already—"

"Dotsy, look!"

Lettie pointed toward the swinging door of a women's restroom. A skinny, haggard woman had just emerged and turned right, toward the station's main exit. She was wearing a green silk blouse, a multi-colored skirt, a gold rope belt and designer shoes.

"She's got Shirley's clothes on," Lettie said.

"Where's Shirley?" I asked, a rhetorical question.

We dashed into the restroom shouting for Shirley. She wasn't there or in any other restroom or waiting room or platform in the station. We looked everywhere. A fast train from Rome pulled into the station and opened its doors, disgorging scores of people and rendering hopeless any chance of finding the woman in Shirley's clothes again.

TEN

IN THE TINY LOBBY of the caserma, I pretended to read the posters on the wall and felt uncomfortable. I wished Captain Quattrocchi's door would open so I could see for sure if he was even there. The man behind the front desk and I had been unable to communicate well, and I was still unsure if he knew I wanted to speak to Quattrocchi personally. Had he told me to wait or go home? He might have said, "Come back later." He glanced at me occasionally, as if my presence was ruining his day.

Quattrocchi popped his head out and smiled when he saw me. He waved me in. "Good day, Mrs. Lamb. I am happy to see you." I was surprised he remembered my name. His office was plain, with a government-issue desk and several straight-backed chairs ranged around the walls. There were no windows and the room smelled of smoke. Seating me in one of the utilitarian chairs for visitors, he rolled out the soft leather chair behind the desk for himself.

"I understand that Shirley Hostetter has already told you about the disappearance of her daughter, Crystal," I began.

"That is correct. She has also notified the police."

It took me a second to recall that there was a difference between the carabinieri and the police. I told him what Lettie and I had seen at the train station—the woman wearing Shirley's clothes. As he took notes in Italian, I went over my story slowly and repeated most of it. His gaze locked on my face in deep concentration.

"Excuse me, did you say you did or did not see Mrs. Hostetter after you saw the woman wearing her clothes?"

"I did not see her." I was relieved to know that he had apparently understood me.

He jotted a few more notes and looked at his wristwatch. He wore it with the watch face inward, over his pulse. "It is time for lunch. Mrs. Lamb. Will you allow me to take you to a restaurant near here? I would like to talk to you some more."

"All...all right," I managed to stammer out. This was a complete surprise. I felt as if I had been asked out on a date, and I was way out of practice. "Will you call me Dotsy?"

"Dotsy? Very good. Then you must call me Marco."

Perhaps I had committed a *faux pas*. To ask him to call me by my first name was to require, for the sake of good manners, that he reciprocate by asking me to do likewise. But perhaps calling carabinieri officers by their first names was not done. I didn't know. Too late, now.

He guided me through narrow streets to a small trattoria, taking my arm gently as we crossed each intersection. The air in this part of the city was freshened by a gentle breeze off the River Arno, just to the south. I relished its coolness as it wound through my hair and dried my wet scalp.

"Dotsy. That's a pretty name. It is a...an above name?" He tried again. "It is not your...baptism name, yes?"

"My baptism name," I said, falling easily into his brand of English, "is Dorothy. But I much prefer Dotsy." I wondered if he saw me as a witness, a potential suspect, or what? He knew I had been sitting outside the elevator yesterday when Meg's body was discovered. But what about when Meg was killed? Was he sure he had the right man in jail and didn't need to look at anyone else? Or did he still want to nail down exactly where everyone was at the time of the murder? And what time was that? I still didn't know. It could have been any time between the phone call from Lettie to Meg, about a quarter to five, and Beth's call to the front desk, about a quarter to six. Wilma Kelly had talked to Meg after Lettie did, but how long after? I slapped a sticky note on my brain to get what I could out of Quattrocchi

Marco—on that point. As I thought about all this, I nearly ran over the woman in front of me on the sidewalk. Marco, ever vigilant, steered me around her.

Inside the trattoria, a waiter seated us at a small table near the window. The room was filled with the aromas of herbs and baking bread, and Marco helped me with the menu. "May I recommend the ribollita? It is a thick sort of..." He rubbed his fingers together as if feeling the texture. "A sort of soup. Minestrone, but with some parmigiano and bread. It is what you Americans call cozy food."

I laughed. "Comfort food, we call it."

Marco ordered for both of us and snapped a napkin across one knee. "So, Dotsy, are you married? Children?"

"Divorced and five children, all grown now."

Marco raised his eyebrows, but thankfully made no comment about my figure or the effect thereon of five pregnancies. I think my body is pretty good for a woman my age. I'm about ten pounds heavier than I would like, but then I always have been ten pounds heavier than I would like.

"What about you?" I asked.

As the waiter plopped a carafe of Chianti in the center of our table, Marco said, "Two boys and one girl. My youngest is still at university and my oldest is preparing to follow in the feet of his...how do you call it...old man. He is...trying, ah...training to become carabinieri." Marco poured wine into both glasses.

As soon as I felt I could reasonably change the subject, I said, "What do you think has happened to Crystal Hostetter?"

"I think she has run away, but she will be back soon. I think she and her mother are not...ah, getting along very well. These kids, eh?" He raised his glass to mine. *"Salute."*

"Cheers," I said.

"I have sent out some men to look through the three main Roma camps outside of town, and everyone on duty today has been given a...ah...description of her."

I imagined that description: *Subject was last seen wearing a black T-shirt with white letters and red blood splatters. On the front it says 'psycho-scum,' and the back has large white spiders. Black capri pants, black leather platform shoes with ankle straps, black-and-white striped knee socks, leather neck band with metal spikes sticking out and silver jewelry on ears, nose, fingers and tongue. Safety pin through right eyebrow; hair in long magenta spikes.*

"I do not believe she has been kidnapped," Marco continued. "That is not the way of the Roma. She may be running around here in town, or she may have gone somewhere with that boy she was seen talking to. Bread?" He passed me a basket of fresh crusty rolls.

"Do you know who that boy was?" I ripped my roll in two, scattering crumbs across my side of the table.

"I have no idea. The man…Ivo…he says he knows nothing about it."

"Do you think Ivo killed Meg Bauer?" I had not meant to be so blunt or to bring it up so soon, but it slipped out.

Marco looked like I had slapped him. He was silent a long moment. "Well, yes," he finally said. "To think that it was anyone else is beyond imagining! We *know* he broke into her room, and a few minutes later she was found murdered!"

"What time do you think it happened?"

"Very close to five-thirty; certainly within a few minutes before or after. We know this by comparing the times given to us by Mrs. Kelly who stopped by her room, by Mrs. Osgood who talked to her on the phone, and by the time of Mrs. Hines's call to the front desk." Quattrocchi squared his hands about six inches apart. "Those three things narrow the time of death to about five-thirty."

"But it doesn't make sense to me. Why would a thief who plans to do a little stealing decide to go ahead and commit a murder while he's at it? It doesn't make sense. Why didn't he run?"

The waiter brought our bowls of ribollita, and Marco showed me how to doctor it up properly with grated parmigiano and a drizzle of olive oil.

"And to use a weapon that he just happened to find on the

scene?" I continued. "What are the chances of finding a knife that's just right for doing the trick at exactly the time you need it?"

I tried the ribollita. It was excellent but still too hot to eat, so I ate a bit more of the bread.

"Ah," Marco said. "So you know about the knife."

"Too bad it wasn't a gun. Then we'd know the time of death, exactly. I mean, I assume in a hotel like that, a shot would be heard."

"Yes, a gunshot would have been heard."

"Where was the knife? I mean, before…"

"Mrs. Hines says she put it in the center drawer of her dresser the night before. She showed it to some people who came by their room, and then she put it back into its little box and put it into the drawer. That is the last time she saw it."

I had to concentrate hard when Marco talked because he had a way of putting the same emphasis on all his words, as if he were reciting a list of nonsense syllables, which to him, English probably was.

Soon, I thought, Marco would become wary of my questions, but I ventured one more. "I've been wondering about those flowers that Beth…Mrs. Hines…got. The pot of white narcissus. Doesn't the timing of that seem a little strange to you?"

"Roma do not usually send flowers before they rob someone."

Quattrocchi grinned, and I felt uneasy. I couldn't tell, through his beard, if it was a companionable grin, or if he was making fun of me.

"Who *did* send them?"

"I do not know. I do not think it is important."

"But if it was important, could you find out?" I tried the soup again and found that it was just right. I tucked into it.

"Sure, sure. We could find out how it was paid for by asking the ah…the florist. If by cash, the buyer would have come in personally, and they would be able to give a description. If by check, we would get a name from that. If by credit card, we would get a number, and from that get the name."

A sudden panic grabbed me by the throat. If he found out I had already been to the florist—already knew who sent the flowers—he would know I wasn't being entirely honest with him, and that I was snooping around on my own. How could I explain that? Now that I'd mentioned it, he'd probably check out the florist as a matter of course. What were the odds he'd talk to the same clerk who waited on Lettie and me? What were the odds she'd mention the two Americans who were in this morning, asking questions about those same flowers? Pretty good, I'd say. I remembered the "loopy in the head" signal from the young girl to someone in the back room. There was a good chance that she'd gone straight to the back room and had a good laugh with whomever else was there; that I had become the story of the day. In that case, even if Marco or his men talked to someone else at the shop, she'd probably mention me.

Quattrocchi wiped soup droplets from his beard and suggested dessert. I said, "Not for me thanks, I'm diabetic."

"Do you take…" He apparently didn't know the right word.

"Insulin? Yes, I do."

"Does it bother you, being so far from home, from your regular doctor?"

"Oh, no. I know how to handle it myself. I'm careful, and I test my blood sugar level several times a day."

"I won't have dessert either, then. Do you mind if I smoke?"

"No, go ahead." I looked at the carafe of Chianti. There was enough left for us to each have a glass, so I held my thumb and forefinger about an inch apart. "Could you pour me a half glass of wine?"

"So why did you and Mrs. Osgood go to the train station this morning?" he asked while pouring. He seemed to want to steer the conversation away from the crime.

"For two reasons, actually. I had a feeling the station would be a likely place to spot Crystal if she's anywhere nearby, and because when we saw Shirley heading that way, Lettie and I both thought she was dressed rather strangely."

"Very good! Maybe I should put you and Lettie on my staff." His brown eyes twinkled. He shifted his cigarette to his left hand, directing the column of smoke away from my face.

"I was shocked to see how many pickpockets ply their trade at the train station. I guess it's the Gypsies…Roma, doing it. Can't you guys do something about it? It's really awful." I told him about the woman handing her bundled baby to a stranger and watched his face as a wall descended in front of it. He tightened his lips and tapped his cigarette against the ashtray.

"What can we do? We crack down on them and the human rights organizations—they come to us and say we are committing genocide. We leave them alone and the tourists complain they are the victims." Quattrocchi moved his stiff hands, palm to palm, from one side of the table to the other. "They tell us we should make them a part of our society, bring them into the mainstream, you know, and the Roma say we are destroying their culture. We leave them alone and they say we are condemning them to starve, preventing them from making a living. Now I ask you, what are we to do?"

"I hadn't thought about it that way. You're kind of stuck in the middle, aren't you?"

"Very much so."

Once we were back out on the street, his anger disappeared as he asked, "What will you do this afternoon?"

"I'm supposed to meet Lettie at the hotel so we can go to the Accademia and see the *David,* but I've heard the lines are terrible."

Quattrocchi's face brightened and he held up a finger. "Aha! I have the perfect solution. Do not stand in the line. Do you have some paper?"

I ripped a page from my little trip diary and he began scribbling with the paper held against a nearby lamppost.

"Sometimes it is good to be a captain," he said. "I have a little weight to throw around, as you Americans say."

He handed me the note and instructed me to go to a side entrance at the Accademia.

"Give them this note, Dotsy. They will let you in immediately…and Lettie, too, of course. You must not wait in that line in the front. Not on a day like this. You would die of the heat before you got in."

I thanked him and walked away, trying not to trip because I could feel his eyes on me.

ELEVEN

"WHAT'S THAT STRAP over his shoulder for?"

"It's his slingshot. Don't you know the story of David and Goliath?"

"Oh! He's *that* David! I never realized…I mean, I just thought Michelangelo did a sculpture of a nice-looking young man whose name was David. It's the one in the Bible, isn't it?"

"Not so loud, Lettie." I figured about half of our fellow gawkers understood English, and I heard a few snickers behind me. Michelangelo's *David* is one of those world-famous things that, when you see it in person, does not disappoint. It was magnificent. The concentration in David's eyes as he contemplates the giant—the tension, the faith, even the veins in the youthful but hard-worked hand. Incredible to think that it had once been a chunk of marble.

In the long hall leading to the *David* room, I found Dick Kramer contemplating one of Michelangelo's so-called "slave sculptures." Arms folded and head on a tilt, Dick shifted from one foot to the other. When he saw me, he drew me into his space with, "Are you of the school of thought that Michelangelo deliberately left these bodies only partially emerged from the stone, or that he didn't finish them?"

"Oh, I'm not qualified to have an opinion on what Michelangelo intended," I said.

"They certainly are powerful." He glanced from one to the other of the four bodies that seemed to struggle to free themselves from the stone. "Are they prisoners or slaves? Is there a difference?"

"Is Michael here?" I asked, but Dick didn't seem to hear me. He was lost in the sculptures. Sunlight poured through the high windows and cast his contorted features in bold relief. As if he himself were inside the stone, writhing to get out. His face looked like a marathon runner forging through a wall of pain.

"Interesting, isn't it," Dick went on, oblivious of my question, "how he carved out the torsos first. The head, the hands, and the legs—well, they would come later, wouldn't they? The brain, the action, they come later. After the guts say, 'Let's do it. We have to be free.'"

He turned again to the next work in the series, some fifteen feet away. "The hell of it is that if you can manage to struggle free of this—" he nodded at the slave in front of him "—you only find yourself stuck in that." He jabbed a finger toward the next one.

I stayed quiet so he would know he could keep talking if he felt like it, but Lettie, returning from the ladies' room, breezed past and motioned for me to follow.

I held up two fingers, which I hoped she'd interpret as "Be with you in two minutes."

"I know what being stuck feels like," I said to Dick. "That's one reason I felt I needed to make this trip. Sometimes we need to force ourselves out of the little ruts we let ourselves get into, don't you think? Did you come on this trip for the same reason, Dick?"

He cleared his throat. "No. Actually, I'm here with Michael to learn more about Italian furnishings and décor…" He cleared his throat again. "I own a furniture business at home, you know. We also do interior decorating, designs, etcetera. I've recently hired Michael to head up the bigger design projects…uh…he's a very talented young man. As you may or may not know, selling furniture is not a matter of selling folks something to sit on. It's a matter of selling them a dream, an image, an ambience, if you will. It's not enough to show them some nice, old-world furnishings. You need to make them see themselves in that old-world setting. Sell them on the feeling, the setting, and they'll buy the furniture."

"So you brought Michael here to help him get a feel for the old world setting?"

"Right. That sort of timeless, relaxed, sunny…"

He paused, looked over my shoulder, and I turned in time to see Elaine King coming toward us. Several yards behind her, pretending to study an air vent, was Paul Vogel.

After raising five kids, I know how to tell when someone is lying. When someone who doesn't lisp starts coming out with sibilant S's, they're either self-conscious or lying—or both. Dick Kramer had been telling the truth when he talked to me about the slave sculptures and how it felt to be trapped. I had no doubt that Dick was imprisoned by something he couldn't escape. But that whole spiel about Michael and soaking up Italian ambience was pure crap.

Down a corridor to the left of the *David*, Lettie and I found a room crammed with hundreds of plaster casts and students' work. This was, after all, an academy for the study of art. I was particularly entranced by a sculpture of a small boy playing with a dog. He had his finger in the dog's mouth, like children often do. It occurred to me that dogs, even two thousand years ago, knew how to bite without hurting. Lettie gave me a nudge, the pressure of the crowd compelling us forward. The room was hot and stuffy; there were too many bodies in too small a space.

Spots began to dance in front of my eyes. I became dizzy. "I have to sit down," was all I needed to say. Lettie took my elbow, guided me into the corridor to a bench where she seated me.

"Where's your candy? In your purse?" Lettie didn't wait for an answer, which was good because I don't believe I said anything. She found a piece of hard candy in my bag, unwrapped it, and stuck it in my mouth.

I rested my head against the cool stone wall and drifted on the edge of lucidity for what could have been any length of time, but the next thing I was consciously aware of was Lettie's shaky hands spilling orange juice down my neck as she held a small cup to my lips.

"It's orange juice, Dotsy. It'll work fast. There, there. Oh dear, I'm so sorry I'm spilling…"

I managed to bring her face into focus. Lettie was crying. She had the most desperate look, and her mouth quivered.

I recovered in a flash. "You can relax now. I'm okay. Where in the world did you get orange juice?"

"I have my sources," she said with a sniffle, swiping her left eye with the collar of her shirt.

"Seriously."

"You remember that back room we came in through? The secret way your friend, the Captain, got us in? It was a sort of workroom and I saw a little cooler. I figured they'd have something to drink in there, so I knocked on the door and asked. Luckily they remembered me. 'Ah! The woman who knows the Captain.' They fell all over themselves offering me stuff."

Who, but Lettie, could walk through a room one time and remember seeing a cooler? "I should know better than to push it like I just did," I told her. "In this heat I need to take breaks and eat a snack every so often."

"I'll make sure you do from now on."

"No, Lettie, it's not your job."

ACHILLE MANEUVERED US down a country lane so narrow and steep it seemed the bus must surely have a flexible midsection. None of us would have found the restaurant on our own, because it was at the end of a dirt road tucked in between a wooded hillside and an old stone bridge over a spring. There was no sign at the main road or anywhere else to advertise that it existed. I was almost embarrassed at the way our garishly painted bus blighted the sylvan setting like a pimple on a baby's face, and I wished I had a big camouflage tarp to throw over it.

They were expecting us. Two or three small parties were already dining, but the eighteen of us were their big business of the night. Mismatched chairs and tables with small bunches of wildflowers, lit by oil table lamps with parchment shades, had already been pushed around so we could sit in fours and sixes.

Beth Hines fell in beside Achille, who seated her gallantly at the table with Amy, Tessa and their dates. Tessa introduced us to her fiancé, Cesare Rossi, and Amy's friend, Gianni Diletti, before they took their seats. These were the same two men I had seen in the lobby after our morning meeting at the hotel. Both were extremely handsome in a Continental sort of way, but Gianni looked considerably younger. Surely, I thought, he couldn't be long out of school. Cesare had a look of rugged assurance, a squared-off stance that bordered on arrogance, and very expensive clothes.

"Tessa's fiancé is an up-and-coming local politician," said Wilma Kelly as she and Jim joined Lettie, the Reese-Burtons and me at a table for six. The Kellys being from Canada and the Reese-Burtons from England, we formed quite an international party.

"A town councilman or something like that," Wilma continued.

"On the Florence town council?"

"No, a little town near Florence. Tessa told me the name of it, but I've forgotten it now. It's the town he grew up in and his whole family still lives there. I think they've always been involved in local government, and Cesare—that's his name, isn't it?—is following in the family tradition."

"Which, in Tuscany, means for the last thousand years, or so." Jim Kelly said.

"Oddun loose lak stul churtpan," Geoffrey said.

"Amy's young man looks like he should still be in short pants," Victoria explained.

Tessa slipped over to help us with the menu. Lettie and I both decided on the broiled trout; I because I love fresh fish, and Tessa assured me this would be freshly caught, and Lettie because it would involve little chewing. Wilma asked Tessa to point out vegetarian dishes and to please tell the waiter she wanted hers prepared with no animal fat.

"*Funghi,* that would be mushrooms." Wilma followed Tessa's finger on the menu.

"It's a mushroom casserole with onions and zucchini. I'll make sure it's prepared vegetarian for you."

"Have you been a vegetarian for a long time?" I asked.

"About twenty years." Wilma nodded her approval of the mushroom casserole to Tessa. "I've been active in animal rights matters since my school days, actually. And then I married a dairy farmer." She glanced toward her husband.

"Mostly so she could make sure I treat the cows properly, I suspect," Jim Kelly said.

"As if there was any question of that! Jim treats his 'girls' better than he treats me. He plays the music they like at milking time, sings to them…get him to show you the pictures in his wallet. You think he carries a picture of me?" Wilma nudged him pointedly.

"Come on, Jim, we want to see your pictures," I prodded.

Geoffrey Reese-Burton pointed to an item on the menu, and Tessa looked over his shoulder. "*Vitello*—that's veal," she said.

Victoria shook her head discreetly and frowned at Geoffrey over the top of her glasses.

"What?" He looked puzzled. "What do you mean? I like veal."

Unfortunately, this was the first thing Geoffrey had said that came out clear as spring water.

"Here's a nice *bistecca,* Geoffrey," Victoria said. "Let's both have that. It says here, it serves two."

Geoffrey didn't seem delighted at the prospect of sharing a steak with his wife, but his face suddenly reflected a recollection that veal is from calves raised in pens, and is at the very top of any animal rights person's "Do not Eat" list.

Jim had his wallet out. "This is Sandra. I call her Sandra because she's blonde and she has big brown eyes, like Sandra Dee. You remember her? Gidget?" He started Sandra's picture around the table, followed by another of Sandra when she was a calf. "And this is Polly. Polly is Sandra's mother." Jim's picture of Polly showed another dozen or so Jersey cows, all more or less identical, in the background.

"But Jim," Lettie said, "*all* your cows are blonde and have brown eyes."

"But Sandra's the one who looks like Sandra Dee—or did, when she was little."

After the waiter had taken our orders, I turned to Wilma. "Do you have any special…" I didn't know what to call it: projects, passions, pet peeves—none of those sounded right. "Any special interests in your animal rights work?"

"When I was in school, I protested against the horrible massacres of newborn harp seals. The pups, you know, the hunters would club them to death, bash in their little heads, right in front of their mothers. They did that to keep from putting a bullet hole in their precious white pelt." Wilma shuddered, her face clouding over. Jim folded his hand over hers.

"You were successful, weren't you?" said Victoria Reese-Burton. "They passed laws against it, didn't they?"

"For a while, yes, but they're easing the restrictions again, and I do worry that we'll go back to square one. The seals' numbers have risen and fishermen are starting to complain."

Jim squeezed her hand and leaned a little toward her. It appeared to be a signal between them, I thought; a signal for Wilma to pipe down before she placed both feet on her soap box.

Paul and Lucille Vogel got stuck at a table by themselves, and neither of them looked too happy about it. As we ate, I glanced their way several times, each time catching Paul with his gaze on our table. I recalled his pointed questions at breakfast about the whereabouts of Jim and Geoffrey at the time of Meg's murder. Did he know something about them, something that would connect either or both of them to Meg? I wondered how many other people he had talked to, and if he had found out everything he wanted.

"I must say I was relieved when they arrested that local bloke for Meg's murder." Victoria realigned her silverware while Geoffrey struggled to divide a large thick steak equitably.

"Relieved?"

"Yes, relieved. Just think of the cross-examination and the surveillance we'd be under right now if these police...whatever they call them...had to figure out which one of *us* did it."

"Do you think they have the right person?" I asked and looked around the table quickly. My question seemed to freeze the entire table; for a second or two, no one moved or spoke.

Jim said, "Do you have anyone else in mind?"

"No," I replied. "It just seems—"

"Well, after all, the most likely suspect has enough troubles of her own, right now, doesn't she?" Victoria used a fork and knife to transfer a portion of steak to her own plate.

"Havta 'splain that, luv," said Geoffrey.

"Well, I mean Shirley. She's the only one in the group that I know of who absolutely hated the woman. Of course, if you ask me," Victoria whispered, leaning forward, "her sister, Beth, had more than ample reason for wanting to do for her as well!"

"I wasn't aware that Shirley and Meg even knew each other," Wilma said.

"They're both nurses," I said. "Didn't Shirley say she had heard about this trip from Meg?"

I recalled Shirley telling me she had visited Meg's hospital recently.

"If Meg told her about the trip," I continued, "and Shirley came and brought her daughter, that doesn't sound like hatred to me."

"I don't know about that," Victoria said, "but I talked to her— to Shirley—on the trip down here from Venice. She filled my ear full of fascinating stuff about Nurse Bauer."

"Like what? Did she say Meg was incompetent?" Wilma asked.

"Incompetent, irresponsible, arrogant, unprofessional, you name it. Shirley told me Meg had made mistakes that killed people. She told me about one case where she had added a…well, basically a disinfectant…a hand cleaner, I believe…to a patient's intravenous tube during surgery. The patient died."

"Oh, my." Wilma's mouth formed an "O."

"Meg didn't get fired. You see, she was quite good at making things appear to be someone else's fault. Usually, the rest of the staff could be persuaded to help sweep a complaint under the rug because they'd be worried about being blamed themselves. Shirley said Meg had violent confrontations with practically all the staff except the ones that could fire her—no coincidence there, I'm sure. Shirley said she saw Meg throw a bag of blood at a patient one time."

"Oh, no!" said Wilma and Lettie at the same time.

"Meg denied it and said the patient was just senile, delusional, which he was, actually. Shirley said there'd been many complaints filed about Meg being rude, arrogant, leaving work early without permission, but nothing ever stuck. The last straw for Shirley was an incident where Meg gave a patient a massive overdose of a cardiac medication. The woman died, and Meg got Shirley blamed for it."

Appropriate expressions of horror rippled all around the table. Lettie said, "I thought you said it was a hand cleaner."

"That was a different woman. Oh, there have been several." Victoria straightened her back and glanced at us under one raised eyebrow. "But this one—the cardiac medicine—it seems that Shirley had taken the call from the woman's doctor. He ordered the medicine because the woman was having heart…you know." Victoria patted her chest. "Shirley wrote out the amount—fifty ccs, say, although I can't remember the amount she told me—and she put down that it was supposed to be given as an injection. Anyway, Meg gave it to her in her IV drip and the IV form of the cardiac medication came in a highly concentrated solution. So the poor woman got something like ten or twenty times more than the doctor had ordered."

"So how did Meg get Shirley blamed?" Lettie asked.

"She stole the order Shirley had written, probably while the whole staff was in a panic over this woman going into cardiac arrest. Meg changed it from 'IM' to 'IV,' or from whatever they use to mean injection to whatever means 'put it into the drip.'"

"How awful!"

"Yes, well, Shirley said that's when Meg threw a wobbly and went on the attack. Shirley pointed out to the hospital officials that the ink Meg had used didn't even match the rest of the note, but it was no use. And since she was pregnant with Crystal at the time, she quit the job. By the time Crystal was old enough for day care, they had moved to another city, and Shirley found a nursing position there. In the neonatal unit, I believe."

"I wonder if her meeting with Meg this spring, the one you mentioned, Dotsy, was the first time their paths had crossed since then," said Wilma.

After dinner, we pushed our chairs, all eighteen of them, into a lopsided oval, in order to talk while we sipped our coffee and various cordials. Tessa slipped out the front door, drawing a cell phone from her purse as she left.

"I bet she's calling about Shirley," said Wilma. "Tessa's worried sick, but who wouldn't be? She's got a teenage girl missing, and now the mother's gone, too."

"Oh, my Lord!" I couldn't believe my own stupidity. I hadn't thought to tell Tessa about the woman in Shirley's clothes. Would Captain Quattrocchi have told her? Would they have been in contact with each other this afternoon? Of course, she would have called Shirley's room sometime this afternoon, especially when she didn't hear any further word about Crystal. I dashed out the door.

Tessa was silhouetted against the moonlight reflected off the shallow spring water on the other side of the road. She was talking on her phone, so I waited at a discreet distance until she finished—a good ten minutes. She paced and used her free hand for sweeping gestures that were wasted on the country air.

"Home office," Tessa said when she saw me. "They've talked

to Shirley's husband. He wants to fly here tonight, but he doesn't have a passport. The tour company is pulling strings to see if they can get one issued to him quickly. They said he's out of his mind. In a total panic."

"I would imagine so. His wife and daughter are in a foreign country and they're both missing! Who wouldn't be panicked?" I told Tessa my story and watched her pace back and forth across the parking area, head down and hands clamped together. "I'm so sorry I didn't tell you earlier, Tessa, but I did tell Captain Quattrocchi. He said his men are already on the lookout for Crystal."

"I know. I've talked to him several times today. Did you check all the bathrooms at the train station? Are you sure she wasn't there?"

"I think we checked them all. The train station is such a big place, I couldn't swear she wasn't in there somewhere, but then again, I couldn't swear she went into the station in the first place. The last I saw of her, she was walking across that plaza in front of the Church of Santa Maria Novella."

"Neither Quattrocchi, nor I, nor the hotel has seen or heard from her since this morning. Obviously, something has happened to her. If not, she would have been calling the caserma and the front desk every ten minutes all day." Tessa paced some more and kicked an old dry stone wall at the entrance to the parking lot. "Her husband thinks they've been kidnapped."

"Oh, dear."

"And Pellegrino Tours has got the jimmyjams, because we're supposed to keep up with our guests. I can't blame Mr. Hostetter. I mean, I'd be panicked, too. Hell, I *am* panicked. Nothing like this has ever happened before!"

"What's your best guess, Tessa? When I saw that woman in Shirley's clothes, it occurred to me that Shirley might have made some kind of trade. After all, they were really nice clothes. Perhaps she's wearing the woman's clothes and figures she'll be able to find out more if she can blend in."

"I don't think either of them has been kidnapped. I know Italian kidnappings have got a lot of bad international press, but trust me, it just doesn't happen to ordinary tourists. Only the very rich. The Hostetters aren't rich, are they?"

"I never met them before this trip," I said, "but Shirley did say she saved up for it. She was anxious to have this time with Crystal in a new place, just mother and daughter, and Shirley works as a nurse. No, I'd say they aren't rich. The rich don't have to save up for a trip."

"Exactly." Tessa's phone beeped. She looked at the message screen. "Damn. That lazy Cesare is paging me…too lazy to walk out here." She took my arm, and we strolled toward the door. "Oh, something else, Dotsy. I have a favor to ask."

"Yes?"

"Wilma Kelly mentioned to me that she thought it would be nice to have a little memorial service for Meg. Something small and simple, you know. I agree. It seems to me that before we go on with our tour, we should have something, I don't know, it just seems appropriate. What do you think?"

"Well, yes." I could feel an assignment coming on.

"The problem is, several in our group didn't really feel all that kindly toward Meg. I'm afraid she left behind a lot of raw nerves and injured feelings. I'm the most logical person to organize it, of course, but Dotsy, you have no idea. I've got more than I can handle right now. I'll be on the phone all night, I'm sure, with the home office, with Shirley's husband, with Meg's brother back home. I'm rooming with Amy, trying to help her get through this, I'm worried about Beth, I'm in the middle of wedding plans and I'm trying very hard not to get fired. I can't organize a memorial service. Could you do it, please?"

Tessa had me firmly by the elbow. I wasn't getting back inside until I made a decision, but this was supposed to be my vacation, damn it. Organizing a memorial service was the sort of thing I did at home. "Well, I didn't really know her," I said. "I met her at the start of this trip."

"So you didn't dislike her. That's why I'm asking you. That, plus the fact that Beth told me you are a super organizer." She gave me an almost comically pathetic look. "I know a church in Florence, an English church, the vicar is from England, and they would probably let us have it there. I'll give him a call tomorrow if you'll go talk to him and take care of it."

"Okay," I said. I have trouble with the word "no."

My coffee was cold when I returned to my chair, and the waiter caught my grimace as I took a sip. Without a word, he brought me a fresh, hot cup. Cesare, his chair pushed back and his legs stretched out, affected a posture of extreme nonchalance and, it seemed to me, an awareness that Amy's date, Gianni, was copying him, right down to the casually crossed ankles. Paul Vogel, elbows on knees, scanned the circle, his eyes pausing for a microsecond on each face. Wilma Kelly kept her feet tucked under her chair, and I wondered if it was because she had compared her own worn canvas shoes with Tessa's and Amy's designer jobs.

"One way or another, Achille will drive us to Pisa on Tuesday morning," Tessa said. "I still don't know if we'll stay there overnight, or drive back here, but we'll definitely see the Leaning Tower either way."

Cesare spoke up, in heavily accented English. "And another thing. I have an invitation to…to offer to you. On Wednesday evening, my town is having a festival…a march…"

"Parade," Tessa corrected him.

"Yes. And I am have…I will have a party before. I would like to invite all of you." He swept his upturned hand, an inclusive gesture, around the circle.

"*Lasiarme loro dice,*" Tessa murmured to him and took over. "Cesare's home town, he's on the town council, has a festival every year on this date. It's a medieval sort of thing with costumes, a parade, and banners—very colorful and fun. Anyway, we can't be positive where we'll all be on Wednesday evening at this point, but if we're in Florence, Achille can take us there. It's about a thirty minute drive, and Cesare would like us all to come to the party he's hosting at the town hall. We're supposed to be in Siena on Wednesday, but whether we spend the night there or in Florence, it's not a long drive from either place."

"Do we have to wear costumes?" Wilma asked.

"No, only the parade people, the marchers, will be in costume. You can wear whatever you want."

TWELVE

BACK AT THE HOTEL, Lettie stopped by Beth's room, and I knocked on Shirley and Crystal's door but got no response. Lettie managed to get a call through to Ollie from a public phone in the lobby by using a phone card.

"I was a fool for even mentioning Meg and Crystal and Shirley to Ollie. Now he'll do nothing but worry 'til I get home," Lettie fretted, kicking her shoes into a corner.

"Did Ollie know Meg?"

"No. He's met Beth once or twice, but not Meg."

"If I were you, I'd call him every night for the next few, just to relieve his mind."

"Good idea," Lettie said. "So what do you think about Victoria's story—about Meg and Shirley and those poor patients? Is it possible that Shirley came on this trip just to get Meg?"

"And then Crystal disappears because...?"

"Huh?"

I slathered a big dollop of cream across my face. "Do you have a theory that explains why a mother would bring a kid on a trip on which she plans to commit a murder? And why the kid then promptly disappears?"

"Well, no."

"I'd say we can scratch Shirley off our list of suspects...if we ever did suspect her."

"Scratch her *off?*"

"Sure. If she had had any idea of killing Meg, why would she have handed Victoria her motive, on a silver platter?"

IT'S ODD HOW WE GO on vacation to get out of the rut we're in and immediately start forming new ruts. Lettie and I walked straight to the patio for breakfast, took the same table we'd had yesterday, and ordered the same things with one exception: I added a large fruit cup to my order, because I had noticed one on my way in and thought it looked delicious. We each sat in the same chair as yesterday.

"I'll go to Tessa's room after I eat and see if she's called that vicar yet. I guess today would be a good time to catch him at the church, right after morning services."

"Do you need me to go with you?" Lettie asked.

I shook my head.

"I sort of told Beth I'd do something with her this morning," Lettie continued. "I think she wanted to go to services at the Duomo, but I'm so worried you'll have another one of your spells like you had yesterday. Don't you want me to go with you?"

"No. In fact, I think I'll see if Amy can go with me. I want to get to know her a little better." I buttered a croissant. "I've been thinking about motives. Paul Vogel is obviously interested in Jim Kelly and Geoffrey Reese-Burton—at least he was yesterday. Why do you suppose that is? Does either of them have a motive?"

"Not that I know of, and you say we can forget about Shirley because she blabbed her motive to Victoria."

"Well, don't you agree that she would hardly have mentioned it, if she had any thought of committing murder?"

"I suppose so. Beth had a motive. The way Meg belittled and embarrassed her all the time could be construed as a motive, don't you think? Especially over time. Living with her. The resentment would build up and build up…" Lettie bit her lip. "But Beth couldn't kill a fly. I'm serious. I've seen her pick up crickets in a napkin and carry them outside."

"Sorry, Lettie, but there's no connection. Crickets are innocent creatures. You can't hate a cricket. Meg was a human who knew what she was doing, knew when she was hurting her sister, and did it deliberately. That's evil. Crickets don't know about good and evil."

"Okay, what about Amy?"

"Motive? None that I know of. Of course, we all did hear her say, 'I hate you, Meg,' when we were boarding the vaporetto in Venice. But that was more in sympathy for poor Beth than for herself. How about Lucille Vogel?"

"Lucille? I don't think they even know…knew each other," Lettie said. "I don't recall ever seeing them together, so what possible motive could she have?"

"Money. If she really is a drug addict, she needs money to support her habit, doesn't she?"

"And she looked like she had money yesterday, didn't she? Lucille might have plenty of her own, though. We have no reason to think she needs to steal."

A city bus roared by on the other side of the hedge that separated us from the street, interrupting conversation and leaving a trail of foul air in its wake. "I told you the main reason I thought that Ivo, the Gypsy man, couldn't have killed Meg— other than the fact that an experienced thief would have better ways of dealing with the situation—was because he wouldn't have known about the knife. Unless it was lying out in plain view, he wouldn't have known about it. Yesterday, Marco said Beth told him she'd put the knife in a dresser drawer."

"Ivo might have been going through the drawer when Meg walked in on him."

"That's possible." I thought about it. Yes, that was possible. "But Lucille *did* know about the knife. Think about it, Lettie. A drug addict, desperate for a fix, notices Meg has a lot of cash in her wallet, knows Meg's sister has just bought a knife that could be hocked or fenced for a decent chunk of change, and knows what room they're staying in."

Lettie nodded, finished her coffee, and headed upstairs to find Beth.

I was on my way to Tessa and Amy's room when, passing through the lobby, I came to a screeching halt. The sign on a little booth advertised the rental of cell phones, pagers, fax machines, printers and various electronic gizmos. I hadn't brought a cell phone with me because I had assumed it wouldn't work in Italy, and I had never used a pager in my life, but here was a possible solution to Lettie's anxiety about me and my diabetes.

It wasn't that easy. The boy who waited on me spoke no English, and his attempts to show me how the pagers worked made no sense at all. I could see, however, that they had little screens and could display either numbers or letters, so I rented two of them for a week and trusted that Tessa could help me. If it turned out that they weren't what I needed, I could bring them back.

Tessa sat with me on the bed and showed me how the two-way pagers worked. Amy was barely awake, her eyes still puffy from sleep, and her voice gravelly. Tessa, her head turbaned in a shampoo-scented towel, punched a message into one device and sent it to me, two feet away.

"Boboli Gardens," I read. "So that would tell me where you are, but not what you want me to do about it."

"Right. If I want to talk to you, I get a phone number from somewhere, maybe a phone booth or the bartender's phone, and just send you the number…like so." Tessa looked at the phone on the nightstand between the two beds. She punched in that number and sent it to me.

"Let me try one." I punched in ROOM 238 and sent it. It was easy. "Have you called that vicar yet? The one you told me about last night?"

Tessa checked her watch and dragged a phone book from under the nightstand. "It's not too early to call on a Sunday, I'm sure, but I bet he's already doing a service. I probably should have called earlier."

While Tessa waited for an answer, I explained everything to

Amy. She seemed too fog-brained to process more than the basics, but I had the idea Tessa had mentioned the possibility of a memorial service to her already. She didn't look surprised.

"If the vicar can see me, would you go with me?" I asked.

"I don't know anything about stuff like that," Amy said.

"But you know what Meg liked and didn't like, I don't even know if she belonged to a church, or had any particular beliefs we should be sensitive to, or—"

"Meg belonged to the church of Meg!" Amy diverted her gaze to the window. "Sorry, I shouldn't have said that. Our parents took us to the Episcopal Church when we were little. I don't believe Meg attended any church regularly since she grew up...not that I know of. So if this is an Anglican Church or Church of England, that will be fine."

Amy pulled a bra and panties from a red suitcase. I debated whether I should repeat my request for her to go with me as she padded, barefoot, to a closet and dragged out a yellow shirt.

"Yeah, okay," she said. "I'll go with you. But I have a date tonight, so I don't want to be gone too long."

AMY NEEDED A FEW MINUTES to dress, so I headed down to my own room. Something made me look out the northwest-facing window in the stairwell. A bedraggled woman pulled herself, hobbling, to the Fountain of the Bloody Knife. Her dirty, flowered skirt was half covered by an equally grimy blue-flowered shirt, and her blonde hair hung in wet strings. She was barefoot. She fell onto the low ledge that surrounded the pool and leaned over, dipping her hands into the water. As she lowered her head to splash it, I saw the bottoms of her feet. They were bleeding and as raw as fresh hamburger. After splashing several handfuls of water into her face, she turned toward the hotel, but I already knew it was Shirley Hostetter.

I dashed down the stairs and out the side door. I glimpsed a few people milling around near her who were apparently afraid to approach her. Shirley appeared dazed, and caution told me not to rush up to her since I might startle her. I simply sat beside her on the edge of the fountain and said, "Shirley?"

She looked at me and smiled, tears beginning to roll.

"I'll get you to your room, Shirley. Sit here a minute while I run in and get some help."

"No. I don't need help. Just let me lean on you. I can walk."

"Your feet, Shirley. Your poor feet. Will you at least wait a minute while I run in and get a pair of slippers for you?" I had the feeling she didn't want to deal with anyone else and would have preferred for me not to have seen her, either, but it was too late for that.

"I've been looking for Crystal," she whispered, "but I couldn't find her."

I was relieved to find the side door into the stairwell could be opened from the outside. I guessed they locked it in the evenings, so after dark it could be used only as an exit, because I had tried it last night after we got off the bus and had found it locked. I dashed down the hall to my room. My own slippers had backs and would not have fit Shirley, I figured, since she's several inches taller than I am. Lettie had brought slip-ins, so I thanked her in her absence for her kind donation and took them out to the fountain.

Shirley refused to go down the hall to the elevator, insisting that we take the stairs—up two floors, four flights of stairs. She put most of her weight on me and the banister, but uttered not a whimper the whole way up. I imagined she wouldn't allow herself that luxury, lest I remind her I had recommended the elevator.

"Do you have your room card?" I asked.

"No, I lost it."

As I was planning how I would need to drop Shirley in the hall, prop her up against the wall and run down to the lobby for help with opening the door, she added, "We put Crystal's card on the ledge above the door because we knew she'd lock herself out, otherwise."

Above each door on the hall was a narrow transom window and a deep ledge. I couldn't reach that high, but by backing up and jumping a few times, I saw the card. I used a sheet of newspaper, rolled lengthwise to coax it off the ledge, then attempted to return the front page of *La Nazione* to an acceptable state of neatness for the occupant of room 357.

I helped Shirley onto a bed and worked on her feet with a wet towel while I convinced her to let me call room service for some breakfast. She lay heavily, like one completely defeated, and tried half-heartedly to cry. Faint traces of mascara and tears still streaked her face, which had faded to the color of bread dough. As we waited for room service to come, Shirley began to talk.

"I went to a Gypsy camp. I found out where the largest one was. There are three big ones outside of town, and I exchanged clothes with this woman I found at the train station. I knew I'd stand out like a sore thumb with my own clothes, and my hair.

"The conditions they live in are horrible…you can't imagine. This camp, there must have been five hundred people there, is just lean-tos. People living in plywood…corrugated tin…cardboard."

Shirley seemed about to doze off, so I prodded her with, "How did you manage to communicate?"

"I didn't. I walked all around the place several times until I had seen everything I could see without walking into someone's…home. Then it got dark, and the music started. The men played guitars and…things. All the women danced around this huge bonfire, and I knew I'd be too conspicuous if I just stood there, but I couldn't possibly let myself go enough to dance unless I got a little drunk first. There was plenty of wine around, in big goatskins…gallon jugs. So I drank until I loosened up. I thought I was doing pretty good, too." Shirley raised one hand and soundlessly snapped her fingers. I saw the faintest hint of a grin on one side of her mouth.

"But I danced right out of my headscarf, and that was it. Game over. I ran out and kept running for about a mile or so, I think, until I looked back and there was no one behind me anymore."

"They actually chased you?"

"Oh, yes. I'm sure they thought I was a spy, a police informant. I tried to get away by walking fast, but there were about ten of them gaining on me, so I broke into a full run."

"It was your blonde hair that did it?" I asked.

"Some of them are blonde, too. I think it was the haircut. Sixty-dollar cuts and moisture-conditioned hair are not the norm in a place like that. Anyway, I walked along the road. I was thinking, all night long, that a bus would come along or a car would stop and pick me up. I knew, at least I thought I knew…at first…then I wasn't so sure, that I was heading in the right direction, back to Florence. But I didn't know how far it was, because I had taken a bus out there yesterday and hadn't paid attention to the distance. I walked all night. Not one bus. A few cars, but they just looked at me as they sped past. I guess I looked like a derelict. I suppose they were afraid to pick me up. Miles and miles and miles. I had flip-flops to begin with, but one of them broke, and I tried shifting the good one from one foot to the other. That made the bare foot hurt worse, so I finally chucked that flip-flop, too."

"You poor baby." I checked her feet again. A doctor needed to take a look at them, but for now I thought it best to leave them open to the air.

"I did find one thing, though." Shirley pulled up her long, grubby over-blouse and fished a brochure-sized piece of plastic from her skirt pocket. In red and green letters, it said "Pellegrino Tours."

I had one just like it in my room, a little folder given to each of us by Tessa to keep tickets and such handy.

"Crystal must have been there," Shirley said.

There was a knock on the door. "That'll be your breakfast," I said.

"Mom? Open up."

THIRTEEN

THE VOICE CAME FROM the other side of the door. Shirley scrambled across the bed and fell against the wall in her haste to get the door open. Shaking with excitement, she pulled her daughter inside. Crystal looked prettier than I would have thought possible. She was really a cute young girl. The harsh makeup was gone, and it seemed to me that a few pieces of facial hardware were gone as well. Her hair had faded from magenta to pink and was pulled back into a ponytail. As Shirley smothered her in kisses, Crystal, a bit self-consciously, hugged her mother back.

She was starved. Shirley gave her the breakfast when it arrived and immediately called in an order for two more of everything. Crystal dribbled juice down her chin in a vain attempt to add a half glass of liquid to a mouth already full of bread. She had freckles. Now that the death-warmed-over makeup was gone, I could see her Irish red-head's complexion—green eyes, chubby cheeks and freckled nose. Shirley pulled up another chair to the table and simply stared at her daughter. I felt I intruded on what ought to be a private moment.

"I'd better be getting on," I said. "Amy Bauer and I are going to this church on the other side of the river to talk to the vicar about a memorial service for Meg."

"Oh! Don't go, Ms....I forgot your name." Crystal spun around and held out one hand.

"Call me Dotsy."

"Okay. That's a cute name. Anyway, don't go yet. I've got some important news."

I saw Shirley's stomach tighten as she caught her breath, and I knew what she was thinking. *Important news? It can't be good.*

"Could you first tell us where you've been since night before last?" Shirley asked, her hands clamped rigidly together in her lap.

"In a Gypsy camp…a couple of Gypsy camps, actually. Now, don't have a hissy fit, Mom, but I was talking to this guy, Chiriklo's his name, outside the hotel the other night and he asked me if I wanted to hang with him and his friends for awhile and I said okay…" Crystal paused.

Shirley opened her mouth and then shut it.

"Anyway," Crystal continued, "he's real hard to talk to because he doesn't really speak Italian. He speaks what they call Romanes—and a little Italian."

Shirley turned to me. "Crystal speaks quite good Italian. She learned it from an exchange student we had and from taking it in school."

"I learned diddly in school. Dafne taught me all the Italian I know," Crystal fired back, and Shirley didn't argue with her. "Anyway, this guy Chiriklo took me to this huge Gypsy camp outside of town, and we just hung out with these other kids. It got real late and I told him I had to get back to town. He asked all around, but nobody had a car or anything, and so we had to stay there all night.

"Chiriklo has a sister who lives in that camp, he and his Mom and a bunch of brothers and sisters live in this other camp, and she let me stay with her. Chiriklo stayed with some of his friends."

Shirley breathed an audible sigh of relief.

"So, here's the big news. You know that guy they arrested for killing Miss Bauer? He's a Gypsy, too. His name is Ivo, and he lives in the same camp as Chiriklo. Anyhow, we finally caught a ride yesterday, but it was to this other camp. I thought he was taking us back here, but no such luck. We saw Ivo's wife, and she didn't know anything about him being arrested for murder.

Isn't that wild? Nobody bothered to call and tell her...well, actually, I guess they couldn't. They don't have a lot of phones in these camps.

"So Mrs. Ivo grabs up a couple of kids and runs off to find someone to give her a ride into town. That left Chiriklo and me at Ivo's trailer with a couple of other kids Mrs. Ivo forgot to take with her, and we couldn't just leave them alone, so we hung out there for a while."

The second round of breakfasts arrived, and Shirley set out the plates, this time taking some for herself. I wished I could prod Crystal to get on with her story. I looked at my watch, but Crystal was absorbed in the buttering of a fresh roll.

Shirley said, "It was nice of you to help with the little ones. I guess Mrs. Ivo just wasn't thinking clearly...understandably."

"Yeah. Well, while we were waiting, I picked up Ivo's guitar and tried to play it, and it went like, bluungghh!" Crystal plunked an air guitar and made a sour face. "So I tried it again, and it went bluungghh. It was strung backwards. So I said to Chiriklo, 'Is Ivo left-handed?' and he said, 'No, Ivo's hand is...' and this part took a while because like I said, Chiriklo doesn't speak good Italian." Crystal paused for a breath. Her green eyes sparkled. "Ivo's right hand doesn't work! These two fingers, Mom..." She held up the index and middle fingers of her right hand. "These two fingers, are stiff. He can't use them. Some kind of accident, I guess. But Chiriklo explained that somehow he can still use his right hand for the fretwork on the guitar, but the strumming and picking he has to do with his left hand. You see what this means, don't you?"

As Crystal said it, I recalled what Marco Quattrocchi had told me the day before. "The murderer was right-handed," I said. The Captain told his assistant that when I gave him the knife. Remember?"

Shirley shook her head.

"No, I guess not," I said. "They were speaking in Italian so you wouldn't have caught it, but I did."

"I can see how it would make it less likely that he would have used his right hand, but not impossible," Shirley said.

"Bit it is impossible. We tried it. Here, you try it." Crystal passed her butter knife to me and nodded toward the one on her mother's plate.

With the knife in my right hand, I held my index and middle fingers out straight. I tried it several times, and discovered that Crystal was right. Without those two fingers, all control of the knife was lost and there was no strength in the grip.

"You've got to go to Captain Quattrocchi's office immediately," I said. "I can go with you."

Shirley glanced at Crystal, then turned her gaze on me. "No, that's all right, Dotsy. You have another mission to accomplish. Crystal and I can find our way over."

Looking at her bare, swelling feet, she added, "We'll take a cab."

AMY AND I HURRIED to get to the church before the second morning service ended. Following Tessa's directions, we dashed across the Ponte Vecchio, an ancient bridge lined with jewelry shops, all closed on Sunday. We passed the imposing Pitti Palace, residence of the Pitti family and, later, the Medici family. "The Boboli Gardens behind the palace are supposed to be wonderful for strolling," I said, pausing for breath.

"Maybe Gianni and I could go there tomorrow," Amy mused out loud.

I had already gathered that Amy was totally smitten with Gianni. Since we'd left the hotel, she had yet to utter a single sentence that didn't have his name in it. Gianni was picking her up tonight at seven, but she was already obsessing over what to wear.

"Gianni does some modeling for a shirt designer, occasionally," she said. That's not his full-time job, of course, but it means he knows fashion. He knows quality, too. I think Italians in general have a good eye for quality, don't you?"

"Maybe." As I picked up speed again, I attempted to change the subject. "Elizabeth Barrett Browning's home is supposed to be near here. I wonder if we could find it."

"I wouldn't want to just drop in on her, though, would you? Not on a Sunday morning."

Amy seemed relieved when I assured her I wouldn't dream of interrupting the Brownings' day of rest.

We found the church and read the message board—it was in English—then wandered around the churchyard to kill time until the late service ended. A stray acolyte advised us that the man we needed to talk to was the Chaplain, Father Quick, and that he should be out shortly. Father Quick, however, was anything but. When we were sure the congregation was all gone, we looked into the nave.

"Could he have got away?" I asked Amy. Then a tall, stooped man in a clerical collar emerged from a side room. "Excuse me," I said. "Might you be Father Quick?"

Father Quick moved, spoke and reacted to my questions like a turtle in cold molasses. He studied my face, his head tilted a little, as I described our situation, and responded with such a long silence, I was afraid I had asked him for the impossible.

Finally, he said, "Yes, of course. When we have a small group such as you have described…" His voice trailed off, as if he had lost his train of thought.

"We'll have about fifteen people, I guess."

"We like to recommend one of the small chapels…just over…follow me, please. Yes."

He shuffled across to a charming little chapel off to one side of the nave. There was an altar, a lovely oil painting of the Madonna and Child, and several rows of seats. It seemed to me that the church had perhaps four of these little chapels, maybe two on each side.

"If you'll come with me to the parish house," Father Quick said, "I can check the book, but we almost never have all the chapels in use at the same time."

"If this one is available tomorrow, it would be lovely," I said and turned to Amy who nodded her assent.

"What about music?" Father Quick asked.

"I supposed, on such short notice, that we wouldn't be able to arrange for music."

"One of our organists—I'll get you her number—is sometimes available to play. For a small fee."

It seemed to take forever, but we booked the little chapel for ten o'clock the following morning and left with the phone number of the sometimes-available organist.

Amy and I paused in the center of the Ponte Vecchio on our way back to the hotel. In the middle, there was a wide gap in the row of little shops that lined both sides of the bridge, affording a wonderful view downstream of the Arno as it flowed lazily westward. We sidled over to the railing where a nice breeze funneled through, cooling my neck and scalp. Amy trapped a passerby and asked him to take our picture with the river in the background.

"How is Beth doing?" I asked when the accommodating stranger ran out of ways to prolong his meeting with Amy and walked on.

"All right, I guess. She's been kind of clammed up about Meg. At least around me, she has. It's great that she has Lettie here with her, though. I think she'll talk to Lettie. She should talk to someone."

"Are you and Beth close? Sorry, that sounds nosy; but I've just been wondering about you three sisters…and you also have a brother, don't you?"

Amy squinted as she gazed down at the water flowing under us. "We were so spread out in ages, you know. When I was born, Meg was already grown, Beth was starting high school, and Joe was nine. Beth babysat me, and I looked up to her like a…well, she used to show me how to put on makeup…let me try on her clothes. But Meg was out of the house and in nurse's training when I was born. I've always thought of her more like an aunt than a sister."

"And Joe? How did he handle being surrounded by sisters?"

"He paid very little attention to any of us. He had his own friends on the soccer team, baseball team, Boy Scouts...stuff like that."

"I've been wondering how Beth will fare financially, now. Lettie told me she was left destitute by that rat of a husband who walked out on her."

"Oh, right." Amy turned and by some tacit agreement, we resumed our stroll northward into the center of Florence. "What a rat he was. I think she'll be okay, now. I talked to Joe last night, and he says Meg left a will. He'll be contacting her lawyer in the next few days, but he thinks she left everything to the three of us, equally. Joe's been worried about Beth, and he doesn't need any more money than he's already got, so he said he'd pass on Meg's money. Beth and I could split it. All Joe wants is a small piece of property Meg had on a lake. It's not too far from where he lives, and there's a small cabin on it. He wants to fix it up as a weekend getaway place."

"Meg's money? Did she have a lot? I mean...I do sound nosy, don't I? But somehow I just assumed, being a nurse and all..." I was shocked at my own brazenness, but this sounded like Meg had left a tidy sum—enough that a piece of lakefront property would be a minor consideration. Perhaps she had come into a bundle via a divorce settlement. "Was Meg ever married?"

"No! What man in his right mind..." Amy left the rest of that sentence unfinished. "Our parents weren't wealthy, but we were comfortable. Dad was a building contractor. Mama was totally naïve about money matters. When Dad died, he left everything to her, and that was the house, of course, and some bonds, some CDs and a nice life insurance policy. So Mama was financially okay, and then Meg came back home to live with her. Beth, Joe and I were glad of that, because what could be better, in her declining years, than to have a nurse living with her? But then Mama died only two or three years later, herself."

"And left everything to Meg?"

"No, not really. That was a funny thing, you know."

Amy and I turned left and took the wide street that led westward along the river. Amy collided with a middle-aged man, apologized, and patted his jacket. The man showed every sign of being delighted to have collided with Amy.

"In Mama's will," she continued, "Mama left all her money— her liquid assets—to Beth, Joe and me. She left Meg no money, but all the real estate. All what real estate, you ask? Well, it seems that over the last few years, Meg gradually insisted Mama invest in more and more land and other property in our part of Baltimore. It was a smart investment because it was all in a part of town where prices were going up fast.

"But with the will made out like it was, that meant that Meg got everything. At the time she talked Mama into making her will like that, it would have meant that Beth, Joe and I would have inherited a lot more than she would have. So Mama probably thought Meg was being a martyr by taking only—well, at that time, it was only our house and a quarter-acre lot. But by the time Mama died, there was no more money. It was all in real estate."

"How awful. I really can't imagine Meg didn't plan it that way from the beginning. Can you?"

"Sure she planned it. She sold off most of that property and made a tidy profit. It wasn't poor Mama's fault. She didn't know enough about finances to realize what Meg was doing. Plus, Meg *was* giving her good advice, and Mama did increase her net worth by following it."

Ahead of us lay a piazza with several streets dead-ending into it. One of those streets, I recognized as the one I had walked along the day before with Marco Quattrocchi. In fact, the little trattoria we had eaten at was just a couple of short blocks to the right and the caserma was straight ahead along the street called Borgo Ognissanti. Several taxis sat idle around the edges of the piazza. A woman on crutches swung unsteadily toward one of them while her companion, a young girl with pink hair, rushed ahead to engage the driver.

"It's the Hostetters," Amy said. "Why is Shirley on crutches?"

"I told you about her feet, didn't I? She must have seen a doctor and he gave her the crutches."

"You said her feet were raw, but I didn't take that literally! Ohmigod, the poor woman."

Crystal spotted us as she held the taxi door open for her mother. She held up one finger to the driver, who reacted by slapping his forehead. Crystal dashed toward Amy and me.

"I can't friggin' believe it!" She raised her hands to the skies. "They're not releasing the poor guy."

I turned Crystal around and pointed her toward the taxi. Amy and I walked over with her, talking rapidly in deference to the steam that seemed to come from the driver's ears. "Did you tell the Captain?" I asked. "Are you sure he understood you?"

"He isn't in today. I told the others…several others. They called the Captain at home, but they wouldn't let me talk to him. They said he told them to do nothing until he got there, and I have no idea when that'll be."

"Actually, I'm not surprised. He'll want to talk to you, I'm sure, personally, before he releases the man."

"But poor Ivo is just sitting in jail, not knowing what's going on. And his poor wife, wherever she is…I guess she took the kids back to the camp. I need to get back out there." Crystal grabbed my arm and bounced with her knees the way kids do when they're begging for something or when they have to go to the bathroom.

"No. You need to stay at the hotel where Captain Quattrocchi can find you." I cringed at the thought of Shirley losing her child again. "If he doesn't call in the next hour, you should find Tessa and explain. She'll know what you should do."

"Tessa's out, I think," Amy said.

"Well then, go to the front desk, Crystal, and ask them what to do. But stay at the hotel, okay?"

The taxi driver hit the steering wheel and let fly a sentence that even attracted Crystal's attention. "Okay," she said as she crawled in beside her mother.

Amy followed me down a little street to the trattoria where I'd had lunch with Marco Quattrocchi yesterday. It was closed, but just ahead in the next block we spotted a self-serve pizzeria that was open. I felt like I needed to eat something. Amy and I took our food to the only unoccupied table in the place.

"Does this—what Crystal found out—mean that Gypsy they arrested definitely didn't kill Meg?" Amy asked.

"Oh, I never did think he did it."

Amy gasped. "Why not?"

"Because if he had any thought of killing somebody, rather than stealing stuff, he would have brought a weapon with him. To have just lucked onto Beth's knife was too much coincidence. No, I thought from the beginning they had the wrong person."

"You think it might have been someone in our group?"

"That's the most likely possibility, isn't it?" Over the top of my water glass, I watched Amy's face closely.

"Do you have any ideas?" she asked.

"Do you?"

"No, of course not." Her gaze darted toward the wall; she was not a good liar. After a long pause she said, "The only person I've had any doubts at all about is Tessa's fiancé, Cesare."

"How so?"

"Oh, nothing definite. It's just that he has a lot of money for a guy who only works on his father's farm and serves on the local city council. I don't know what the council position pays; it wouldn't be much, if anything." Amy pulled something out of her *panini* and scowled at it.

"I've noticed he wears expensive clothes."

"Very expensive," Amy said. "So I've wondered where he gets all that money. He drives a Ferrari and takes Tessa out to expensive restaurants all the time. You know what I mean?"

"Yes, I do. But when it comes to who killed Meg, would Cesare have a reason? Did he ever meet Meg?"

Amy pulled another offending item out of her panini. "He met

Meg in Venice that night when he and Gianni came to pick us up, our first date…" She paused, as if savoring the memory. "But that was no more than a 'hi-nice-to-meet-you.'"

"Who else knew Meg? I mean, before we came over here."

"She and Shirley Hostetter knew each other as nurses. I think they were at the same hospital at one time. I don't know that she'd ever met Crystal." Amy frowned thoughtfully. "She knew your friend Lettie, slightly, through Beth. That's about it. Nobody else knew her that I'm aware of. Tessa, of course, heard me talk about her when we were in college together, but I don't think they ever met. I went to Tessa's home a couple of times during semester breaks, but I don't think Tessa ever came to my house."

"The whole thing makes no sense," I said.

"I could probably find you a thousand people who didn't like Meg, but there's a big difference between don't like and murder."

"Exactly." I had to go back to the counter to get another glass of water, as there was no table service. "Amy," I asked, when I returned, "do you know whether Meg had much money with her—I mean, cash—when she was killed?"

"I went to the bank with her as soon as we got here, the afternoon we flew in. She got a thousand dollars worth of euros. She should have had most of that, I think, because she hadn't bought anything much."

Amy reached under her chair for her purse. "Oh! You were asking about what our family was like when we were growing up." She pulled out her wallet and riffled through a half dozen photos. "I brought this along to show Meg and Beth. I found it in a bunch of old letters a week or so ago." Her voice softened as she added, "I never showed it to Meg."

It was a snapshot of the Bauer family at Christmas. They all stood in front of the wreath-trimmed front door of a brick house. Amy, the shortest, stood in front of the others. She was pretty even in the middle of that awkward, pre-teen growth spurt. Joe looked about sixteen and embarrassed. Obviously, he didn't want to stand on the front porch with his family. Beth was a young woman, bright-eyed and lively. A scowling Meg, bundled in a sleek white fur coat and matching hat, looked like a constipated polar bear. Their father, bald and mustached, looked as sturdy as his wife looked frail. Father and mother stood close together—a strong oak and a clinging vine.

I looked at Amy. "Nineteen eighty, I'd say, based on the cut of the jeans."

"Wow, you're good." She tucked the photo back in her wallet.

"Amy, the first day we were here, when you and Tessa picked up Lettie and me at the airport, Tessa called you by another name…a Spanish name, I think it was."

"A Spanish name?" She seemed momentarily at a loss. "Oh, Perez?"

I nodded.

"That's because when I knew Tessa to begin with, when we were in college, I was Amy Perez. When I graduated from high school, I made a stupid mistake. I was even dumber then than I am now, and that's not easy. I married this boy I was going with. I was afraid if I went off to college, he'd forget about me. So, instead of college, I spent my first year out of high school playing house with this kid who was no more ready for marriage than I was.

"He wasn't a bad guy, really, but…" Amy shivered. "So when I met Tessa, I was still going by Amy Perez. I took my maiden name back after college."

"There were no children?" I asked.

Amy realigned her cutlery before answering, "No."

WE PASSED A SHOE STORE on our way back to the Hotel Fontana and Amy yanked me to a halt. "This is the shop where Tessa ordered our bridesmaids' shoes. I wish I could show them to you, but they're on order. They probably won't be in for another few weeks, but they're a gorgeous green with tiny straps."

"You're in Tessa's wedding? I didn't know that."

"Yes. In August. How about that, huh? Two trips to Italy in one year."

"I didn't realize you and Tessa were that close," I said. "You haven't seen each other since—"

"One of her other bridesmaids dropped out a couple of days ago. I kind of invited myself to be the replacement."

And, incidentally, give yourself an excuse to see Gianni again.

Something needled me all the way back to the hotel. It hit me as I punched the elevator button. *If the bridesmaids' shoes are on order, what were those green shoes Tessa showed Lettie yesterday morning?*

FOURTEEN

"AMY, YOU CAME TO the parking lot Friday evening with Tessa. Did you run into her downtown, or what?"

Engrossed in watching the elevator lights progress upward, she took a few seconds to answer. "I ran into Tessa down near the Duomo, and we visited that little shoe store I just showed you. She was ordering the bridesmaids' shoes, or checking on the order, or something."

"But that must have been after five o'clock. Weren't you planning to go up to the Piazza Michelangelo with us? We were supposed to have left the hotel at five."

"But Tessa changed it to six. Didn't you get the message?"

"Yes. After I got back to the hotel, Lettie told me. But how did you know? Tessa didn't tell anyone about the time change until four-thirty or so, and if you were downtown…"

"Oh, I see what you mean." The elevator opened onto the third floor hallway and Amy stepped out. I followed her. She stopped to fumble through her bag for her room card. "I wasn't planning to go up to that piazza with the group, anyway. I was supposed to meet Gianni for dinner. I was going to stay here and wash my hair."

"I see. So you and Tessa visited the shoe store together and then came straight back here?"

"Sort of. She talked to the store manager for a few minutes, and then we stopped at an ATM machine because Tessa had to get some cash. Then we came back here." Amy inserted her card in the door slot. "Want to come in?"

"If Tessa's still here, I'd like to tell her about our plans for tomorrow," I said, but Tessa wasn't there. I took the opportunity to get another look out their window. The Fountain of the Bloody Knife looked so close from this angle, I almost felt I could jump out the window and land in it. Seeing the fountain reminded me of Shirley and her poor feet. "I think I'll drop by and check on Shirley," I said on my way out.

I took the stairs down one floor. Shirley and Crystal's room on the second floor was next door to Jim and Wilma Kelly. A half dozen or so doors down from them and on the same side of the hall was Dick and Michael's room and next to that was Walter and Elaine's. Beth's new room, the one they'd moved her into when the first one became a crime scene, was on the opposite side of the hall.

With the handle of the stairwell door still in my hand, I stopped. A man in a blue T-shirt and plaid shorts slipped out from a room near the other end of the hall. It was hard to see him because the light slanting in from the stairwell window on the far end of the hall made him appear dark, outlined fuzzily by the glare, but I was pretty sure it was Paul Vogel. He pulled a handkerchief from his shorts pocket and closed the door, giving the knob an extra swipe with the cloth. As he turned, thankfully toward the stairs on the far end of the hall, I allowed myself to exhale. If he had decided to take the elevator, he would have found me peeking around the door in a manner that couldn't possibly be construed as anything but furtive. Paul Vogel walked in a way that reminded me of the little pointy-nosed "Spy vs. Spy" characters from *Mad* magazine. I now had no doubt it was he.

As soon as he was safely gone, I slipped down the hall while keeping my gaze on the door he had emerged from. It was the third one from the end, number 366. I knocked; no answer. Assuming this was either Dick and Michael's room or Walter and Elaine's, I gingerly knocked on the door of number 368, aware that there was a fifty-fifty chance it belonged to someone I'd never seen before. I was relieved to get no answer again.

Pushing my luck, I backed up two doors and tried number 364.
Nothing.

So Paul Vogel was snooping around in the room of one half
of the Curious Quartet; definitely snooping, because he had
been in there alone. Was there any connection at all between the
Vogels and these folks? None, that I knew of. I'd have to ask
Lettie to clarify the room numbers for me—Lettie with her practically photographic memory.

No one was in Shirley and Crystal's room, so I walked to my
own room. Lettie was back from services at the Duomo and
bubbling over with details. I grabbed a box of orange juice,
kicked off my shoes, and tossed Lettie a pager. "My security
blanket," I announced. "We'll both carry one of these so we can
find each other if we need to."

"I don't know how to use this thing."

We practiced for a while, sending each other phone numbers
and short messages. We agreed that a phone number would
mean "Call this number" and a room number would mean "This
is where I am" and be preceded by the word "room."

"Okay, I'm sending you a number." I punched in my own
home phone number, for no particular reason, and sent it.

"Oh no, Dotsy! That's your home number. Do you know
how much that's going to cost?"

"Lettie, I'm not calling that number. I just sent it to you.
Across the room. I promise you my phone at home isn't ringing.
There's no one there to answer anyway."

Lettie blushed and lowered her head. "Are you going to tell
everyone I said that?"

"Only if there's a lull in the dinner conversation."

"Please don't," she begged.

"It's time to reevaluate our list, Lettie. This morning I've
learned about some more possible motives people might have
had for killing Meg." I quickly filled Lettie in on the return of
Shirley and of Crystal to the safety of the Fontana Hotel, my visit
with Amy to the English church, and our chance encounter with

the Hostetters. "Amy, Beth and Joe were all more or less screwed out of their inheritance by Meg's conniving. That's one thing. Now that Meg's dead, Amy and Beth will finally get what should have been theirs to begin with—that is, if Amy told me the truth. Also, Amy has noticed, as I already had, that Tessa's boyfriend tosses around more money than you'd expect from a small-time farmer."

"So maybe he's involved in some shady business. What would that have to do with Meg?"

"Good question. Maybe drugs? She's a nurse. Aren't there sometimes connections between hospital staff and black market drugs?"

"I don't know." Lettie stretched out on her bed and laced her hands across her chest.

"And Meg apparently had the better part of a thousand dollars in cash at the time of the murder."

"Really. Who has it now?"

"Ivo? Didn't they say he had a lot of money on him at the time of his arrest? They probably took it away from him when they arrested him."

"If not, then whoever killed her probably took the money," Lettie said.

"Here's what we need to do: forget motives. They're too confusing, and we're perpetually discovering motives we didn't know about before, so it stands to reason that there are yet more motives out there that we still don't know about."

"Okay."

"Let's go through the list again, and this time try to think exactly where each person was at about five-thirty. Marco—Captain Quattrocchi—says he has it narrowed down to a few minutes on either side of five-thirty. When we made the first list, we put down where we thought everyone was between four-thirty and a quarter to six."

I found my original list behind an ice bucket, grabbed a clean sheet of paper, and wrote:

Dotsy and Lettie—sitting in front of the elevator on the ground floor

Meg—in her room, getting murdered

Beth—entering, or about to enter, that same room, carrying a pot of flowers

Amy—downtown with Tessa

Tessa—downtown with Amy

Victoria and Geoffrey Reese-Burton—in hotel, having recently taken the elevator

Crystal—outside somewhere

Shirley—outside, looking for Crystal

Dick, Michael, Walter and Elaine—downtown and together (at least they all came to the parking lot from that direction and they were all together)

Paul—downtown (he came to the parking lot just behind the gruesome foursome)

Lucille—with us, trying to call the elevator down, shortly after Beth's call came in to the front desk, but neither Lettie nor I saw what direction Lucille had come from

Wilma—outside, but had stopped by Meg's room before going downstairs

Jim—in his and Wilma's room

Achille—in the parking lot, by the bus

Ivo—somewhere in the area, perhaps just entering or exiting the hotel

Cesare—?

Gianni (Amy's new love)—?

After much discussion, Lettie and I agreed we could mark eleven people off the list of suspects: ourselves, of course; Amy and Tessa, since they could vouch for each other's whereabouts; Crystal and Shirley, since they had their own little melodrama going; Dick, Michael, Walter and Elaine, since they were apparently all together (but maybe they weren't; we needed to check on that); and, of course, Ivo, since he was physically incapable of cutting a throat with his right hand.

We agreed that just because Paul Vogel had approached the group in the parking lot along with the gruesome foursome, it didn't mean he had been with them at 5:30—a good thirty minutes earlier. Lucille Vogel was not eliminated because we hadn't seen what direction she had come from, but I suggested it was highly unlikely she could have presented herself, smiling and completely free of blood spatters, only a few minutes after the murder.

"In fact, Lettie, that whole blood thing still bothers me. This would be a messy affair." I saw the grimace creep down from Lettie's forehead to her mouth and told her firmly, "Yes, messy."

She gulped. "If the person was standing behind Meg, wouldn't the blood have squirted out the other way? Toward the front?"

"I suppose so. But it would have virtually poured out. And blood is under pressure, you know, when it goes up your neck."

Lettie put her fingers against her own carotid artery and nodded weakly. "It would have gotten all over his or her hands."

"And I have a great feeling at least some of it would have gotten on the killer's clothes."

"So the killer had time to clean up."

"And the means of cleaning up. I doubt he or she would have hung around in that room to wash up. He or she would have run out immediately. That makes the people who were supposedly in their rooms, or who could have dashed into their rooms quickly, seem most likely."

"Not really," Lettie sat up. "If it was Cesare and he left the hotel unobserved, he had hours to clean up. Same goes for Gianni."

I couldn't decide if we had made progress or not. Things were still a bit of a muddle, but at least we had eliminated a few folks. "Lettie," I remembered at last to ask, "who's in room three sixty-six, across the hall from Beth's new room?"

"Walter Everard and Elaine King, the married couple you say aren't married, and Dick Kramer and Michael Melon are in room three sixty-eight, next door."

So now I had to find Paul Vogel and make him a proposition.

FIFTEEN

PAUL AND LUCILLE WERE both in their room down the hall from us. Lucille had a surprising offer; she wanted to sing at the memorial service tomorrow.

"That would be lovely, Lucille. Thanks," I said. "Do you have any particular song in mind?

"I like to do the 'Ave Maria,' but I'll ask Beth or Amy if that would be all right, or if they'd prefer something else."

"Excellent. But I don't know yet if we'll have an organist to accompany you. I have a phone number."

"Fine if you do, fine if you don't," she said, heading for the door. "I don't mind doing it a cappella, if the organist doesn't work out." With a toss of her little round head, she was gone.

"Who's your client, Paul?" I asked.

"I don't know what you're talking about."

"Who's paying you to spy on Walter and Elaine?"

"You've been watching too much TV."

I had to give him credit. Paul could stay calm under pressure. He turned to the window. Talking to the back of his head, I said, "When you told me the other morning that you were in security, photography, and location—or whatever euphemisms you used—I should have translated that as 'private detective,' right?"

Paul remained in the same position and volunteered nothing.

"I saw you come out of Walter and Elaine's room a few minutes ago," I continued. "If you weren't spying on them, why were you so careful to wipe your prints off the doorknob?"

"You didn't see me come out of Walter's room," he said, turning and facing me. "I've never been in Walter's room in my life."

"Room 366."

"Room 366 is Dick Kramer and Elaine King's room."

"Is that a fact?" I said, as if I dealt with this sort of stuff every day.

"You asked who my client was. It's Dick Kramer's wife. She knows he and Elaine have been having an affair for some time, but she wants proof to improve her position in the divorce she intends to file for."

"What a lovely job you have, Paul."

Ignoring my jab, he said, "Kramer's wife has all the money in the family. She set him up in the furniture business, and if she pulls her money out of it now, Kramer is S.O.L. This, Mrs. Kramer figures, is exactly what he deserves, but she needs to make sure he won't get enough in the divorce settlement to stay afloat.

"Walter and Michael are gay," Paul continued. "They stay in the room next door, regardless of what the hotel register says. In order to make his little holiday with Elaine appear to be a business trip with an employee, Dick offered to pay for both Walter's and Michael's trips. So Dick Kramer, or Dick Kramer's business, I don't know exactly what account he's using for this, is paying for all four trips."

"You said 'an employee.' Which one is his employee?"

"Walter. He's a graphic designer, and he works for Dick Kramer's company."

It was hard, I found, to rework my concepts of the curious quartet. This meant that I needed to go back over my talk with Dick Kramer in front of the slave sculptures at the Accademia yesterday. Should I simply fill in "Walter" in place of "Michael" in that conversation? The anguish I had seen on Dick's face—was it from struggling with his conscience? Or was it from being torn between two women? Or from being torn between his business and his true love? Perhaps he had been faking the whole thing, to divert my attention from the fact that Elaine King, not Michael Melon, was coming back from the rest room to rejoin him. I remembered, now, seeing Paul there, too. He had pretended to be engrossed in a masterpiece that was actually an air vent on the wall.

Why did I keep running into so many cheating husbands?

"Walter and Michael share an apartment in Washington," Paul said. "As far as I know, this is a free vacation for them. I really couldn't care less about those two."

"Have you gotten all the proof you need?" I didn't even try to keep the sarcasm out of my voice.

"I'm afraid I'm going to have to insist that you keep this just between us," Paul countered.

"*You* have to insist? The last time I checked, I was in the driver's seat. I believe I'm perfectly free to tell everything or tell nothing. Can you give me a good reason why I should keep my mouth shut? Or did you intend for me to interpret that word 'insist' as a threat?" I prayed that I sounded more intimidating than I felt.

"I could interpret *that* as a threat!"

I just stared at him with my jaw clamped tight.

"Or," Paul said, "did you intend it as blackmail?"

"I don't like the word blackmail. I meant to suggest that, if you could do something for me, we could be more like partners than adversaries." I sounded, even to myself, like a character in a B movie—that last line should have been delivered with my thumbs hooked under my suspenders.

"I'm listening," he said.

"You have contacts back home. It's part of your business. I want to find out everything about Meg Bauer's work history— lawsuits, threatened lawsuits, lawsuits settled by her hospital, reprimands, what's in her folder at work, and, especially, the name or names of anyone Meg has been accused of harming or killing, and the names of their next of kin. No, make that the names of everyone in their family. I want to know if Meg is straight with the IRS, and I want to know if she's removing more than a paycheck from her hospital…you know, drugs, that kind of thing."

"You think she was killed by someone who came here specifically for that purpose?"

"It's a thought," I said, and allowed myself a deep breath. Since my entire dissertation on what I wanted had been delivered with one lungful of air, I felt a little dizzy.

"I think you may be right." Paul jammed his fist into his plaid shorts pockets.

"Why were you asking Lettie and me questions about Jim Kelly and Geoffrey Reese-Burton the other morning? Do you suspect them, or are they having affairs with Elaine, too?"

Paul gave me a sidelong glance and the corner of his mouth quivered in what might have been a smile. "I think this murder must have been committed by a man. Quite a bit of strength would have been needed, you know. Meg Bauer was hardly what I'd call a delicate little flower."

"But a determined woman…" I began, then decided to let it go.

"I hate my job," Paul said. "Most of what I do is stuff like you saw this morning. All-night stakeouts in motel parking lots make you feel like a slime bag."

"I can imagine."

"So when I run across a real murder, the kind of thing I used to dream about doing, my radar starts beeping."

He wiggled his fingers in my face, and I thought about what Lettie had said about my antennae beeping. Were Paul and I alike? God forbid.

"So you want me to put my sources to work," he clarified, unnecessarily. "It'll probably take 'em a couple of days, but I'll see what I can do."

MARCO QUATTROCCHI WAS NOT a happy man; I could see that from the hand gesture he flung at the hotel manager, a thin young man who couldn't possibly bow or scrape more humbly than he was already doing. It was dinnertime when Lettie got the call that Quattrocchi wanted to see her in the conference room adjoining the lobby, a call we had been expecting all afternoon. I figured he'd need to interview us all again, in light of today's developments, so I had gone down with Lettie in the quickly-dashed hope that I might suggest he join us for dinner and interview both of us over our meal. Given the look on his face, I didn't care to cross him by suggesting anything. He looked as if he was ready to chew nails and spit horseshoes.

Fortunately, Victoria and Geoffrey Reese-Burton passed by just then and asked me to dine with them. I slipped over to the desk to tell Lettie where I'd be, but Marco had her by the arm, funneling her into the conference room, and I just pointed my finger in a roughly southeasterly direction, a gesture that meant nothing much, even to me. Victoria suggested a small restaurant she and Geoffrey had discovered earlier, and we left by the main lobby doors.

In the middle of the ever-revolving row of taxis in front of the hotel was a thoroughly banged-up blue Fiat, and Gianni Diletti sprawled casually behind the wheel. No doubt he was waiting for Amy.

Achille approached the car from the front and slammed his hand playfully on the Fiat's curbside fender. Gianni sat up as Achille made monkey faces through the windshield at him.

Beth was with Achille. She wore a blue sundress with a white shawl, so it looked to me as if they might be just leaving for a night on the town. As Achille and Gianni clasped hands and exchanged a few jibes, apparently humorous, in Italian, Beth smiled.

Victoria and I asked for another table in the little restaurant because the headwaiter first seated us in the middle of a noisy crowd. Since I normally had a hard time understanding Geoffrey, I knew that it would be impossible under these conditions. The headwaiter found us a table covered with red-and-white checked oilcloth behind a room divider topped with fake plants.

"I understand Crystal has returned bearing information that's got the Gypsy man released," Victoria said.

"The Gypsy man has a lame right hand, and the murder, according to the police, was done by a right-handed person." I told them all I knew about the adventures of Shirley and Crystal. "Have you heard for sure that he's been released?"

"Tessa says they let him go." Victoria realigned her cutlery, a mildly irritating quirk, especially since, most of the time, she only moved it a millimeter or two. "I've been wondering if Shirley would think it too strange if I asked Crystal to go with me to San Gimignano one day," she said. "To the medieval torture museum."

I must have gasped audibly, because Victoria quickly added, "Here's my reasoning. I already told you it's an area of interest for me because of my bookshop. I like to stock what sells, and I've learned that people don't want to know about the clean air and verdant woodlands of medieval times. They want to read about the gore. Man's inhumanity to man. Of course, there are things going on today that are as bad or worse than anything they thought of back then, but people are blind to that."

I nodded and said, "Teenagers, especially, faced with the reality of growing up and dealing with the hard, cruel world—leaving the cozy simplicity of childhood—are drawn to the dark side of man's nature. That's part of the fascination they have for the Gothic thing: vampires, the occult, witchcraft."

"That's exactly what I mean." Victoria seemed delighted that I understood. "I think perhaps they actually need to deal with the dark side of life."

"Maybe you should talk to Shirley, first. Right now, she's just glad to have her little girl back, with hair that's faded down to a medium pink."

"Right. She probably doesn't want to take any chances, but I found out there's a bus one can take from Florence to San Gimignano. It's not a long ride."

Geoffrey said nothing until the meal was almost done. He seemed enclosed in his own world, but when our coffee arrived, he finally spoke up. "So no-ow we haaf a real mystery on our hands."

"Have you a solution?" I asked.

"A lot of people had motives, I think." Geoffrey harrumphed

a couple of times. It seemed to me he was making a concerted effort to speak clearly, each word emerging from his mouth in its own little package. "And a lot of us could have had the opportunity, too."

"Geoffrey and I talked about it. It must be someone in our group. Don't you think it had to be?" Victoria peered at me over her glasses.

"If we include Cesare and Gianni in our group," I said.

"Gianni?"

"Amy's new love. I have no reason to suspect him, but Lettie and I were talking about it this afternoon and we decided to put him, and Cesare, on our list of suspects." I poured a lot of milk into my coffee. "Lettie and I decided we could scratch you and Geoffrey off the list, and Amy and Tessa, people we know were together at the time of the murder and can vouch for each other."

"Can't do that," Geoffrey said. "What if the two are in it together?"

"Oh, dear. Did you have to say that?"

Before we parted, back at the hotel, I reminded Victoria and Geoffrey about the memorial service tomorrow morning at 10, and Victoria suggested that a shared taxi to the church might make sense since it was a twenty to twenty-five minute walk.

"If we leave here by cab about thirty minutes before, we should be in plenty of time," I said.

"See you half-nine, then," Geoffrey said, as he turned toward the elevator.

Half-nine. Funny, the way the English say things. Half-nine. Nine-thirty.

I liked half-nine better. It sounded…pithier.

THERE WAS A BAR TUCKED in beside the restaurant off the lobby, and I saw Tessa at a table by herself. She looked exhausted and defeated, clutching her drink glass in both hands. "Mind if I join you?" I asked.

"Please, do," she said. "I've been given a brief reprieve.

Captain Quattrocchi is interviewing Achille right now, so my translating services aren't needed—for a few minutes at least."

"I thought Achille was out with Beth."

"They're back," Tessa said. "I think you may be next, Dotsy. He has to talk to everyone again, you know, and this time he's going into more depth. Has to."

"Has Ivo definitely been released?"

"Yes, but Quattrocchi didn't let him go until about two hours ago. He didn't want to at all, but he had to. The coroner, the prison doctor and every medical authority Quattrocchi could find tried to trick Ivo into using his right hand. Quattrocchi grilled the coroner for an hour, and the prison doctor examined Ivo's hand six ways from Sunday."

"Apparently there's no way he could have killed Meg with that knife," I said.

"Apparently." Tessa retreated into silence, and I asked the waiter for a cappuccino. He didn't seem to understand me, even after I repeated it two more times. Tessa lightly touched my hand and muttered, "They never drink cappuccino after dinner. It just isn't done."

I changed my order to an espresso, remembered I'd already had enough caffeine—an espresso would have launched me into orbit for the rest of the night—and finally settled on a glass of wine.

"I had a nice talk with Amy today," I said. "She told me a good bit about her family and showed me a picture that was taken, I'm sure, before you knew her."

Tessa nodded.

"She told me she visited your home, occasionally, when you were in college together, but did you ever visit her family?"

"No." Tessa sipped her drink. "I hardly ever visited anyone from school, because I needed—wanted—to go home every chance I got. My mom had to take care of my brother, twenty-four seven, poor woman. So when I came home, I relieved her a bit so she could go out shopping."

"What a lot of patience that must have taken."

"Dad wasn't much help. He was in the military—gone from home a lot—plus, he considered child care woman's work." Tessa snorted. "That's why my mother never learned English, you know. She never left the house long enough to learn. Funny thing is, I guess I owe my job to her. If she'd spoken English to me at home, I'd never have learned Italian. As it is, I learned both languages from babyhood."

"What sort of handicap did your brother have?" I immediately wished I'd phrased that better. I took a big gulp of my wine. "I mean, was it from birth? Or…"

"Yes. From birth. There was an accident when he was born."

A cold chill ran all over me. Was it possible that Tessa's mother had given birth in the hospital where Meg worked? That Tessa's mother and her baby had been the victims of one of Meg's careless screw-ups? Hadn't the note Amy dropped in the Milan airport said "crushed the baby's skull"? But regardless of the events surrounding the birth of Tessa's poor little brother, if Tessa had felt compelled to seek revenge, she would have done something before now.

"My dad is marrying again. Did you know that?" Tessa pulled me out of my reverie. "He's retired, he's moving to Italy, and he's marrying a woman I can't stand. I just hope Mama can't see through the clouds."

Marco Quattrocchi charged into the bar with a gruff, "May I see you now, Mrs. Lamb?"

So we were back to last names again.

To Tessa he said, "Mrs. Lamb *ed andiamo per una passeggiata.*"

Tessa looked at me, her face devoid of any expression. "He says the two of you are going for a walk."

SIXTEEN

I RAN TO KEEP UP as Marco Quattrocchi tramped down the sidewalk that ran eastward from our hotel to the Duomo. He took my elbow at crossings but said nothing for a full three blocks. I stayed as quiet as a kid being escorted to the principal's office, but I'd done nothing wrong, so why did I feel I had to cower?

"I had to let him go," Marco finally said. "I guess you have heard that already."

"Yes. I heard you really gave him the third degree before you let him go."

"The third degree?"

I explained what that meant.

"Of course I did! Of course I gave him the third degree. I would not have let him go at all if I had any way to hold him. You know why? Because I will never see Ivo Ramovic again, that is why. I told him not to leave the area, but he is already in Milan or Rome by now, I am sure. He was probably gone within the hour. Finding a Roma is not like finding a dentist. They do not have addresses. They are not officially even here."

"I hadn't thought about it like that," I said.

"I have to think about it like that. What I have now is the murder of a tourist from America, and a group of possible suspects and possible motives and…" He stopped and turned to me. He lowered his voice. "There is a strong possibility that I will have to arrest an American, or a Canadian, or a citizen of the U.K. for the murder of an American citizen. Do you know what that will involve with the embassies…possibly extraditions…it makes my head hurt to think about it."

"I'm sorry."

"The American Embassy is not fun to work with. I avoid it whenever I can."

Ahead of us was a gelateria bustling with customers.

"Have you had dinner already?" Marco asked. "Would you like a gelato?"

I nodded.

"I am sorry. I forgot your diabetes."

"It's okay, one gelato won't hurt." I asked him to get me a cone with one scoop of strawberry. "What are you having?"

"Nothing. I do not want any."

It occurred to me that a carabinieri officer might feel silly licking an ice cream cone in public, but surely he could eat a dish of gelato without sacrificing his dignity. Maybe he was too upset to eat anything. After raising four boys and trying to keep a husband happy for thirty years (albeit unsuccessfully, apparently) I have some feel for what a man's ego requires. I changed my order to two scoops of strawberry in a dish and, while Marco paid for it, I picked up two spoons.

"Did Ivo have a lot of money on him when you arrested him?" I asked.

"Almost nine hundred Euros."

"Did you take it away from him?"

"Of course. Do you think we would let him keep it?"

"But after you let him go…I mean, how do you know it wasn't his money, legitimately?"

"Because he admitted he took it from Meg Bauer's room."

"So he admits he was there?"

"He did, after we had questioned him for several hours. He said he got into the room using the card he had earlier stolen from Mrs. Hines's…"

"Waist pack?"

"Yes. He said he found Miss Bauer lying near the bathroom door in a pool of blood. He said the contents of someone's purse lay scattered on the bed, and there was a wallet with a lot of money in it. He grabbed the wallet and ran out. He does not remember if he closed the door or not, but he still had the room card in his pocket when we found him."

"And the wallet?"

"He had thrown it in a trash box behind a restaurant. We have it now."

"How about the purse?"

"We have not found it."

I handed Marco a spoonful of gelato. He ate it and smiled. The gelato seemed to cool him down a bit. I saw his eyes relax. "People expect a lot of you, don't they?"

"A lot more than stupid idiots like us can live up to." He let me refill his spoon. "Dotsy, do you know what people think about us? About the carabinieri?"

"No," I said, happy I was Dotsy again.

"They think that we are all in the Sicilian Mafia, they think that we are all gangsters, they think that we are all below average in intelligence. I, for one, am not from Sicily. I have lived my whole life in Tuscany." Marco drew his hands to his chest. "I am not in the mob. I am honest, and I deal very severely with anyone who I discover is not honest."

I smiled, but I could have cried for him.

"I may, however, be below average in intelligence," he added.

We both laughed. Marco had the eyes we used to call bedroom eyes. My knees felt weak.

His face turned serious. "I will tell you who is in the mob. Cesare, Tessa D'Angelo's fiancé. Did you know that?"

"I've heard it suggested."

"I have to ask you some questions, now." He found a small table on the sidewalk outside the gelateria and pulled out a chair for me. He leaned forward in his own chair, his hands tucked between his knees. "How long did you sit in the lobby in front of the elevator?"

"I already told you. I was there from a little after five until a quarter to six or so. Lettie, Lucille Vogel, and I tried to catch the elevator about that time, but apparently it was being held on the third floor. Oh! I have something you might not know."

I told him about Lucille Vogel and the mysterious transaction Lettie and I had seen in the train station. While I was at it, I filled him in on Amy's version of the Bauer family inheritance.

"Do you want to come to work for me? You would be a good detective," he said. "Another thing. When did Mrs. Hines go up in the elevator? You did see her go up, did you not?"

"Oh yes, with a pot of flowers. It was a few minutes before…it was about five-thirty, I guess."

In other words, I thought, Beth could have reached her room in time to kill her sister, toss the knife out the window, and call the front desk in an ersatz panic. I felt like a traitor—as if I had just convicted Beth. Lettie would hate me.

"Marco, who do you think it was? I know you don't know yet, but you must have some idea."

"I do not know. I really do not. The obvious first choice is, of course, Beth Hines. She had the motive, actually two motives considering what you just told me about Meg getting all of their mother's money, and she had the opportunity. She would have known exactly where to find the knife; it was *her* knife. But there is a lot we still have to learn."

"Don't you think it would have been hard for Beth to have committed a very bloody murder at five-thirty and clean up fast enough to invite the folks from the front desk up at five forty-five?"

Marco tapped his forehead and winked at me. "I know that Meg Bauer had a lot of enemies. She was apparently a very careless and…uh…unfeeling nurse. I keep discovering all these little connections…possible motives."

"Yes. And tonight Tessa told me her younger brother's handicap was due to a problem with his birth, and it struck me…what if Meg was the nurse? Of course, what are the odds of that?"

"You know what I mean then," Marco said. "Things like that just keep coming up. But Tessa has a very good alibi."

"I know. She was with the victim's sister at the time of the murder."

"Also, she has a receipt from a cash machine that says she was downtown at five-thirty-two p.m."

"That let's out Amy, too."

"Yes. They both agree they were at the cash machine together. And Amy has also told me that Meg was a very active supporter of…what do you call the kind of abortion that pulls the baby…" Marco twisted one hand into a forceps-like curl.

"Partial-birth abortion," I said.

"Right. And Mrs. Wilma Kelly is quite active in the movement *against* partial-birth abortions. She has had her picture in the paper protesting against it."

My brain was in danger of crashing from information overload. "How did you find this out?" I asked.

"Mrs. Shirley Hostetter mentioned it."

IF I SLEPT A WHOLE HOUR that Sunday night, it certainly wasn't more than that. I had too much to think about. I pretended to be asleep so Lettie wouldn't talk to me and so I could think things out by myself. Sometimes, it's good to bounce your ideas off someone else, sometimes it's good to listen, and sometimes you have to work it out in your own head. I started by imagining Beth Hines as her sister's killer. I tried, as they say, "wearing that for a while."

I imagined being at the mercy of a shrewish sister at a time in my life when I had always imagined I'd be free and financially secure. I'd drive home—no, I'd drive to *her* home—from work every day in the old clunker my husband left me, only to spend the evening with a never-ending discourse on all my flaws and shortcomings. I would think, now and again, that if I had gotten my fair share of my mother's money, I wouldn't be a charity case. Perhaps I'd dwell on that. Perhaps I'd obsess about it.

I imagined how Beth must have felt when Meg embarrassed her in Venice, in front of Achille, perhaps the first man to show an interest in her as a woman since her divorce. On that fateful Friday, having just dealt with the loss of her money and credit cards, she would have had to listen to a lengthy harangue from Meg about her stupidity in allowing herself to be robbed. How would she feel, after a trek through sweltering afternoon streets, dripping with sweat, to discover that what she had hoped was a gift—maybe even from an admirer—was one more cruel insult from Meg?

If I had bought that knife for a completely innocent purpose, for a gift, I would certainly remember it. I would think about its potential. I would realize that, with one well-placed slice, my "Coltello d'Amore"—knife of love—would silence that hateful voice forever. Would I be able to resist the temptation? If there was ever a straw that broke the camel's back, wouldn't the card on that pot of flowers, the card that said, "Vanity, vanity" be that straw?

If I were Beth, I could have slipped into the bathroom when Meg was preoccupied with her own ugly face in the mirror, grabbed her hair in my left hand, jerked it backward—

The memorial service. My mind suddenly jumped to the memorial service and the fact that I had totally forgotten to call the organist. I punched the little light on my wristwatch; it was 11:05. Was it too late to call? Italians do tend to have long dinners and to stay up later in the evenings. I didn't want to awaken Lettie, so I slipped on my slacks and shirt in the dark, ran my feet under the bed until I found my shoes, and felt around on the floor under a chair for my purse.

I'd also need a Bible. I had meant to check our room for a Gideon Bible before going to bed, but, like the call to the organist, I had been so preoccupied with my thoughts of Beth, I had forgotten. I needed a Bible—in English—to pick out a couple of things to read tomorrow. I didn't plan to make a speech. I hoped one or two people might volunteer to say a few words, and I could come up with a kind sentence or two myself, but a couple of scriptural passages would definitely be needed if the service was to last more than five minutes.

The woman at the concierge desk led me through a warren of computers, fax machines and a central phone bank which appeared to have buttons for dozens of extensions. She unlocked a small office door, entered, and ran her fingers along the top row of books on a shelf while I waited at the doorway.

"Grazie," I said as she handed me an English-language Bible. *"Ritorno domani?"* I added, feeling incredibly bilingual.

From a phone in the lobby, I dialed the number of the organist and braced myself for an avalanche of verbal abuse. A woman answered, *"Pronto."*

"Il mio nome è Mrs. Lamb." I switched to English, figuring that if the woman didn't understand me, I had the wrong number. She was, indeed, the organist I was looking for, I had not awakened her, and she would have played for us tomorrow if I'd called earlier. She had another engagement.

So it would be a plain and simple service. But at least we'd have one song from Lucille Vogel, who had said she didn't mind singing a cappella.

I parked myself in the same chair in front of the elevator that I had sat in on Friday afternoon. In a cold rush, the horror swept over me again. The confusion at the desk, the scurry, and the curt orders spat out by the hotel manager as he rushed past us. I shook myself back to the present and flipped through the Bible, sticking scraps of paper at Psalm cxxi and I Corinthians xv. I thought those passages would sound good.

Gathering my stuff together in preparation for returning to my room, I saw Amy and Gianni approach the elevator, their arms wrapped around each other. Amy carried her high-heeled sandals hooked over her fingers. Her head was tucked into the hollow of Gianni's neck, and he lightly kissed her hair. I wondered if she had taken the shoes off so she'd be shorter than Gianni for the goodnight kiss. He held her against the wall beside the brass panel of buttons and kissed her over and over. I think I could have yelled "Fire" and neither would have moved.

Back in my bed, I resumed my tossing and turning. So Ivo

had actually been in Meg's room and had seen her lying there in a pool of blood. I could understand why he had not reported it, but to take the time to swipe the wallet before he ran out? I couldn't imagine thinking about money at a time like that.

Paul Vogel had been asking about the men in our group only because he assumed a woman wouldn't have had the strength to do it. Could I have done it? If yes, any woman in our group could have murdered Meg. I decided if I was mad enough, or determined enough, I could. The hardest part would be steeling the nerves to actually press and drag that blade across the neck. It might be easier, I thought, for someone who'd had experience with blades and flesh. A chicken or pig farmer, perhaps, or a hunter, or a butcher, or a doctor—or a nurse.

I thought about Shirley Hostetter. She had a motive. She had been forced to quit her job because Meg surreptitiously altered her note detailing the doctor's orders. But why would Shirley have told the story to Victoria Reese-Burton? Wouldn't she have tried to hide the fact that she had reason to hate Meg? Marco said Shirley had told him about Wilma versus Meg in the battle over partial-birth abortion. Might Shirley have mentioned that in order to throw suspicion on someone else? Might she have told her story to Victoria because she knew it was bound to come out anyway, once Meg's murder was investigated? Put the story out there so it wouldn't seem as if you were hiding it?

I worried that I was becoming way too suspicious.

What about Jim and Wilma? Jim had no motive and no alibi. He was supposedly in his room throughout the relevant time, and I had already learned not to put too much stock in an apparent lack of motive. Motives had a way of popping up.

Wilma Kelly was certainly an intense, issue-oriented sort of person. The sort that would love to throw fake blood on a woman wearing a fur coat. But murder? I couldn't see it. Murder would be a refutation of everything she stood for.

Geoffrey and Victoria Reese-Burton had no possible motives. Okay, Victoria had a fairly weird hobby—medieval torture—but that was strictly armchair torture, I was sure. I rose to my feet, went to the bathroom, drank a box of orange juice, and brushed my teeth again to get the sweet juice off.

Amy and Tessa. Tessa and Amy. Friends since college. Amy had a motive—money. Tessa might have had a motive. Paul's contacts back home might dig up something, but the problem with Amy and Tessa was that at the time of the murder, they were definitely together, so either they were in it together, or they weren't in it at all. And, of course, there was the time problem. Unless Marco was wrong about the time of the murder, Amy and Tessa couldn't have done it unless they could get from the hotel to downtown Florence in two minutes. Make that eight to ten minutes. Marco had said, "Give or take a few minutes." But still. No way.

I wasted a half-hour trying to consciously will myself to sleep by relaxing every part of my body, starting with my head and working my way down to my toes. After a dozen attempts, I gave up. So I analyzed everything I knew about Gianni—a kid, a copycat—that was about it. Cesare—arrogant? No, that was unfair. I thought he looked arrogant, but I had no evidence that he was. Well, almost no evidence. He was the sort of man who'd rather send an electronic message to his fiancée a few yards away than get up and stick his head out the door. Cesare was probably connected with the mob-controlled underworld in some way. I had heard that from two independent sources, and he was awfully young to be holding political office. Did he owe that position to the criminal element? Might they have demanded repayment?

Lucille Vogel: motive, money for drugs; opportunity, practically none. I couldn't see how she could have killed Meg and met us in the lobby just a few minutes later. Paul Vogel: motive, none; opportunity, who knows? But Paul was such a sneaky guy, he could easily have killed Meg, circled around the hotel, and followed the gruesome foursome into the parking lot. That way, it would appear that he, too, had come from downtown.

Speaking of the gruesome foursome, in spite of their little deception as to who was bedding whom, I knew of no connection between any of them and Meg Bauer, except that Elaine King, Dick Kramer's paramour, was acquainted with Beth and had heard about this tour from her. If there was another connection, perhaps Paul's sources back home would uncover it.

When my wake-up call came at 7:30 a.m., I clicked the receiver and tackled one more worrisome thought. *Suppose Paul Vogel does have a motive, and his connections back home discover it. He certainly won't report it to me, will he? And the same would go for his sister, Lucille.*

SEVENTEEN

WE ALMOST FILLED THE little chapel on the left side of the nave. I counted twenty of us, including Gianni and Cesare, and we arrived in a Ferrari, a Fiat and three taxis. The curious quartet moseyed in on eight feet, having opted to walk. Father Quick had forgotten all about our request, but it didn't matter. There was no one else scheduled to use the chapel.

Crystal Hostetter shocked me. She arrived with an acoustic guitar she had rented and asked me if she could play a song during the service. I glanced at her mother, hoping for some assurance that it would be okay, because I immediately flashed on a vision of Crystal and her guitar bouncing vintage Sex Pistols off the Norman arches, shattering the stained glass windows. Shirley gave me a nod.

I started with my first reading and then called on Crystal to play. She seated herself atop a stool off to one side and began to play—simply, beautifully—a melody that brought tears to most of our eyes. Her pink head bent down over the neck of the guitar, her right hand expertly plucked intricate variations on each chord. I wondered if I was the only one who recognized "Girlfriend in a Coma," a song recorded by The Smiths sometime in the eighties. I had heard it hundreds of times, pounding through one or the other of my kids' bedroom doors. The funny thing was that Crystal wouldn't have even been born at the time that record was released. *Don't tell me "Girlfriend in a Coma" is already a classic,* I thought, as I glanced across the aisle toward Tessa, Amy, and their boyfriends. They were mostly of an age to have been teens at about that time. Only Amy showed signs of recognition, her grin discreetly concealed by a tissue.

Tessa said a few appropriate words, and Amy followed suit. She didn't go so far as to say she'd miss her sister, but she came up with some nice things to say about her—nice, without being too disingenuous. Beth sat, motionless and withdrawn, her hands lying softly in her lap. She was so small and vulnerable, I thought.

Lucille, looking more than usual like a dwarf bowling pin, came to the altar, folded her fat little hands in front of her and sang the "Ave Maria" in a deep, rich, contralto voice like liquid silver. It seemed to me that the very walls of the church sang with her. There was not a dry eye in the chapel when she finished. After my last reading, Lucille finished the service with "Amazing Grace." The whole service had turned out so much better than I had imagined. On our way out, everyone gave Crystal and Lucille hugs and thanked them.

Lettie and I walked downtown immediately after the memorial service, with the vague idea of shopping, browsing, or eating lunch. I wanted to go back to the Museo Archeologico, but I didn't think it would interest Lettie, so we found ourselves winding up and down rows of stalls that sold leather goods, clothing and jewelry in a large open-air market near the Church of Santa Croce. I know nothing about how to tell real Gucci purses and Rolex watches from fake ones, but from the prices I saw on most, I thought I could assume they were fake. Still, some of the leather jackets were gorgeous and bargain-priced. I had to try on one or two of them, in spite of the heat. I didn't need a leather jacket, but at these prices…

"Dotsy! Here's Meg's purse!" Lettie called from a nearby purse and wallet stall.

I handed the jacket back to the vendor and dashed over. Lettie held up a brown Fendi handbag with a large, silver buckle on the side. I vaguely remembered Meg wrenching a very similar bag out of Lettie's hand as we were getting on the bus in Scarperia. Lettie had tried to clean off the ice cream that she had accidentally spilled on the purse, but Meg wouldn't let her. I cringed a little at the memory.

"It does look quite similar," I said. "Meg's was a Fendi, too, wasn't it? How much do they want for it?"

"No, Dotsy." Lettie shook the bag in my face. "This isn't *like* Meg's purse, this *is* Meg's purse! Look. The dried ice cream is still right here at the bottom of the strap. See?" She pointed to a small, yellowish, jelly-like glob.

"But how? I mean, it can't be! Scuzi?" I held up the purse and showed it to the man behind a table piled with handbags. "Where...*dove*...where did you get this?"

But he didn't understand, or didn't want to understand. I tried several more times, and Lettie tried, too, with an energetic sort of charades version of *where-did-you-get-this?*

"It's hopeless," I said at last. "I'll have to buy it. Fortunately, it's a bargain." It was marked 150 Euros, but I talked him down to a hundred and Lettie split the cost with me.

"We have to take this to Captain Quattrocchi," I said, and then I remembered fingerprints. "We have to get it there without getting any more fingerprints on it."

"We need a bag to put it in, Dotsy."

The vendor had no bags large enough for it. "One of us needs to stay here and hold the bag just like this." I held it with two fingers under the strap. "While the other one finds a bag to put it in."

"But heaven knows how many people have handled it since Meg."

Lettie's voice sounded shaky, and I wondered if she was picturing the purse lying on Meg's bed, Meg's dead body on the floor.

"No reason for us to make it any worse by adding more fingerprints than we have to," I said. "Why don't you wait here? I'll find a plastic bag."

I left Lettie holding the purse in front of her, by two fingers. I imagined she'd have to endure a lot of strange looks before I got back. My first thought was to simply ask the merchant in the next stall for a bag, and then it occurred to me that this purse was crucial evidence, and the bag we put it in should be free from stray hairs and dirt-anything that might contaminate it. I should buy a box of new bags, straight from the factory and never opened, but where? I couldn't find any such place in the open-air market, but on a narrow street nearby I found a little store that had what I needed. By the time I returned to Lettie, she sat on the stone curb, her middle finger dangling the purse, her elbow digging into her knee.

Checking my city map, I saw that we were within walking distance of the caserma on Borgo Ognissanti, but Lettie and I decided to indulge in a taxi ride. The driver stared after us as we left the cab with our trash bag and its mysterious contents. I wished I could tell him, "It's a human head. We didn't want to get our clothes bloody," but I knew the humor would get lost in the translation.

Marco Quattrocchi waved us into his office almost immediately. It took a while to convince him that the purse was Meg's purse, not one like it. Lettie suggested that the lab might analyze the dried ice cream to see if it was lemon. She was positive they'd find that it was.

Marco slipped on latex gloves and removed the purse from the plastic bag. The purse had an overlapping magnetic button closure. Without touching the surface of the purse, he ran a pencil underneath the flap and peered inside. "Blood," he said, and invited me to look. "Traces of blood, see? Here?" He used the tip of his pencil to point. "And here?"

It wasn't a lot, but I could see a rust-brown smear that partially obliterated the FF monogram on the interior pocket. Plus, a number of smaller spots on the lining. "How can you tell it's blood?"

"I cannot tell for sure. It will have to be tested. But I would bet it is blood, wouldn't you?"

"The question now is, why was it for sale on the street and how did it get there?"

"Probably, it was found by someone who simply sold or traded it to the vendor of the stall where you found it. Some of the designer goods in these markets are the real thing, and some are reproductions or…how do you say…?"

"Knockoffs," I suggested. "Counterfeit."

"Right." He motioned Lettie and me to visitors' chairs and took the leather swivel chair for himself. "Sometimes they are authentic, but they have not been obtained in the…normal way."

"Stolen."

"Yes. But in this case, I am suspecting that it was discarded and then discovered by someone unconnected to the murder of Meg Bauer."

"That makes sense. I wonder if the murderer would have been so bold as to sell a purse he or she had taken from his or her victim."

"I doubt it. No, I think someone may have found it, tossed away by the murderer or possibly by the Roma man, Ivo, although he says he never saw the purse."

"Might the blood inside have been from some sort of protective clothing the murderer wore while killing Meg? It could have been folded up with the soiled side inward and stuffed into the purse."

Marco tapped his forehead. "I told you before. You would make a good detective."

I tried to accept the compliment graciously, but I feared my face looked smug. "If it was one of those very thin plastic rain coats, you know, like they sell for emergencies, it would fit easily into that purse…even if it was bloody."

"And what would that tell us?"

Marco sat back and tented his fingers in front of his beard. I could see a slight twinkle in his eyes.

"That the murder was premeditated," Lettie put in.

"Correct."

"The killer came to the room with protective clothing, all ready to go!" Lettie sat forward, fairly bouncing with excitement.

"Do you think they'll find any useful fingerprints on it?" I asked.

Marco pointed to the leather parts of the purse, the handles and the wide closure strap, with his pencil. "These parts will, but these—" he indicated the monogrammed fabric on the sides "—no prints are likely here. But fingerprints may or may not help us. Whose will we find? Your own, probably."

"We were as careful as we could be," Lettie said. "We tried to hold it by the middle of one strap, but I'm afraid we both handled it before we even thought about fingerprints."

"There will probably be prints from the vendor, the person who gave it to the vendor, maybe a print or two remaining from Meg Bauer." Marco exhaled loudly. "Even if we find the prints of another member of your group, what would that prove? Nothing. Any of you may have handled that purse for any number of reasons."

"The man at the leather stall is Paulo Palermo. He's a little guy, gray hair, about fifty," Lettie said.

Good old Lettie. It hadn't occurred to me to get the vendor's name.

"But the bloodstains," Marco said. "With luck we may be able to identify the blood as Meg Bauer's blood. Perhaps the killer cut himself, too, and some of his blood might be mixed in." Marco winked at us. "But that is a bit too much to hope for."

"If you found prints from an unknown person, could you identify them?" I asked.

"Only if they belong to someone with a criminal record. Otherwise, they would not be in our data bank. We will, of course, compare any prints that we do find with the prints of Ivo, of the vendor you bought this from, and of all the people in your tour group."

I stared at Marco. "And if you find prints that belong to someone who does have a record?"

"Then we will locate that person and ask him where he found this purse."

"Duh." Lettie gave me a cross-eyed doofus look.

"I will take this to the laboratory now. Thank you," Marco said, and melted me with his smile.

EIGHTEEN

ACHILLE DROVE US UP a big hill south of the Arno to the Piazzale Michelangelo at 5 p.m. It was the same time of day but three days later than we had originally planned to go. The bus wound up a narrow road past the eleventh-century Church of San Miniato to a broad flat terrace centered by a much-larger-than-life bronze replica of Michelangelo's *David*. Although hot, there was a nice breeze out of the west.

On stiletto heels, Amy Bauer clicked off across the pavement until she reached a railing of the overlook, where she was joined by Tessa.

Geoffrey and Victoria Reese-Burton headed for a building at the back of the piazza, possibly a restaurant or lounge.

Paul Vogel put his camera to work.

Crystal, whose hair had suddenly turned grass-green, sat on a concrete balustrade at the edge of the pavement, which seemed to have nothing but thin air on the other side. Shirley warned her to get off. Behind Crystal was the famous vista that everyone recognizes as Florence—the Duomo, the Church of Santa Croce, the tile roofs, the Arno. The piazza wrapped around on both sides to forested walkways and roads on the west and to farmland and houses on the hillsides to the east.

I took a few photos from the balustrade and, looking down, saw that two broad staircases led from the top level, where we were now, then fanned out left and right to yet more overlooks, flower gardens, and a winding path that disappeared into the trees below.

Jim and Wilma Kelly called to us from the bronze statue. I

took a picture of them standing on the steps below the statue. They snapped Lettie and me doing the same. Jim got one of Wilma, Lettie and me.

Beth and Achille disappeared down the stairway. It appeared to me that he slipped his arm around her shoulder as soon as they descended a few steps. Amy and Tessa soon followed, but I couldn't see whether they took the left or the right wing of steps. Since our driver and our guide had both wandered away, I figured we would be here a while.

"Tessa said thirty minutes, didn't you hear her?" Lettie told me.

The curious quartet replaced us at the statue, and Michael Melon, who I now knew was Walter's lover and not Dick Kramer's employee, stretched his cat-like self out languidly along its base for a photo op. If Paul Vogel could get this shot, I thought, he could sell it to a men's fashion magazine, but Paul seemed to have disappeared.

"Who's missing, Lettie? There's someone missing."

"Lucille Vogel. She stayed in town."

Lettie and I strolled down the left branch of the stairs and found another overlook, even better, I thought, than the one above. The sun, sinking in the western sky, cast a tangerine glow across the river. We walked to the rail. From there I could glimpse a road winding up the hill through the pines. A small blue car crept up and disappeared behind the hill.

"Looks like Gianni's car," Lettie said. "Do you suppose it is?"

Turning, I looked up the slope. From the winding road below, the car could climb to the parking area on top, or it might continue on around the road our bus had taken and descend the hill to the south. I turned back to enjoy the view and the breeze. A minute or two later, Dick Kramer and Michael Melon appeared on the stairs above us. They seemed to be debating whether to go left or right when a chilling scream, a woman's scream, pierced the golden afternoon air.

I paused long enough to point myself in the probable right

direction. Lettie was right with me as I raced around, not up, the wide double staircase. Another balustrade at the boundary of a flower-lined terrace led off the east side. Tessa stood at the balustrade, leaning over. She appeared to be choking. I dashed over and touched her shoulder gently, so as not to frighten her. Tessa pointed downward.

It was a sheer drop from the balustrade to a grassy slope. At the base of the slope, Amy lay in a contorted position, her head downhill from her feet. It was obvious to me that her neck was broken. She lay on her right side, her left arm behind her back. Her legs were in a sort of climbing position, but her head faced the other way. Tessa kept making choking sounds.

"Oh, my God!" I darted a few steps left, then right, searching for a route down the hill. The only way, it seemed, was to go back up the stairs and across the piazza. Elaine, joined quickly by Dick, dashed across and looked down in horror. "Watch Tessa," I shouted to them as Lettie and I rushed up the stairs.

The race across the piazza and the parking area beside it seemed to take hours. By the time we got to the slope I hoped would take us down to Amy, we were joined by Crystal and both Kellys. A car motor coughed to life somewhere below us. I skidded to a stop, sliding a little on the grass, and saw the blue car as it rounded the backside of the hill.

"Damn. I wonder if that could have been a Fiat," I mused out loud.

"It was a Fiat. Blue. The last three parts of the license were '10 M' or 'IO M.'" Lettie tossed this over her shoulder as she edged down, planting each step firmly into the slope.

Kneeling beside Amy, Jim Kelly said, "She's dead."

"Where can we make a call?" Wilma looked up the slope to the balustrade above.

My gaze followed hers. Shirley leaned over, calling to Crystal to come back up.

Amy's eyes were open. They stared out sightlessly behind her at an angle she could never have achieved in life. I swallowed hard and tried to think what to do.

One of Amy's high-heeled shoes lay ten yards or so uphill from her feet.

Lettie shoved Crystal in the back. "Your mother is calling you," Lettie said, then followed at Crystal's heels like a shepherd corralling a wayward sheep.

"How can we call an ambulance from here?" Wilma turned around as if she expected a phone booth to materialize on the slope. "Shall I run up and find a phone?"

"Please do." It occurred to me that Tessa would be the best one to make the call, but I doubted if she would be able to, given the state she was in. "If you see Achille, you might ask him to help you."

I was left alone with Amy's body. Her pretty face, so lively and animated until a few minutes ago, was now scrubbed of all personality. I thought of our walk to the church together yesterday, how her shiny hair swung as she bounced along the street, oblivious to the leers and stares she got from the men she passed. How she worried that I would barge in on the Barrett-Brownings and interrupt Elizabeth's Sunday morning tea.

Amy's shirt was bunched up in front, exposing her thin midriff and the lower part of her bra. I wanted to pull it down for her. I knew she'd want me to. But I also knew I mustn't tamper with anything.

The corner of a piece of paper peeked out of Amy's pants pocket, and I remembered the note she'd made a frantic dive for when we had butted heads at the Milan airport. Could this be the same one? I wrestled with my conscience. Could I justify pulling the paper out and reading it? Assuming this was an accident—and there was no reason to think it was anything else—there'd be no harm in taking a quick peek. If Amy's fall wasn't an accident, I'd get my fingerprints on the paper, but then my prints could already be on it from the airport encounter.

I looked up to the balustrade. Dick, Shirley and Crystal were all staring down at Amy's body. I considered moving to the left

far enough to block their view of Amy's pocket, and then thought
I'd just boldly take the note out and read it, not even try to hide
it. After all, what could the repercussions be? A tongue-lashing?
Someone called down from the upper level and all three turned
away. I seized the chance and slid the paper out of Amy's pocket.
It was a small sheet, probably torn from a pocket-sized planner.
Written with a dull pencil, the loopy handwriting was hard to read,
but there wasn't much there—as if it had been cryptically jotted
down by the note taker while someone else was talking. It said:

Hosp dir Dr Spring
Syntometrine inj uterine contractions
Case
Filed 9/6/81
crushed the baby's skull
Seal
Hearing 1/16/82

I repeated the word "syntometrine" several times to myself,
associating it in my mind with synonym and metric. Dr. Spring,
I supposed, was a hospital director. The date might refer to a
complaint, to a criminal charge, or maybe a civil suit. That made
sense, since the date for "filed" was about four months earlier
than the date for "hearing."

But more important than the words on this small slip of paper
was the fact that Amy had it in her pocket today. It was in her
purse last week. She had risked a cracked head to get it away
from me, and it was with her today. I refolded the paper and put
it back. There was nothing else in her small, shallow pocket.

The ambulance shrilled across the parking lot and stopped so
close to the edge that I could see its rotating beam from my
position below. As paramedics rushed down with a stretcher, I
climbed the hill, staying well out of their way.

Beth insisted she'd ride in the ambulance. She wouldn't hear
of letting Amy leave without her. But there was a language

problem. The ambulance driver and Achille were gesticulating wildly, yelling in Italian. With a tight grip on Beth's arm, Lettie said, "If you're riding in that ambulance, I am, too."

I understood that Lettie didn't want to let Beth deal with this alone. I wanted to go as well, if I could.

The free-for-all of frantic English and Italian threatened to turn nasty, but Tessa intervened, both hands raised in a gesture of peace. She seemed to have regained her composure. She said something to the ambulance driver. Achille interrupted her and she glared at him. He shut up.

"They can take two people, maximum, in the back," Tessa said. "Beth, you can ride to the hospital with your sister, and I think I should—"

"I want to go, too," Lettie interrupted. "I really must. We'll do okay with the language thing, don't worry."

Tessa helped Beth and Lettie into the back of the ambulance and explained things to the paramedics who, by this time, had secured Amy's body to a gurney and were sliding it in. Beth and Lettie were directed to sit along the wall and out of the way.

The ambulance sped out, leaving the rest of us to stare after it, still not quite believing.

Later, Lettie told me she had found Tessa, shivering uncontrollably, swaddled in several sweaters and wraps that Elaine had rounded up for her. Lettie had also found Beth, wandering aimlessly around a flowerbed, a blank, uncomprehending look in her eyes. So, naturally, Lettie had sat with her and held her hand until the ambulance showed up.

Right now, Michael Melon peered over the balustrade at the approximate spot Amy had gone over. By now, the lights around the piazza were on, and the city below was winking to life.

"It was those shoes—those damned shoes!" Michael said.

"What do you mean?" I asked as I joined him.

"Center of gravity too high. Haven't you ever walked in stiletto heels?"

"Yes, of course I have."

"Then you know it raises your center of gravity. It also shrinks your baseline, the length of foot that touches the ground. Amy was tall, five ten or so." Michael stepped close to the concrete balustrade and stood on his toes. It put the top of the balustrade below the bend of his hips. He leaned forward and the mother in me automatically grabbed the tail of his shirt. "If your center of gravity is about here," he said, indicating his waistline, "it goes outside your baseline and you fall. It's that simple. And in four-inch heels, it's easy to lose your balance. If Amy's torso went over as far as this…" He leaned over again, and I grabbed his shirt again. "She would have tumbled over, and unless she could have grabbed onto the rail, very unlikely, she wouldn't have had any way to stop herself."

"But why would she have leaned over that far?" Glancing around, I recalled seeing Crystal Hostetter teetering on the upper balustrade a little while ago. Crystal, I could see doing it, but Amy?

Michael said, "She either tripped, lost her balance, or—"

"Somebody pushed her," I said.

NINETEEN

IT WAS DARK WHEN we climbed onto the bus. I sat about halfway back, by myself. Tessa took her usual seat opposite the driver, with sound system controls and microphone handily placed beside her, but she didn't say a word. I could see her face in profile when an oncoming car's headlights swept across the windshield. She looked numb. She picked up her microphone, but didn't do anything with it. Dangling from her slack hand by its cord, the microphone swung with the movement of the bus.

The bus was eerily quiet. I tried to imagine what Beth and Lettie were going through at the hospital. Surely a doctor would pronounce Amy dead within a few minutes of her arrival—a mere formality in this case. Then Lettie would sit with Beth and try to comfort her while the hospital staff shoved papers at Beth to sign. They would ask her what she wanted them to do with the body. No, no. It wouldn't be like that. They would probably hold the body or do an autopsy before they released it, given the traumatic nature of the accident. Then they'd need to call Beth's brother, Joe. Would Beth be able to do that herself, or would Lettie do it for her?

With a sudden thud in the pit of my stomach, I realized that the four Bauer siblings were reduced to half their former number. Only Beth and Joe remained. If Beth had accepted Meg's murder without apparent undue anguish, she certainly wouldn't be able to do that with Amy's death. Amy was the little sister Beth had baby-sat; the kid she let try on her clothes and taught to do makeup.

How close were Amy and Tessa? Friends in college. Close

enough so that Amy went home with Tessa over several weekends, and close enough so that Amy planned to fly back to Italy in August to be a bridesmaid in Tessa's wedding. On the other hand, they hadn't seen each other or even kept in contact since college. Tessa had called her Amy Perez, as if the name Bauer—which Amy had been using for several years—was new to her, and Amy had indicated that she had kind of gotten herself invited to be in the wedding party. Maybe they sent each other cards at Christmas, or maybe the travel convention meeting they mentioned was their first contact in years.

Perhaps Tessa was mainly concerned about what this might mean when it came to her job with Pellegrino Tours. What was it she'd said to me outside that little country inn Saturday night? *I'm trying not to lose my job,* she'd said. What would Pellegrino Tours say when they learned she was now minus *two* people?

As Achille swung the bus into the hotel parking area, I caught Tessa's face in the blue-white light from a lamppost. Her eyes tightly shut, she covered her mouth with her hands and shook all over, as if she were forcing herself back into the here and now.

My stomach reminded me that I needed something to eat. It was after 7 p.m.

Jim and Wilma Kelly caught up with me before I reached the hotel door. "We're going to the restaurant downstairs now. Want to join us?" Wilma asked.

"Yes," I said, "I'd like that." It hadn't occurred to me until just then that I would be alone for dinner. How nice of them to have thought of it first. "I'll just dash upstairs and take my insulin. Won't be a minute."

My blood sugar tested quite low. When it's like that, I need to eat without delay or I'm likely to get hypoglycemic. I ran a brush through my hair and dashed down to the restaurant.

"I feel so horrible for poor Beth," Wilma said, after we'd placed our order. "And that sweet, pretty Amy. It's too, too much."

I agreed, then asked, "Did you have a chance to get to know

either Meg or Amy? I had a nice talk with Amy yesterday. It doesn't seem real to me yet…that she's gone."

"I'd only had a couple of brief chats with Amy," Wilma said. "Now, Meg, well, I don't want to speak ill of the dead, but I would be less than honest if I said I liked her."

"Did you know her before this trip?"

"No…" Wilma paused and glanced toward her husband. "Well, our paths had, in a way, crossed a few times, but I don't believe I had ever actually met her until this trip."

"Wilma is very active in protecting the rights of those who can't protect themselves," Jim said.

"Like animals," I said. "Yes. I remember our talk about the baby harp seals."

"And babies in general." Wilma took a sip of water and touched her napkin to her mouth. "I used to live in Baltimore, some years ago. I was active in a group that endeavored to protect the rights of the unborn…" Her voice sort of trailed off. "Nurse Margaret Bauer's name came up frequently, usually at the end of a quote that would make your blood run cold."

"A hard woman," I said. "That's the impression I got."

Wilma smiled, as if she had found a compatriot. I wouldn't have gone that far, but it didn't hurt to have her think that way. I turned to Jim. "Did you see Amy fall, Jim? I was on the other side of the piazza, so all I heard was a scream."

His face reddened down into his collar. He cleared his throat and glanced at Wilma. "No," he said. "I was on the upper level, you know, where we took those pictures by the statue of the David. Well, not there exactly, but on that level…on the other side, though. Wilma was with me, weren't you, love?"

"Oh, yes. Yes, I was. We were on the other side of that upper level, you know, where we couldn't see anything, but we heard. Just as you did."

Wow, that was way more than I had asked for. A simple "No" would have been sufficient.

"Not to change the subject, but according to our itinerary, we are supposed to leave for Pisa tomorrow," Jim said. "Do you have any idea what we're doing?"

"No, I think tomorrow is supposed to be Siena," Wilma said.

"I doubt if Tessa has even thought about it yet," I said. "Let me know if you hear anything."

The pager inside my purse startled me. Jim and Wilma both jumped. I scratched around until I found it and read: room 367. Lettie, letting me know she was in Beth's room now.

I CALLED TESSA'S ROOM when I got back to my own, but there was no answer. I called Beth's room, and Lettie answered. In a whisper she said she would spend the night there, try and get Beth to rest. Lettie said, "Joe will be flying over tonight. He'll probably be here by tomorrow morning."

Faced with an evening alone, with nowhere to go and an urgent need to do something, I washed my hair, repacked my suitcase, and was running a basin of water to do some hand laundry when my phone rang. Marco Quattrocchi wanted me to meet him on the roof.

"Nobody is able to talk to me tonight," he said. "Tessa is not answering her phone, and Beth Hines is…well, your friend, Mrs. Osgood, says she cannot be disturbed."

"My hair is wet."

"Perfect. There is a nice warm breeze on the roof. You will not need the hair dryer."

I ripped a fresh shirt and slacks out of my neatly packed bag and dabbed on a little foundation and mascara. As I stepped off the elevator onto the roof, my heart skipped a beat. Marco was at the railing with the floodlit Duomo behind him. What a perfect picture. This was what I had come to Italy for. No, this was way better than anything I had imagined I'd find in Italy. If only I could simply enjoy it. But the reality of two tragic deaths was there, and it wouldn't go away.

Marco said, "Your hair looks very nice wet."

"Thank you. What have you heard about Amy Bauer? I mean,

I know she's dead, of course, but are they going to do an autopsy? Are you convinced it was an accident?"

"Yes and yes. They have to do an autopsy in a case like this. Of course it was an accident. There is no evidence of anything else."

"But you haven't talked to the people who were there yet. Don't you need to do that first?" I glanced at Marco. The Duomo was reflected in his tired-looking eyes.

"I have talked to Dick Kramer and Michael Melon and to the couple…"

"Elaine and Walter?"

"Yes. They seem to always be together, don't they?"

"I call them the curious quartet," I said, and Marco laughed. *Oh, please, don't let him ask me what else I know about them!* The sleeping arrangements of that little group had no bearing on Marco's investigation, and I'd promised Paul I'd keep my mouth shut. I decide to change the subject. "Have you talked to Paul Vogel? Shirley Hostetter was nearby, too, I think."

"I have talked to both of them. What did you see, Dotsy? From your viewpoint, what happened?"

"I heard a scream, but I didn't see anything. I was on the overlook on the lower level, but on the opposite side from the staircase. Do you know how it is up there?"

"Of course. I have been there a hundred times."

He walked toward the southern end of the roof, and I followed. From here, we looked toward the Arno, and the Fountain of the Bloody Knife was to our right. The breeze on this side blew my wet hair across my face. Lifting it gently away from my lips, Marco smiled at me, jerked his hand away quickly as if he had committed a minor sin.

"You see my problem, don't you?" he said. "My prime suspect is in a genuine state of grief. I can't question her now. If she's guilty of killing her sister Meg, she is still grieving for her sister Amy. And if she is guilty, you can bet she will prolong this state of grief as long as she can, to delay the questioning."

I was shocked at his bluntness, but strangely flattered that he was confiding in me.

He grabbed the railing with both hands, so tightly his knuckles stood up in bold relief. "I cannot keep your group here much longer. I've questioned all of you, and unless I can arrest someone, I have to let you go on your way. You have all paid for a tour of Italy, right?"

"Right."

"I have to know who killed Meg Bauer. It was a brutal killing." Marco spat the words out.

I felt exactly the same way. Never mind what Meg was or wasn't; it was a brutal killing. From Marco's point of view, it was his job to find out who did it. From my own, it was the only way my innocent friends could get out from under the cloud of suspicion that lay over all of us.

Marco took a deep breath. "I know Mrs. Hines is a close friend of your friend, Lettie, but look at what I have here. Beth Hines, who had good reasons to hate her sister Meg, stands to benefit financially by her death. Beth is seen entering an elevator. She is angry because her sister has pulled another one of her cruel tricks, and a few minutes later, that same sister is found dead, killed with the knife Beth bought the day before and left in a drawer by the door. Now, I can make up stories that will put someone else, like Lettie, or you, or Paul Vogel, or even Achille, at the handle end of that knife, but compared to the simple, obvious case against Beth Hines, all the other stories I can make up are…" And here his English failed him.

"Like straining at gnats?"

"What?"

"Never mind. I do see what you mean." I held back my hair with my hands. "Have you considered Jim Kelly, Marco? I can't think of a sufficient motive, but out of all our group, Jim is the only one with no alibi. He was in his room, he says. His wife was out."

"Jim Kelly has a better alibi than anyone. In fact, he has a perfect alibi. From four forty-one p.m. until five-thirty-five, he was on the phone with the United States Secretary of Agriculture. They were discussing the safety of Canadian beef, and there are tapes and backup tapes of the entire conversation in Washington, D.C."

"Okay. What about Paul Vogel?"

Marco put his hand against my cheek and turned my face toward him. The kiss was warm and sweet and traveled to the very heart of the lonesome part of me. I didn't want to think about what this meant, or if it meant anything. I simply wanted it to last.

"Paul Vogel couldn't cut a cooked chicken," Marco whispered, pushing the hair out of my left eye. "Meg Bauer would have had him pinned to the floor in two seconds."

TWENTY

LIKE A CYCLONE, Joe Bauer blew into the lobby, rained chaos down upon the front desk, and thundered into the elevator, taking most of the air with him. Lettie had slipped out of Beth's room, leaving her asleep, to get a bite of breakfast with me. We were waiting to be seated when the hubbub arose.

"Oh, dear, he's going straight up to Beth's room," Lettie said. "I'd better head him off at the pass. She needs to sleep."

I grabbed her collar as she tried to run out. "Let him go. You couldn't stop him anyway."

Tessa, clean and nicely dressed, popped in. Her sunglasses, normally on top of her head, were across her eyes today, but other than that, she looked the same as usual. "Meeting in the conference room at nine-thirty," she said and popped out again.

EXCEPT FOR THE BAUERS, we were all there by 9:30, and the meeting only lasted a few minutes.

"I know that some of you want to get on with our tour and some of you don't," Tessa said. "I have to stay here today, as I'm sure you'll understand, but that doesn't mean the rest of you can't go to Pisa as originally planned. Achille will meet you in the parking lot at ten-thirty, or as Geoffrey would say, 'half-ten.' The drive takes about an hour and a half. You can have lunch there, and you should be back here by six o'clock. If you're not in the parking lot by ten-thirty, Achille will assume you don't want to go and leave without you."

"I'm staying here," I told Lettie on the way out. "What about you?"

"Me, too. I want to be handy in case Beth needs me. Do you mind if I don't go with you wherever you go today?"

"Of course not," I said.

Marco Quattrocchi and Joe Bauer stepped off the elevator, steam pouring out of all four of their ears. They sidled off to the little seating area, the same one where Lettie and I had sat last Friday while Meg was being murdered.

"I have to talk to her today. Whether we do it here or at my office, I do not care," Marco said, gesturing firmness with his hands. His voice was cold and measured.

"After what she's been through? You've got to be kidding!" Joe, a big, barrel-chested man squeaked on that last word. He looked as if he was about to lose control, if he hadn't already.

"I have a murder to solve."

"It's out of the question."

"Your sister has been murdered. You should both be trying to help me!"

"Beth is in a state of shock. You saw her. She's a zombie! You will have to wait."

The way Joe said it, I thought Marco would be smart to back off. Lettie and I sneaked over to the plate glass window in front of the gift shop and pretended to study the shawls on display. We could still hear the two men.

"I can have her picked up and taken to my office in a squad car for questioning."

"You do, and I'll sue."

"You are an alien, remember?"

"What do you mean by that?"

"What I mean is," Marco hissed through clamped teeth, "by the time you figure out how to sue the carabinieri—in Italy—you will have to apply for a visa, or maybe even citizenship. I have to find out who killed your sister, and I have to do it while these people are still in Italy."

"You've had *three days* to talk to Beth. Meg was killed on Friday!"

"And I did talk to her, several times. But I need to talk to her some more."

It was time for Lettie and me to go upstairs. Soon Marco and Joe were bound to notice us hanging around, and we couldn't pretend to be interested in shawls forever. I hadn't told Lettie about the kiss, and I don't exactly know why I hadn't. I suspect it was because I enjoyed keeping it to myself. Or maybe it was because I wanted to be free to distance myself from Marco if Lettie and the Bauers declared war on the carabinieri.

As soon as the elevator doors closed, Lettie said, "I'm going up to Beth's room now. In case the captain and brother Joe move their battle upstairs, I want to be there to protect Beth. She can't take any more conflict; she'd go right round the bend. Do you want to come with me?"

"I'm going to visit Paul Vogel."

"Why?"

"I'll tell you later. We'll have a lot to talk about tonight."

I rode up to the second floor with Lettie and held the door open for Victoria Reese-Burton and Crystal Hostetter who were rushing down the hall together. Victoria raised one finger—the universal hold-the-door signal—as Crystal, a few steps behind her, lifted a couple of complimentary shampoo bottles off the maid's cart.

"We're going to Pisa today, Crystal and I. Shirley wants to take it easy and stay here," Victoria said.

"I don't blame her. Her feet are still healing, I'm sure. How *are* her feet, Crystal?"

If Crystal had any guilt over her mother's lacerated feet, she didn't show it. "They're okay, I think. She says she's going to return the crutches to the doctor's office today."

"What about San Gimignano? I thought you wanted to go to the…" I let my voice trail off. I realized, when I was halfway through that sentence, that Victoria might have decided not to mention the medieval torture museum. She might have decided it was not appropriate.

"Oh, the torture museum," Victoria said, and the gleam in Crystal's eyes told me that she had already mentioned it. "Tessa says we'll probably have another day trip to Siena tomorrow. San Gimignano is between here and Siena, so we might have the bus drop us off on the way."

"Don't forget, Pisa is the home of Pinocchio. I understand you can get some wonderful puppets there." I deliberately said that so I could watch Crystal's eyes roll, and she didn't disappoint me.

Paul and Lucille's room was on the first floor, only a few doors down from mine. Paul answered my knock and looked a little uncomfortable as I invited myself in. Lucille was in the bathroom with the door open, so neither of us could actually say, "Where can we talk in private?"

But Lucille was dressed, her ample waist already girded by a denim travel pack, which I took to mean that she was on her way out.

"Your songs at the memorial service yesterday were wonderful, Lucille. I can't thank you enough."

"Oh, that's okay," she muttered, hitching up her waist pack.

"I don't think there was a dry eye in the chapel when you sat down. I know my own weren't."

"'Amazing Grace' always gets 'em," Lucille tossed over her shoulder as she walked out and slammed the door.

Paul jammed his hands into his shorts pockets, then sheepishly studied his feet. "My sister is not as hard as she pretends to be."

"Have you heard anything from your contacts back home?"

"Not yet. Maybe today. I'm still not sure what you're looking for," he said.

"I'm looking for a connection between Meg Bauer and somebody on this trip. Something other than the obvious sister or fellow nurse or whatever. I know Meg had problems and conflicts as a nurse. She caused Shirley Hostetter to quit her job. She had views that ran counter to those of Wilma Kelly, a political activist. Meg had a reputation for sloppiness. Tessa has a younger brother who suffered some sort of problem at birth that resulted in a severe handicap, and Amy had an early marriage that ended quickly. I have it on good authority that Tessa's fiancé, Cesare, is likely in the Mafia, and one can't really ignore their well-known dealings in drugs, or the fact that nurses have been known to pilfer drugs."

"You're seeing motives everywhere you look, aren't you?" Paul couldn't hide his grin.

I think I must have blushed. "Well, they do seem to be popping up all over the place."

"Have you found a motive for me, yet? I feel left out."

I didn't dare approach the subject of his sister, Lucille, and the possible nurse/drug addict connection. We didn't need to go into that. But I felt like countering his sarcasm with a little impertinence of my own. "I don't really have a motive for you yet, Paul, but it has occurred to me that if your sources back home uncover one, you certainly won't pass it along to me."

"I don't believe you! You are the most...the most..." He spluttered and spun on his heel.

"Oh, but I don't suspect everybody. I've eliminated Jim Kelly. Captain Quattrocchi told me that Jim was certifiably on the phone to the U.S. Agriculture Department throughout the time of Meg's murder. They have tapes and everything."

That got Paul's attention. He didn't admit it, but his face told me it was news to him.

"I've been thinking about what I said, that the murderer had to be a man," he muttered. "That was probably a bit sexist. Actually, if a woman—"

"Wait! If you're about to say hell hath no fury like a woman scorned, may I suggest that that would be even more sexist?"

"I doubt Meg was killed because someone got scorned. can't imagine a woman being jealous of her."

"Paul, do you think Amy fell by accident yesterday?"

"No."

"Me, either."

"A lot of people have a fear of heights, you know. Acrophobia. Very common. People walk up to the edge of a cliff or an overlook or something, like that place yesterday, and they don't want to get too close to the edge because they're afraid they'll fall. Some people are afraid they'll suddenly be overcome by an irresistible urge to jump. But nobody ever does actually fall. Can you name me one example where somebody accidentally fell off a cliff or the edge of an overlook? I'm not talking about mountain-climbers, guys hanging onto the side of a cliff with ropes, of course they fall sometimes. I'm talking about somebody just enjoying the view, and whoops!" Paul's left hand described a trajectory that smacked it into his right.

"That's sort of what I thought. Michael Melon thinks Amy lost her balance because her shoes were too high-heeled."

"I probably don't know as much about high heels as he does, but I do know that women learn how to navigate on those things, somehow. Haven't you learned how to compensate?" He stuck his hands out to the side as if he were walking a tightrope. "I saw Amy take off, running across that plaza. Obviously, she had a lot of practice in high heels."

"Quite right," I said. "Paul, you took pictures up there yesterday. Could you get them developed? Like today?"

"No way. I have to use the developers I work with back home." He pulled a desk drawer open. A dozen labeled film cans already littered the bottom. He looked at them wistfully, as if they all held shocking secrets just screaming to be brought to light. "I really need to go digital."

"Who does have a digital camera?"

"Walter." Paul looked at me. We were both thinking the same thing. "If we could hook it up to a computer… They have computers for rent downstairs, don't they?"

I raced up the stairs alone. Paul refused to go with me to the rooms he had explored surreptitiously, because, I expect, he feared saying something that would expose him for the spy he was. If the curious quartet was going to Pisa, they would be leaving soon or they might have already left.

Should I knock on room 366 or 368? It gave me a headache to think about it.

Walter was supposedly staying in 366, but, according to Paul, he was actually in 368. But I wasn't supposed to know that. Therefore, if I was here to see Walter, I should try 366 and, whoever answered, it would be all right. Elaine opened the door and told me Walter was visiting Michael, next door. A towel draped her shoulders. She brushed her thick hair and slipped a scrunchy around her unruly mass of curls. "But they may have already gone down to the bus," she added.

Walter surprised me. He showed more enthusiasm for putting his pictures into a computer than for making it to Pisa. He suggested we go downstairs immediately to see about getting a computer. As we dashed to the elevator, he checked his watch. "Ten minutes before the bus leaves," he said. "Think we can do this in ten minutes?"

"I have no earthly idea."

I paid the rental fee on the laptop computer while Walter took it to the little seating area in front of the elevator. He attached his camera to the computer with a cord he'd brought with him and, after a minute, said, "Damn." He ran back to the rental desk and engaged the young clerk in a frantic conversation that I didn't understand. I gathered the computer we had lacked the software program Walter needed for seeing the pictures. Walter and the clerk booted up several more computers and looked at what was on their hard drives. The fourth one they checked generated a smile from the clerk and a nod from Walter. Three minutes until bus time.

After what seemed like years, Walter pulled up a picture from yesterday's trip to the piazza. He scrolled past several shots of Michael sprawled out under the bronze *David*. "I really need to get out of here," he said, checking his watch.

"Oh, please," I begged. "Just a couple more."

The next shot showed Amy, Tessa and two other people standing at a balustrade. "Yes, yes!" I shouted. "That's it. Can we make a copy?"

"I'm saving it on the computer. You figure out how to print a copy. I've got to go. I can help you some more tonight."

"For now, would you save that one? And the next two?" I figured I couldn't push it more than that.

"Do you want the time and date on the pictures?"

"Oh, yes." That possibility hadn't even occurred to me.

Walter swept the cursor around the screen and clicked on a few things. Then he grabbed his camera, yanked out his wires, and headed for the side door.

"Printer?" I asked the young clerk, who already looked like he had dealt with as many problems as he could handle for one day. "Color printer? I want to make a copy of some pictures."

Even with his help, I printed pictures of some people I'd never seen before—pictures apparently left on the computer by someone else. Then I printed the right pictures, but smaller than a postage stamp, then the upper left quadrant of pictures blown up much too big. Finally, twelve Euros and a sinful amount of wasted paper later, I returned the laptop and walked out with three photos, taken consecutively at the piazza yesterday.

TWENTY-ONE

I FLAGGED DOWN A cab in front of the hotel. The trip to the piazzale Michelangelo was bound to cost a lot, and I hoped I had enough cash. As the driver wound up the hillside through umbrella pines, I tried to figure out where, exactly, the blue Fiat had been yesterday when we saw it from the overlook. There was more than one road it could have been on.

I spread the three pictures on my lap, in chronological order. The time printed on the first picture was 17:40, or 5:40 p.m. In it were four people: Beth, Achille, Amy and Tessa. Beth sat on the stone border of a flowerbed, and Achille, standing beside her, looked out into the distance. Amy and Tessa stood side by side at the balustrade, their backs to the camera.

In the second picture, stamped 17:41, Lettie and I stood at an iron railing with the top of the Duomo visible in the distance. Jim Kelly's head, out of focus, was in the bottom right side of the photo—as if he had just slipped into the frame and Walter had got him by accident. The third picture, taken four minutes later, at 17:45, showed Achille and Tessa at the stone balustrade, apparently the same one as in the first shot, but Beth and Amy were not there.

I had just enough cash to pay the driver, so before I did anything else, I needed to find an ATM machine or some place I could acquire enough cash to get me back to town. At the back of the piazza there was a lovely building which, on closer inspection, proved to be a restaurant—not open yet. Inside, a man was setting tables, so I figured I could cash a traveler's check there later, if I ordered something.

Walking to the northern edge of the upper level, I set about figuring out where Walter had stood to take each picture. How different it looked this morning. The sun was high in the southeastern sky and the pavement was already hot. To the north, cool, blue mountains beyond the city contrasted sharply with the hot stuccos and orange tiles below. A few little cumulus clouds bounced along the mountaintops, daring the sun to vaporize them. Walter's pictures from yesterday evening were filled with long shadows and the rosy cast of the setting sun. It looked like a different place.

I held the pictures out in front of me and one of them was instantly whisked out of my hand by the wind. It tumbled across the flagstones, a few feet ahead of my grasping hands. A teenage boy, smoking with some friends near the statue, rushed out and trapped it for me. *"Grazie,"* I said.

Back to the overlook. I found the spot from which Walter had taken the first shot. He had been aiming down onto the eastern overlook, which was largely shadowed by the staircase and by the tops of nearby trees. Amy and Tessa had their backs to the camera and nothing in their posture gave any hint of what, if anything, they were doing other than enjoying the view. Beth, seated at the edge of a begonia bed, looked down at her feet, while Achille, lightly touching her shoulder, looked off into the distance.

For the second picture, Walter had moved left, to the western side of the piazza, but I couldn't get the photo to align properly with what I saw before me. After trying several spots, I realized that he had stood, not at the upper balustrade, but on the left wing of the stairs. I found the exact place about halfway down. In the photo, Lettie pointed toward something in the town near the Duomo, and I was holding my breeze-blown hair out of my face. Our long shadows stretched across the brick pavement. Jim Kelly had, obviously, just walked down the stairs.

There was a four-minute gap between the second and third photos. I thought of what that meant. Walter could have walked back up the stairs and down the ones on the other side, or he could have gone around the front, to get to the eastern overlook. There would have been plenty of time. In those four minutes, the population of both overlooks might have changed completely. People didn't tend to stay in one place very long up here.

Walter had stood at or near the bottom of the right wing of the staircase for the last shot. *How odd,* I thought. Achille and Tessa stood, backs to the camera at almost the exact same spot where Amy and Tessa had stood in the first picture, but neither Beth nor Amy was there now. As soon as I located the spot, I saw that the balustrade and pavement wrapped around to the south, extending way around the side. This was not apparent until you walked right up to the edge. Amy might have been there when the third picture was taken.

I walked around that way as far as I could and looked out across the farmlands dotted with tall cypress trees and stucco houses. At the bottom of the slope and beyond a thin clump of trees, a narrow road wound around the hill. In a flash, I realized that this was the road the blue Fiat had been on yesterday as we had picked our way down the slope to Amy's body.

Charging up the steps and across the parking area on the upper level, I stepped down and across the slope and grabbed onto the strongest-looking plants on my upslope side for a little bit of anchorage. I found the spot where the body had lain; there was a bit of blood still on the grass. I hadn't noticed any blood yesterday, but Amy's head had been twisted in such a way that if she had bled from the mouth or the left side of her head, I wouldn't have seen it. I paused a minute and thought about Amy. So young and healthy one minute. So dead the next. I hoped she was in a better place.

From here, I couldn't pinpoint the exact spot from which Amy had fallen. I needed to go back up and put a marker or something at the place Tessa had been standing when I saw her, choking and gasping for breath. I doubted she had moved away, once Amy had fallen, but that didn't mean that Tessa was right beside Amy when she fell, did it?

The spot from which I thought I had heard the blue Fiat rev up and peel off was just below here and a little to the right. I walked up and down the road for about a quarter mile in both directions. It was too narrow, along most of this stretch, for two cars to pass without one of them pulling onto the shoulder. There was one place where the outside shoulder was wide enough for a car to park. I stood there and looked up the hill. It gave a perfect view of the southern end of the balustrade. The spot where Amy had landed was almost directly between here and there.

If it was Gianni, and I would have bet good money that it was, what was he here for? Could he have been the reason Amy fell? He might have told Amy earlier, "I'll meet you at the piazza." It would have been shortly after work, if he worked at a regular nine-to-five job, but I had no idea what hours he worked—or *if* he worked. Amy had mentioned that he did some modeling occasionally, but that wasn't a steady job.

Suppose he parked here until he saw Amy at the balustrade. If he had a motive for doing away with her, he could have simply walked up the slope—unseen by anyone but her—and pulled her over. Maybe not. I climbed back up the slope until I reached the part that was too steep to go any farther, and looked up. Unless Gianni was part mountain goat, I didn't see how he could have done it. At best, he could have clambered up to the base of the wall, possibly grabbed the bottom of the balustrade, reached up and...

Forget it. Amy would have had to be a willing participant in her own killing!

There was another possibility. Suppose Amy thought he was scrambling up to kiss her, à la Romeo and Juliet. Then she would have leaned over the balustrade eagerly.

I thought about Amy and Gianni. Who was he, anyway? A friend of Cesare? A friend of Tessa? How did he and Amy meet? A blind date? Somehow, I had the impression neither Tessa nor Cesare knew him very well. If that was true, had Gianni finagled an introduction to Amy so he could ask her out? If someone wanted Amy dead, this could have all been planned before any of us even arrived.

Oh, God. Paul is right, I'm finding snakes under every rock.

I returned one more time to the east overlook and stood on tiptoes to get the feeling of wearing high heels as I imagined myself falling over, pulled over by someone on the other side, or pushed over by someone on this side. I couldn't quite imagine tumbling over in any of those cases, but I chalked it up to being several inches shorter than Amy. I didn't go so far as to test Michael's center-of-gravity theory by leaning over the concrete balustrade myself. I'm not that dumb.

I sat a table in the restaurant I had spotted earlier—a delightful respite from the blaring sun. I ordered a sort of bruschetta and a big glass of water, repeating the last part with hand gestures to make it plain that I needed a *big* glass of water. It seemed to me that Italians should adopt iced tea the same way we Americans have embraced their cappuccino and latte. I asked them to call a taxi for me and, when it came, I told the driver, "To the Borgo Ognissanti, please. To the caserma of the carabinieri."

"I HAVE A CAR FOR YOU to check out. It's a blue Fiat, and the license number ends with either 10 M or I-O-M. It was parked very suspiciously at the bottom of the hill yesterday when Amy fell, and it sped off right after."

Marco wrote that down and glanced at me. "How does one park suspiciously?"

"What I mean is, I saw the car drive up a few minutes before, and as soon as we started down to see about Amy, it tore off in a huge hurry."

"Dotsy, you aren't trying to make Amy's accident into another murder, are you?"

"I think it should be considered."

Marco sat stock still, his gaze glued to the corner of his desk calendar. At last he said, "No. It was an accident, and let me tell you why. I know you will think I want it to be an accident because it makes my job easier and because we have no evidence to the contrary. But that is not so. It would actually make my job easier if it was murder and I could prove it."

"You'll have to explain that."

"Beth Hines stands to inherit quite a lot of money. According to her brother Joe—" Marco forced the name through his teeth "—Meg had accumulated a small fortune, not entirely by means we would all approve of, but there it is. She has left it to Amy and Beth equally. Joe tells me that he told Meg to leave him a small piece of real estate, a cabin on a lake I believe he said, and that was all he wanted. Apparently he has enough money already.

"So, you see, Beth now inherits the whole thing. If she killed her older sister to get half a fortune, wouldn't she also kill her younger sister to get a whole fortune?"

Every cell in my body wanted to scream at him. I knew Lettie would, if she was here, but if I expected him to treat me like a partner, I had to maintain a façade of objectivity. "Go on," I said.

"It can't be murder because it was very bad luck it was even a death. The height from which she fell—the distance—she was very unlucky to have been killed. Most times, a fall like that would break some bones, perhaps collapse lungs, perhaps fracture the skull. But most times, a healthy young person like that would survive. Yes, she was very unlucky. To commit a murder you must do something that is fatal, Dotsy. If your victim survives, you are in deep…you know."

"I hadn't thought of that." I stared at my feet for a while. What he said made sense.

When I looked up, I caught him smiling at me, his cheek resting on his knuckles.

"When this mess is all cleaned up," he said, "I want to take you someplace where we can have a nice dinner, a nice evening together…just enjoy. Would you like that?"

"Well, yes." This was the first time I'd been asked for a date in more than thirty-five years. I probably turned a very unattractive red. "I hope this mess is all cleaned up while I'm still in Italy. Have you heard anything from the lab about the purse?"

"The blood is of the same type as Meg's, but we will know for certain if it is her blood when the DNA tests are completed."

"It occurred to me that the killer might have used one of those thin disposable raincoats. It would have protected his clothes, and it could have been stuffed into the purse quickly."

Marco winked at me. "I am ahead of you. I have men looking through all the trash containers, dumps—anywhere trash is found—within a one-mile radius of the hotel."

"Why one mile? Why not more?"

"Because we have to start somewhere. If this search turns up nothing, we will keep expanding."

"Are you going to check out that car?"

"The blue Fiat? Yes. We will get a list of plates that match your description and see if any of them are registered to anyone we know. Do you recall Gianni's surname?"

"No, but I imagine Tessa can tell us."

"That's all right. I have it in my notes somewhere." Marco thumbed through a notepad. "Diletti—there it is. Gianni Diletti. What else do you know about him? He did not know Amy Bauer before this trip, did he?"

I told Marco everything I could remember about what Amy had said about Gianni on Sunday. Then I gave Marco my impression of Gianni, based on our evening at the restaurant in the country. Marco listened, his forefingers pressed against his seductive lips, and I wondered what he looked like without the beard.

The three photos began to burn a hole in my purse. Marco was so certain Amy's death was an accident, he saw no need to investigate. But I was here because I thought it wasn't an accident, and if I really believed that, then I was withholding evidence in a felony crime, wasn't I?

The phone rang, and before Marco finished that conversation, a uniformed officer popped in with a note for him. He glanced at it and responded. That gave me time to consider what would happen if he discovered Amy had indeed been murdered. He would find out that I had been sleuthing, and he'd find out about the pictures. He'd have to question all of us again, and if I didn't tell him about the pictures, Walter would.

"Could we go out for a walk? I need to get out of here for a little while," he said.

I waited until we had wound through traffic and down to the street that ran along the Arno. Marco lit a cigarette and took a deep drag.

"I have some pictures Walter Everard made yesterday, just before Amy…fell." I pulled them out of my bag. "Do you want them?"

"What did you do? How did you get these?" He snatched the pictures from me.

"Walter used a digital camera, so I asked him to print them for me."

"Why?"

"Because," I began, deliberately not looking at his face, "I wanted to figure out what happened. I went up there this morning." I pointed across the river to the southeast. The piazzale Michelangelo capped the big hill just beyond the Ponte Vecchio. If the bronze *David* were closer to the front of the overlook, I think I could have seen it from where we stood.

"You what?"

I explained. He ground out his cigarette on the sidewalk. "Did you go to the hospital yesterday?" I asked. "Did you see Amy or talk to the doctors?"

"Yes. Yes." He walked a while in silence. "They have probably already done the autopsy because one has to be done in a case like this. I saw the body at the hospital, and I saw your friend Lettie. She was with Beth Hines."

We had come to an intersection, and Marco paused to take my arm. I wondered if he knew I could cross a street by myself.

"Did they give you the contents of her pockets," I asked, "or would they have given them to Beth?"

"To me, but there weren't any."

"Yes, there was. A slip of paper in Amy's pocket."

"Her pockets were empty."

"Marco, I saw the paper sticking out of her pocket when she was lying on the slope, and I stayed with her body until the ambulance arrived."

"Her personal effects consisted of a Swatch watch, very colorful, a Greek key bracelet, and a pair of small gold hoop earrings. That was all."

"No money?"

"Lettie thought she had left her purse on the bus."

Feeling like the worst kind of snoop, I told him what the note in Amy's pocket said. Perhaps the strangeness of the note would make him consider the possibility that Amy's death was not an accident.

Back at his office, Marco slipped the three pictures in a manila folder marked BAUER, asked me to spell "syntometrine," and peeked out into the hall. He closed the door again and took my hand. Pulling me gently to him, he lifted my chin and kissed me lightly.

"This is a terrible thing, Dotsy. I know it is difficult for you and for Lettie." He stroked my cheek with one finger. "But it will all be over soon."

Over soon? How could he say that?

TWENTY-TWO

I TOOK A TAXI to the hotel and sent Lettie the message "Room 220" with my pager. That was to inform her that I was back in our room, but almost as soon as I opened the door, the telephone rang.

"Have you had lunch yet?" Lettie asked. "I need to get out and do something."

"What about Beth?"

"She and Joe are going out for a bite. She's getting dressed now."

After I freshened up, I walked to Beth's room. As Lettie let me in, I glimpsed Beth, at the bathroom sink, sweeping blush onto her cheeks with a large brush. Having prepared myself for a pale and wan Beth with swollen eyes, I was shocked by how good she looked. Lettie grabbed her Florence guidebook and pushed me out the door. "Let's go," she said. "I need to get out of here."

Moseying vaguely in the direction of the city center, we decided to eat, then head for the Uffizi gallery. We found a trattoria with a free table near the Piazza della Repubblica, roughly halfway to the Uffizi. "How is Beth doing?" I asked, as soon as we had ordered.

Lettie jiggled her hands and bounced in her chair as if she didn't know where to begin. "She's devastated, of course. We talked, she cried, and I cried until the wee hours. But Dotsy, Achille called her about every fifteen minutes all night and this morning! I don't know how she stands it. I finally talked to him myself about an hour ago, and I told him, 'Quit calling. Beth needs to rest.'"

"Didn't he take the group to Pisa today?"

"Yes, but he has a cell phone with him. Every time they make a stop, he calls. He's in love with her."

"And Beth? Is she in love with him?"

"She doesn't know. She can't think about anything right now, except Amy and Meg. And then there's Joe. He isn't helping much. The phone rings and Joe stands there tapping his foot and going, 'Who is this joker, anyway?' Joe almost had a fist fight with Captain Quattrocchi this morning, and he's threatening to sue the tour company and the carabinieri and...oh, I don't know. He's trying to help, but he's like a big old bulldozer. He's making things worse."

"Did Beth see Amy fall?"

"No. She said she and Achille were on the same overlook with Amy and Tessa, you know, the one on the other side from where we were, and she left to find a place to get a drink. She was looking for a bar or a water fountain or whatever. She heard the scream like we did, but she didn't see anything."

"I went back up there this morning," I said. I told her all about Walter's pictures and the computers and about walking up and down the road where the blue Fiat had been. "So I visited the caserma and asked Marco to find out who owns a blue Fiat with a license that ends in 10 M or I-O-M."

"You talked to Captain Quattrocchi today?" Lettie, wide eyed, leaned forward too far and got a swipe of marinara sauce on her blouse, at the point of her left breast. She dipped her napkin in her water glass and worked on the smudge.

I knew it was time to tell her about Marco and me, before i got to the point where I was deliberately leaving it out. "Marco kissed me last night...and again today."

"Oh, how wonderful!" Lettie clapped her hands noiselessly because there was a wet napkin in one hand. "A summer romance. A Latin lover. What is it they say? La dolce vita."

"Contain yourself, Lettie. I'm not sure how I feel about it There's so much tension, so much happening." I searche

Lettie's face for a hint of anything other than simple schoolgirl delight and found nothing. "With Marco and Joe going at it tooth and toenail, and a murder investigation and all, I think it's crazy to complicate things further."

"How did it feel when he kissed you?"

I laughed. "You've seen those pictures of a guy crawling across desert sands, haven't you? All skin and bones and dying of thirst, and suddenly there's this great big glass of ice water? It felt like that." I looked at my plate of spaghetti—twisted and tangled, but not more than the current state of my mind. I had lost my appetite. "Did Beth sleep at all last night?"

"We talked until about two a.m. I was totally worn out, but every time I thought Beth was about to wind down, she'd start crying again." Lettie put the back of her hand beside her mouth in that curious little stage-whisper way she does. "So I slipped her a mickey."

"You what?"

"I put some sleeping pills in her ginger ale."

"That was dangerous. What if she was allergic to the pills or something?"

"No chance. I got 'em out of her own toiletries kit. She told me, back home, that she was bringing some pills so she could sleep on the plane."

"Did that do the trick?"

"You bet. As soon as she dozed off, I went to the lobby and called Ollie and cried on his shoulder. It wasn't even bedtime at home, yet."

IN FLORENCE, THERE'S A REAL danger of art overload. This is a state of depravity in which the poor visitor has sunk so low that he schleps by Botticelli's *Birth of Venus,* giving it only a quick glance while adjusting his sunglasses. The Uffizi Gallery is so huge and so crammed with masterpieces, the only way one can avoid going completely numb is to take in a small part at one time. I steered Lettie to a bench in an open-air courtyard as soon as I noticed her eyes had glazed over. Kicking off my shoes, I stretched my legs out in front of me.

"Did you talk to Tessa last night?" I asked.

"We called her room several times but there was no answer. Why?"

"This is bound to be tough on her. She might lose her job, especially if Joe sues the company."

"She's also lost a bridesmaid and a friend," Lettie added.

"When you rode to the hospital yesterday in the ambulance, they let you and Beth ride in the back, didn't they? With Amy?"

"Yes." Lettie grimaced as if the memory was still painful.

"Now, think carefully. Did you see a piece of paper sticking out of Amy's pants pocket? Did a piece of paper fall on the floor or on the gurney?"

"A piece of paper? No, I don't think so."

"Think carefully, please, because I found a piece of paper in her pocket when I was on the hillside with her, when we were all waiting for the ambulance. I read the note and stuck it back in her pocket. It would have been in her left pocket." I told Lettie what the note said, and she looked at me, stunned. "And it wasn't the first time I'd seen that same piece of paper, either. Amy dropped it in the airport in Milan. She just about cracked my skull diving for it."

"I don't remember that. In the Milan airport?"

"You were being—" I lowered my voice "—strip-searched at the time."

"Oh," she said. "But what can it mean?"

"I don't know, but think again. Were you sitting beside Amy beside the gurney on the way to the hospital?"

"There was a sort of bench along one side. I sat there and Beth did, too, for part of the way. Then she knelt on the floor and put her arms around Amy's head. It was so horrible." Lettie frowned and turned her face away.

"But you didn't see a piece of paper?"

"No." Lettie stared across the courtyard until I stood up.

"Ready for a few more masterpieces?" I studied a floor plan of the second floor and set out in search of Michelangelo's *Holy Family*. Lettie followed me.

"Beth says something was bothering Amy," she said. "Last night she told me that Amy hasn't been herself since she got here."

"I don't know how she was normally, but I had a long talk with her on Sunday, and she seemed cheerful enough then. Surprisingly cheerful, in fact, for someone whose sister had just been murdered."

"I don't think Amy was the sort to pretend to be sad. And I don't think she was that upset over Meg." Lettie stopped in front of a wonderful Titian. "And then there was Gianni. Amy really flipped out over Gianni."

"Does Beth know who it involved? This thing that was bothering Amy?"

"No, but she says it started right after they arrived. They got here a day or two earlier than we did, you know. Beth said there was a phone call—she thinks Amy was the one who made the call—and there was a violent argument between Meg and Amy that Beth overheard. It was while they were at the hotel in Venice. Beth couldn't make out what they were yelling about, and neither Amy nor Meg would talk about it later."

"Odd. I wonder what that was all about?"

My mind raced. If the piece of paper had fallen out of Amy's pocket, Lettie would have remembered; she never missed things like that. If the piece of paper had been in Amy's pocket, the hospital would have given it to Marco. Except, nobody had thought Amy's fall anything other than an accident, so a hospital employee could have found the note…and trashed it.

LETTIE AND I TOOK A small detour on our way back to the hotel, to visit the Duomo. On a narrow cobblestone side street, a cool guy on a Vespa grazed my leg as he bumped by, weaving against the traffic, which was all pedestrians because the street was clearly closed to motor vehicles. The Italian love of traffic rules is wonderful to behold. Rules are made to be broken. If there were no traffic laws to break, driving would be no fun.

While catching my breath from that close call, I noticed that we were on the corner where Ivo had displayed his dancing puppets last Friday. Ivo, I surmised, had set up shop elsewhere, because there was a scarf concession there now.

Around the corner, we dodged two uniformed carabinieri on white horses. Lettie looked at me and grinned. "They're all so handsome. Oh, not as handsome as your Marco, of course, but—"

"Shut up, Lettie."

The inside of the Duomo is cavernous. With seats removed to accommodate tourist traffic on weekdays, it has the hollow sound of a train station. Our voices and footsteps echoed dully, then were lost in the air. I lit a candle for Amy, but my conscience bothered me. I should light one for Meg, too. And one for Beth, since she was more sorely in need of help right now than either of her sisters. So I expanded the candle's responsibility to cover the whole Bauer family.

The frescoed interior of Brunelleschi's famous dome depicts the last judgment. On one side, souls condemned to hell tumbled terrified, into the pit, prodded by horned demons with fiery pitch-forks.

How effectively the medieval powers-that-were kept folks in line by scaring the bejeebers out of them, I thought.

Lettie had a fit of vertigo from looking up too long, and I had to lead her to a seat. As she shook the kink out of her neck, she said, "Wow, it's too much, isn't it?"

But it was just starting.

ACHILLE PACED BACK AND forth across the lobby, his cap twisted in his hands like a wet dishtowel. "Lettie, Lettie, please. You go see Beth, now. Tell her let me see. I need to see her." He clasped his hands and his cap over his heart so pathetically it was almost comic

"Achille, she needs to rest," Lettie said. "I already told you that. I don't think she's in her room now, anyway. She left to eat with her brother Joe."

"No good for her. No good. Joe, he…" Achille frowned and made frantic motions with his hands.

I got the idea. He didn't like Joe. I was also willing to bet Joe didn't like him, either.

"How was Pisa, Achille?" I asked, attempting to lighten things up a bit.

"Same like always," he said, holding his forearm at an angle. "Still not straight."

Lettie and I took the elevator up to Beth's room. There was an embarrassing moment when the door opened onto the second floor. Elaine King was waiting beside the elevator and crying. I didn't feel I knew her well enough to intrude on her personal space. On the other hand, I had visited her room this morning. When in doubt, err on the side of friendliness; that's what I always say.

"Elaine? Can I help?" I held the door open while I waited for an answer.

"No."

She shook her head and sniffled, so I let the door close and caught up with Lettie in the hall. Somewhere along our walk to the Uffizi, I had filled Lettie in on the curious quartet according to Paul Vogel. Lettie had trouble getting the new scenario straight, mainly because Dick Kramer would seem to be the least likely lothario. Walter and Michael were both urbane and handsome, whereas Dick was a bit of a lump. The sort of man whose hair looks worse after he combs it; the sort of man who looks better if he *doesn't* shave; the sort of man whose clothes hang a bit awkwardly.

So when Lettie mumbled something about Walter, I reminded her that Dick would more likely be the reason for Elaine's tears.

"Oh, dear. I can't get that straight in my head. It still seems like it should be Walter and Elaine." Lettie knocked on Beth's door. "So, who actually does work for Dick? Or is it Walter who's the boss?"

"It's Dick. Walter works for him. I don't know what Michael does."

Beth opened the door. "Joe has gone off to find…well, I'm not really sure. He's looking for a bilingual lawyer, and he wants to see if the American Embassy can do anything for us. He thinks the carabinieri—in particular that Captain Quattrocchi—are harassing me."

I winced at that.

Beth flopped down crosswise on her bed and rested her back against the wall beside it. "I told Joe they're just doing their job. Somebody killed Meg, and they have to find out who. Joe seems to think they could let it slide."

"Did you have a nice lunch?" Lettie asked. "Are you going to lie down and rest for awhile? Is there anything Dotsy and I can get you?"

Beth made a time-out sign with her hands. "I'm fine, Lettie. Well, of course, not really fine, but…"

"Did Joe get a room here at the hotel?"

"Yes. A suite. Joe doesn't do anything halfway. He asked me to share the suite with him, but I'd rather stay here."

"Beth," I said, "if you find it too hard to talk about this, say so, but I know Amy married right after she graduated high school. A young man named Perez, I believe. She told me about it last Sunday."

Lettie glanced at me warily, as if I was stampeding into a delicate subject. I would not normally have broached it at this particular time, but time was what we didn't have much of, and I was desperate to make connections between Meg and Amy and that note.

"Yes, Perez," Beth replied. "Our parents weren't too happy about it, but they accepted it."

"Was Amy pregnant?"

Beth reddened and Lettie scowled at me. "Yes, she was," Beth said.

"What happened to the baby?"

"Harvey was in the service and, after we got married, they sent us to Alaska. In those days phone calls to Alaska cost a lot, so I didn't talk to the family very often. Mom gave me edited highlights of Amy's situation."

Beth cleared her throat. "Amy got pregnant in her senior year of high school, and she told people she'd been married since Christmas, you know, like kids usually do. She went into early labor about two months before her due date, or it may not have been early at all because she was never real clear about the date of conception." Beth leaned forward, tucking her rigid hands between her outstretched legs. "Anyway, the baby didn't make it, and Amy and—oh, I've forgotten what his first name was, young Perez—didn't have much of a marriage going anyway, so they split up."

"I know this is going to sound impertinent," I said, "but when Amy lost the baby, was Meg the nurse in attendance?"

I really should have eased into that question a little better. My question sounded, even to me, like a well-lobbed hand grenade. I was afraid to look at Lettie.

"No," Beth said. "I mean, I can't be sure, because I wasn't there at the time, As I said, Mom and Dad were just giving me edited highlights of Amy's trials and tribulations. When they called me, they tried to keep the conversation cheerful. I think Amy wasn't in the same hospital where Meg worked, but I could be wrong."

"Lettie says you believe something had been bothering Amy since we got to Italy."

"Oh, yes. I'm sure of that. If only I had made her tell me what it was."

"But that wouldn't have made any difference, would it?"

I stifled a gasp. Was Beth suggesting Amy might have committed suicide? That whatever was bothering her might have induced her to jump?

Lettie stood up and shook out her pants legs. I could tell she was anxious to leave.

Beth slid to the edge of the bed. "I might have been able to make her feel better; it might have helped if she'd just been able to talk to someone. No, it wouldn't have made any difference in…in what happened, but her last few days might have been happier."

"I think they were happy days, Beth," I said. "Something may have been bothering Amy, but I had the definite feeling that Gianni outshone everything else in her mind."

"Speaking of Italian men," Lettie said, heading for the door, "Achille is downstairs in the lobby, pining his heart out."

"Why didn't you say so?" Beth jumped up and dashed to the bathroom mirror. "Do I look all right? I hope he's still there."

"What about Joe? Won't he be back soon?" Lettie asked.

"Screw Joe," she said.

TWENTY-THREE

TESSA PAID LETTIE and me a visit as I was opening my French windows to the early evening air. Lettie polished her nails, and I preferred the smells of the city to acetone. Our balcony was big enough to stand on, but not large enough for chairs, so I stood at the railing and Tessa joined me. She looked very, very tired. "I dropped by to tell you about tomorrow," she said, "although anything or everything could change between now and then." Draping her arms over the balcony rail, she sighed. "Achille will take whomever wants to go, to Siena about ten o'clock tomorrow morning. It's a beautiful medieval town, hardly changed at all since the fourteenth century. They have the Palio, a horse race, around the center of town every year. If you want to go, meet Achille in the parking lot. No need to tell him in advance."

"Are you going?"

"No. I have to stay here. My bosses are not too happy…"

Her voice trailed off. It seemed to me that she was too tired to keep her mind on a subject long enough to finish a sentence.

"Captain Quattrocchi wants me to stay here to do any translating necessary," she continued. "He seems to think my services will be needed. But I don't know why, really. He speaks English pretty well, himself."

"I guess when it comes to formal questioning, they have to be sure."

"That's what he says."

"I don't understand these translating duties. What would he have done if you had been out of town when all this happened?"

"They—and the police, as well—don't need a translator that

often. When they do, they call my roommate, Francesca, or me. Francesca also works for Pellegrino Tours, and we're both in and out of town a lot. It's funny, but even though we share an apartment, sometimes we don't see each other for weeks. Francesca is in the south this week, taking a group around Naples and Pompeii, so I was elected. Of course, I was already here anyway. On the spot, you might say."

Tessa's phone rang. I couldn't tell who she was talking to because the conversation was in Italian, but from her tone of voice, I surmised that it might be her boss.

When she rang off, I asked, "What would happen if they needed a translator and you and Francesca were both out of town?"

"I don't know. I suspect they have more people on their list than just us. I never thought about it. They don't even need us that often. They don't call us for every little traffic or disturbing- the-peace problem involving an English-speaking visitor. Their own English is good enough for that."

"I see," I said. "All they need to know how to say is, 'Shut up before you get yourself in really big trouble.'"

Tessa managed a grin as we walked back into the room. Lettie had finished her nails and was cutting her hair with nail clippers. I didn't say anything. Lettie's red hair was cut in what might be described as a random-length or chaos style, so I didn't see how it could possibly matter if she used nail clippers on it or not.

"I've been thinking about Amy and Gianni," I said. "It was nice that she had so much fun with him in her last few days." I pulled my blood sugar monitor out of my bag and did a forearm test; sugar level, okay. "What I mean, of course, is that she didn't know they were her last few days, but I think she really had fun with him, don't you?"

"She was completely gaga over him, couldn't even see straight," Tessa said.

"Who was it that introduced them? You or Cesare?"

Tessa seemed to need a minute to figure that one out.

"Neither of us, actually," she finally said. "Gianni introduced himself to Cesare in the bar at our hotel in Venice. He had seen Amy walking through the lobby and decided he had to meet her. He told Cesare he worked in men's clothing. I mean, his job had something to do with men's clothing. Naturally, he worked while wearing men's clothing."

"Go on," I said.

"Cesare and I both thought it would be all right to ask Amy if she wanted to go out with him as long as we four were together. That way it would be safe, even if we didn't know him."

"I assumed that he was an old friend," I said. "What does Cesare think of him?"

"That he is very young. That he is not very sophisticated."

Tessa's phone rang again. Lettie and I stared at each other, waiting quietly for the conversation in Italian to end. This time, something told me it was Cesare calling.

"Ciao," Tessa said, and slipped the phone back in her pocket.

"Do you remember the other night when Cesare asked everyone to his town festival and the parade?" Tessa asked Lettie and me. We nodded. "It's tomorrow night. I told him some people might think it was inappropriate to attend a festival, under the circumstances, but he says most of the group had no connection with the Bauers, and they are probably itching do something other than hang around here. After all, the trip you paid for calls for us to be on the road again by now. What do you think?"

My first thought was that it would be a little strange to attend a celebration, but then I thought of the Kellys and the Reese-Burtons and the curious quartet who didn't even know the Bauers.

"Why can't we do it the same way we're doing Siena tomorrow?" I said.

Since it was almost seven o'clock, Lettie asked Tessa to go to dinner with us, but Tessa said she had too much to do and she would be lucky if she ate before midnight.

I slipped into the bathroom and took my insulin. Then I grabbed my purse and gave Lettie the high sign. The restaurant downstairs always filled up before eight.

Tessa's phone rang again. *"Pronto,"* she said. *"Si...si..."* The caller talked for a full minute. Every bit of color drained from Tessa's face. She turned shakily to the door and opened it, mumbling an almost inaudible *"Scuzi"* to Lettie and me as she stumbled out.

"THEY'VE ARRESTED BETH," said Wilma Kelly.

She stood at the door. Lettie and I were trying for the fourth time to leave for dinner, and if Wilma had been thirty seconds later, she wouldn't have caught us.

Lettie and I had gone back to the room for Lettie's room card. Then we returned for my pager. Then, standing at the elevator, I mentioned to Lettie that she was wearing bedroom slippers, and before we could leave the room for the third time, the phone rang. Shirley Hostetter had lost Crystal again.

"I was in the lobby when Beth and Achille came in," Wilma said. "Apparently, they'd been out somewhere together. Anyway, you remember that Captain what's-his-name? The one who's handling the investigation of Meg's murder? Well, he stepped out from wherever he'd been, I hadn't noticed him until then, and he had a couple of uniformed men with him, and he said, 'Elizabeth Bauer Hines, I am arresting you.' I forget whether he said 'for the murder of,' or 'on suspicion of murder.'"

"I said, "For the murder of whom?"

"Margaret Bauer, of course."

Lettie blanched and fell into a chair.

Wilma closed the door behind herself. "Well, my mouth fell open, and Jim's did, too, and Beth, she looked like she was going to pass out. She stared at Achille and her lips were trembling, and he, Achille, looked so helpless. Looked like he wanted to attack the Captain. Protect Beth. Slay the dragon." Wilma took up an *en garde* position and brandished an air sword. "But he'd just get himself arrested, too, if he did anything."

"So they took her away?" Lettie asked. "Did they put hand-cuffs on her? Please tell me they didn't."

"No. No handcuffs. They led her out the front doors and left Achille standing there, looking helpless." Wilma glanced at me, then at Lettie, as if we knew more than she did. "They've got it wrong, haven't they? Beth *couldn't* have killed her own sister, could she?"

"Of course she didn't," Lettie and I said together.

"Does Tessa know about this?" I asked. "Does Joe Bauer know?"

Wilma shrugged.

I called Tessa's room, Beth's room and Joe's suite.

No answer.

Wilma ran off to spread the news to the other members of the group, while Lettie and I dashed out and snagged the first taxi we saw.

"To the caserma," I said.

I DON'T KNOW WHY I expected to find an inflamed mob at the caserma, but as our cab careened through the narrow streets, I imagined myself elbowing my way through a raucous throng of newsmen in loud ties with press cards stuck under their hatbands. Notepads, pencils, and microphones flying around. "Can you give us a quote, Mrs. Lamb? Did she do it? Did she kill her sister, Mrs. Lamb? Did she kill both of her sisters?" I forgot that Beth was not famous, and neither was I. To the Florence press, this was not the big story of the summer.

In fact, the reception area was as quiet as a lead-lined tomb. Once we had swallowed hard and marched brazenly past the Uzi-packing sentry at the door, Lettie and I found no one awaiting us but a small, uniformed man engrossed in his computer screen and Achille, sitting alone by the far wall, wringing his poor cap into a trapezoidal shadow of its former self. He jumped up when he saw us.

"*Buon giorno,*" I said to the uniformed man at the desk. "We are friends of Beth Bauer. I mean, Elizabeth Hines." It sounded as if I didn't know who I was a friend of. It didn't matter anyway; he just looked at me blankly. "Can we see her?" I asked.

"No," the man said.

"We brought her something she has to have," Lettie said.

She would be in big trouble if he asked her what that was. I wondered if I could pass off a bottle of Advil as medicine she would die without. Fortunately, the man showed no interest in what that something was. In fact, he showed no interest in us at all.

Achille walked meekly to the desk. "*So queste donne. Posso spiegare?*" And to us he said, "Beth is back there." He pointed down the hall to the left of the reception desk. "They are asking her questions. Tessa is with her, but they will not let anyone else go back."

The front door banged open and Joe Bauer thundered in.

What sort of man walks past a soldier with an Uzi—in a foreign country, yet—and acts like he owns the place?

"Where's my sister?" he demanded. "You've got my sister and I want to see her. Now!"

The man behind the desk threw his chair backward and stood up to his full height, which was still an inch shy of Joe Bauer's chin.

"Uh oh." Lettie muttered.

Sometimes I amaze myself. I guess it comes from staring down a few Rottweilers and evading a few suspicious men at bus stops when my kids were little, but I'm good at handling potentially dangerous situations like this one. I held out my hand to Joe and oozed, in my best old Virginia accent, "You must be Beth's dear brother, Joe. I've heard so much about you. I'm Dotsy Lamb."

He, of course, had to shake my hand, and that gave me an opportunity to lead him away from the desk and whisper, as if we were old and trusted confidantes, "They're not going to let us back there right now, but if you don't mind my making a little suggestion—"

"Mrs. Lamb?" Marco materialized halfway down the hall and waved me into his office.

I handed Joe Bauer over to Lettie.

Marco exhaled noisily as he closed the door behind us. He walked to the window, avoiding eye contact, and with his back to me, squared his shoulders.

"Does Beth have a lawyer with her?" I asked.

"I've told her she should have one. She needs a bilingual lawyer. Here is a good one." He turned and scribbled on a memo pad, still avoiding eye contact. "Do not worry. I do not get a…a kick-back from him."

Marco returned to the window. I stayed silent. His back muscles were so tense it made a gap between his spine and his belt.

"I thought honesty was important to you," he finally said, "but now I find you asked Paul Vogel to send his…his goonies…"

"Goons," I muttered.

"His *goons* snooping in the States, to 'dig up' information on Meg Bauer."

I felt faint, but managed to stay on my feet.

"Dotsy, I have my own people doing that! Legally, too, I might add." He turned toward me, his face contorted with anger. "How will the persons who are questioned know the difference between my legal investigators and Paul Vogel's goons?"

"I'm sorry, Marco. I hadn't thought of that."

"You should have thought of that. It could ruin my whole case." He put his forearms against the window and lowered his head to the glass. "You visited the florist, did you not? I sent some of my men to Fiorestocana and they tell me two women looked at the order for Beth's flowers. That was you and Lettie, was it not?"

"Yes." I wished I could melt into the floor.

"Here's something you may not know. The phone call Beth says she got from the hotel front desk was never made. She lied about that. Seems you are both good liars."

"Marco, I never lied to you. I—"

"Get out of my office."

Somehow, I managed to grab the memo sheet he'd written the lawyer's name on and stumble out of the office.

Lettie had wisely maneuvered Joe out to the street. I could see them through the glass-paneled front door. Walking outside and handing Joe the memo sheet, I realized there was no way he would use Marco's name when he called the lawyer. He couldn't even say the name without spitting.

"Joe," I said, "I don't think you're taking full advantage of what could be a very useful ally."

"Ally?"

"Yes. Achille."

Joe snorted. "That little bus driver?"

"That 'little bus driver' speaks Italian and English. And he has your sister's best interests at heart. Beth needs a lawyer, and it only makes sense if Achille helps you make the call. He has a cell phone."

Tessa popped out the door, pushing her hair back from her face. "Break time," she said. She took Lettie's hands in her own. "I'm so sorry, Lettie. I would have told you about the arrest, but I didn't know about it myself." Dropping Lettie's hands, Tessa said, "Anybody want a soda?"

"I'm going back to the hotel," I said quickly, before I broke into sobs.

TWENTY-FOUR

I WALKED BACK TO the hotel alone, but I don't remember the first part of the trip. I don't remember anything until I passed the corner where Marco and I had stopped for ice cream the night before last. The shop was filled with lovers. The sidewalk was filled with lovers, too. I was the only person out that night who wasn't with a lover.

And the worst of it was that Marco was right. He had trusted me, told me more than he should have. He'd told me about Jim Kelly's phone call to the Department of Agriculture. He'd told me about the time of Meg's murder.

I couldn't think of any out-and-out lie I'd told him, but that was beside the point, wasn't it? Omitting the whole truth is as bad as lying. I had warned my kids about the sins of omission, told them to be forthright and open. If you want people to trust you, you must be trustworthy, I had said. I was a fraud.

The night I found out my husband was having an affair, I had screamed, "Our marriage isn't wrecked because I found out. It was wrecked the minute you started lying to me."

He had looked at me with a straight face and said, "I never lied to you. I never told you I wasn't having an affair. You never asked."

And I had told him it was the same thing, and it was.

As I dragged myself to the main entrance of the Hotel Fontana, Lettie's cab pulled up alongside the curb. "There you are," she said, stating the obvious. "Want to get some dinner? We haven't eaten yet, you know."

"I've lost my appetite," I said. "I'm going up to the roof."

"Want some company?"

"Sure."

On the elevator ride up, I told Lettie what had happened. As I stepped out, I focused on the floodlit Duomo. It seemed to float on waving streaks of light. In truth, it was lamplight drawn out into long slanting beams by the film of not quite tears between my eyes and the city.

Lettie said, "I'm sorry, Dotsy. I know it hurts."

"My own fault."

"I was in on it, too."

"Don't try to share the blame, Lettie. This is all my fault. Why did I have to be so sneaky?"

"You had to be sneaky because if you'd told him what you wanted to do, he'd have told you not to."

Lettie edged over to the south side of the roof. Since that would have put me in the same spot where Marco and I had stood last night when he kissed me, I didn't follow her.

"When I left the caserma," Lettie said, "Achille and Joe were calling that lawyer, the one on the piece of paper you gave Joe."

Gradually, Lettie moved back toward me. As she did, she said, "Tessa told me about what the girl at the reception desk said to Captain Quattrocchi. What do you think, Dotsy? Beth wouldn't have made it up, would she?"

"Whatever happened with the message, the flowers were real enough. She did get them from that florist, and they really were from Meg. They were charged to Meg's credit card." I caught myself. They were charged to her card, but did that mean they were from her. If the order had been called in, anyone who had access to Meg's card number and expiration date could have charged them to Meg's card. Beth would have certainly had that access. But I didn't feel like mentioning this to Lettie.

"What about Gianni? Tessa said she didn't know him."

"Surprised me," I said. "It's not strange that a man would see a girl walking through a lobby and say to himself, 'I have to meet that girl.' It happens sometimes. I suppose he saw Amy, saw her talking to Tessa and Cesare, and struck up a conversation with Cesare as a way to get an introduction."

"Yes, and Amy was very beautiful, so I guess it wasn't that strange."

"But as long as we're looking under rocks to see what crawls out, we may as well imagine that he could have had other motives."

"You mean that, from the beginning, he had ulterior motives for getting together with her?"

"It's possible, isn't it?" I pulled out a plastic chair from one of the tables and sat, but that was a mistake. Enough dew had collected on the chair to wet the back of my slacks. "Oh, hell." I retrieved a handkerchief from my bag and wiped down the chair, but it was too late for my slacks. "Let's go back to the room," I said.

As Lettie slipped her room card into the slot, I thought I heard a guitar. "Wasn't Shirley looking for Crystal a while ago?" I asked.

"Two hours ago, at least."

"You go inside, Lettie. I'll check on Shirley and Crystal."

Their room was roughly above ours but one floor up, and the guitar music was indeed coming from their room. Crystal opened the door, guitar in one hand, and said that Shirley was in the shower, but everything was cool. She seemed a bit peeved about her mother calling us.

"Lovely music, Crystal," I said. "And I loved what you played at the memorial service. Where did you get the guitar?"

"Rented it. I have to take it back tomorrow morning."

My purse felt too light. As I walked back down the hall, I peeked inside. My wallet was missing. My first thought was that I had been victimized by a pickpocket. We'd all been sensitized to that ever-present threat. My second thought was that if my wallet had been snitched before I visited the roof, I would have noticed the weight difference before now. I decided not to panic until I looked on the roof.

Taking the elevator back up, I found the wallet lying beside the chair I had briefly sat in. It had probably fallen out of my purse when I retrieved the handkerchief. I picked it up and sat for a minute, letting the breeze play with my hair.

What did my list of suspects look like now? I had revised it the other night, based on new information, but now things had changed again. It seemed to me that I had quit thinking about Shirley, Wilma, or Victoria as possibilities, and yet nothing about their status had changed. They were still possibilities. Jim Kelly was out, however. Marco said there was a tape of his phone call to the U.S. Agriculture Department, and that he had been on the phone during Meg's murder. I never had considered Geoffrey Reese-Burton as a possibility—or Victoria, either, for that matter—and I still didn't. What about Crystal? I shuddered to think of one so young...no! She was responsible for Ivo's release. If she had done the deed herself, she'd hardly have gone running in with the evidence that cleared Ivo.

Gianni and Cesare were now on my list, and I had no more idea than a goat where either of them had been when Meg was killed. They could have been anywhere, including the third floor of the hotel. Cesare could have been acting on Mafia orders, or something like that, and Gianni—who knows? Was there an ulterior motive behind his introduction to Amy?

Marco popped into my head, and I pushed him out. Was this it for my love life? Was this the way it would be for the rest of my life? What were the chances I'd be kissed by a man again, ever? On the other hand, I hadn't come to Italy looking for romance. If I'd never met Marco, I wouldn't have thought there was anything missing from my vacation. I certainly didn't need a man in my life.

What hurt was that he had been right and I had been wrong. Not only wrong from his viewpoint, but from my own. What had compelled me to play super-sleuth? Was it my own hatred of lies? The importance, to me, of finding out the truth?

My mind flashed back to Marco's face when he ordered me

out of his office. It was frightening how furious he'd looked. The veins had stood out on his temples. But that was the Italian temperament, wasn't it? Hot one minute, cold the next? Even when we ate ice cream together, he'd changed from sullen to cheerful in an instant.

I stood up, shook myself back to the present, and stumbled sideways. My heart pounded in my ears. To steady myself, I grabbed the iron railing with my hands. I felt dizzy, an unpleasant sort of dizziness, like seasickness.

In the parking lot below and to the right of the fountain, a girl ran across to meet a man in dark clothing, with his collar turned up and his cap pulled down low on his face. Obviously, he was waiting for her. Seated on a low wall at the edge of the lot, he stood up as she approached. The girl was Tessa. The flowered dress and clunky shoes were the same clothes I'd seen her wearing at the caserma earlier. In the dim half-light of the lamp posts, colors were mostly shades of blue, and spots danced before my eyes, but Tessa's mop of curls, the flowered dress, the clunky shoes, the way she ran—it was definitely Tessa.

She couldn't have exchanged more than two sentences with the man. She handed him an envelope, turned, and ran back the way she had come. The man opened the envelope and appeared to check its contents. He watched her retreating figure for a minute, then ambled—almost a swagger, it seemed—to his car. I was about to throw up, but through waves of nausea, I strained to get a good look at the car. It looked like a Fiat, but I couldn't determine the color. Everything in the parking lot looked blue.

I strained to see the license plate, but the front end of the car, the end facing me, was in shadow. It could be Gianni. There was nothing about him that couldn't be Gianni, but with the cap, I couldn't see his face at all. On the way to the Uffizi gallery today, Lettie and I had remarked on how many Fiats there were; far more than in America. And blue was a common color.

What would Tessa have given to Gianni? What could have been in that envelope? A payoff? A memento? Something to remember Amy by? I couldn't think. In a dim sort of way, I realized I needed to get downstairs—to get some sugar. The elevator doors seemed a mile away, but I reached it, somehow, and punched the button. There was only the one button, unnecessarily marked with an arrow pointing down. I waited. Nothing.

I pushed the button again and waited. Sweat beaded up on my forehead. It was hard to estimate how long I had been standing there, or to decide how long I should wait. There was always the staircase. I didn't think I could make it down the stairs, but at least I could start. Once inside the building, I could yell for help. Would anyone hear me? The stairwell was separated from each floor by a set of double doors, but perhaps someone would be on the stairway—if only I could yell loud enough. My voice, I felt, would be too weak. I weaved my way to the stairwell door, my purse slapping annoyingly against my side as I lurched forward. I grabbed the door and pulled. Nothing. Locked.

My palms were sweating, and I was about to lose my grip on my purse. I knew I couldn't make it to the elevator again. My brain was fading in and out. It seemed important to get to the edge of the roof. I was about to throw up and I didn't want to get the roof messy. My lips had gone numb.

The pager! That's why I'd rented the pagers. Logically, it seemed wise to lie flat. I needed to be prone, as flat as possible, because I couldn't fall down if I was already down.

I sank to the rough tile and dumped the contents of my purse. My hand found the pager and I flicked it on. There was a low-wattage floodlight mounted on the brick exterior of the elevator shaft. Blessed light, enough to see by, despite the spots dancing across my field of vision. I crawled nearer to the light. It was angled so that its beam shone in an oval across the tiles and part of the railing. When at last I twisted the pager into a position where I could see the screen, I entered "roof" and sent the message, hopefully to Lettie, wherever she was.

The pager slipped from my hand and skidded under the railing. I wiggled forward on my stomach and ran my hand under the iron railing, only to push the pager over the edge with my fingers. Next stop, the flowerbed.

With my last wisp of consciousness, I realized that I had pushed "roo" but not the letter "f."

TWENTY-FIVE

"WELL, YES, IT took some time," a voice stated. "Nobody really knows exactly how long."

A second voice said, "At least an hour, don't you think?"

"How long have you been here?" the first voice asked. "Do you want to get something to eat?"

"I would like a break. Just a short one. Do you mind?"

"That's what I'm here for, dear," the first voice said.

"Wait. I thought I saw her move."

"I don't think so."

Actually, I think I had moved, but I didn't feel like joining this particular universe quite yet, so I lay still. To wake up was to enter the world with all its problems and questions, questions, questions. I wasn't ready.

The first voice said, "You should have been in the lobby last night when Captain Quattrocchi came in."

"I guess we were in the ambulance by that time," the second voice said. *Lettie!* "Why? What happened?"

"The man at the front desk admitted that you can't get into the stairs from the roof because that door only opens from the inside. The Captain went all red in the face, yelling, 'I'll have your guts for garters!'"

"I'll have your guts for garters?"

"Well, he was yelling in Italian, of course, but that was the gist of it."

I tried to move my head slightly, so as not to attract attention. It felt as if my brain was full of marbles, and they all shifted. I waited a few minutes. There was no more conversation, so I thought I might be alone. Opening one eye enough to glance down my body, I could see a plastic tube, a white sheet, the tip of a red toenail. Obviously, I was in a hospital bed. I tightened my neck muscles and moved my head a little more. It wasn't as bad this time. I didn't pass out from the pain.

I opened both eyes. Might as well get this over with, although I rather hoped I'd be able to lie there a few more minutes before I had to make any important decisions.

Victoria Reese-Burton sat in an upholstered chair against a white wall. She flipped through an Italian language magazine. She looked up and smiled.

"Welcome back, dear," she said in a suitably soft voice.

The marbles in my brain thanked her for not yelling. "I went hypoglycemic, didn't I?"

"Oh, yes. In a big way. We've had quite a night with you. Oh, I'm just so glad you're awake. Lettie's downstairs, getting a bite of breakfast. Do you want me to find her? She'll be so happy."

"No, thanks. Let her eat. What's in the IV?"

"A saline solution, dear. They gave you something last night, an injection they called…glucose? No, but gluco-something."

"Glucagon, I bet. What time is it?"

Victoria checked her watch. "About half-seven…a.m. You've been here all night."

"What happened?" I tried, feverishly, to remember the events leading up to this pretty predicament. I flashed on Michelangelo's *Holy Family*, dashing down the street with Lettie, two carabinieri on white horses, the caserma, the floodlit Duomo. "I was on the roof, wasn't I?"

"You were indeed on the roof, but it took the brains of a dozen people about an hour to figure that out. Lettie got a message on her pager that said 'roo,' and at first she thought you were telling her you were in Shirley and Crystal's room. That you had meant to send 'room' and whatever their room number is." Victoria waved her hand dismissively. "Lettie said that was your signal to let her know where you were, but that if you had wanted her to call the room, you would have sent the message 'call room whatever.'"

"Right. But since I hadn't given any room number, how did she interpret that?"

"That you had changed your mind about sending the message, but had accidentally sent it anyway. That's why she waited quite a while before she did anything."

"I see."

"So after a while, she called Shirley, who said that you weren't there, and Crystal told her you'd come to the door some time ago, but you hadn't come in."

I dimly recalled doing that. If I had a few minutes to think about it, I felt like I could bring it all back. I could see Crystal standing there, holding her guitar by its neck. I walked down the hall, my purse felt too light—yes, it was coming back.

"Lettie and Shirley called room after room. Then the rest of us got in on it. We all—well, several of us at least—ended up in your room. Yak, yak, yakking. Some were of the opinion that you had started to tell Lettie what room you were in, and then you decided to go out somewhere, but sent a part of the message by mistake. Then Tessa had the brainstorm. She said, 'Roof! That's it. Not room, roof!' And Lettie said, 'Of course. That's where we were earlier. She may have gone back for some reason.' So we all dashed up straight away, and there you were."

"I owe all of you a big one."

"Are you hungry, Dotsy? I can call for some breakfast for you."

"Not just yet. What's on the agenda for today?"

"Some are going to Siena, but Crystal and Shirley and I are going to San Gimignano. Achille says he can drop us off on the way and pick us up later."

"How was Pisa yesterday?"

"Oh, lovely. Crystal and I went together, and Shirley stayed in the hotel. Geoffrey wanted to browse the Boboli Gardens. He's a keen gardener at home, you know."

"After spending the day with Crystal, what do you think? Is she doing a normal teen rebellion thing, or are there bigger problems?"

"To tell you the truth, compared to some of the youngsters you see on the street in London, Crystal is an advert for Laura Ashley." Eyes twinkling, Victoria laughed. "Crystal is an exceptional girl, I think. She has a gift for looking at the world differently; from various angles. I think she gets irritated with her mother because Shirley sees things from a conventional angle." Victoria sliced the air in front of her face with a knife-rigid hand.

I thought of "Girlfriend in a Coma," the song Crystal had played at Meg's memorial service. A bit of a tongue-in-cheek joke on the older crowd? On her mother? If so, it was both clever and harmless.

"Yesterday, we took pictures of the leaning tower," Victoria continued. "Well, everybody does, of course. What else would one do at Pisa? I've seen people standing in front of it with their hands up—like they're holding it up, you know. They do that all the time. I've seen people turn the camera, so the tower looks like it's up straight, but then the grass is on an angle. But do you know what Crystal did? She walked around ninety degrees and took a photo from there. How clever."

"Dotsy! Oh, oh, you're awake." Lettie clapped her hands. Two tears ran down her cheeks, and she grabbed a tissue from my bedside stand.

Taking leave of us to go back to the hotel, Victoria pshawed my profuse thanks for her help.

Lettie jammed her fists on her hips. "Well, Dotsy, the next time you send 'roo' you'd better be talking about Kanga's baby. We were at our wit's end."

"I'm sorry. I guess you didn't find my pager, did you?"

"It wasn't there."

"I know. I think I knocked it over the edge. We'll have to check around the building when we get back. When are they going to release me? Do I have a doctor?"

"I'll find out what I can. But are you strong enough to leave?"

"All I need is some ibuprofen and I'll be fine."

Lettie disappeared for several minutes. When she returned, she told me the nurse thought I'd be able to leave as soon as the doctor knew I was awake. The nurse was on her way to locate him.

I asked, "What do you want to do today? Some of the group are going to Siena."

"Do you think you're well enough to make a trip like that?"

"Of course I'm well enough, but I don't want to go. This may be our last day in Florence and I have yet to spend more than a few minutes at the archaeology museum, which is the main thing I came here to see. I want to go there and spend at least a couple of hours."

"Do you need me to go with you? I told two friends back home I'd price some gold chains. They supposedly have some nice bargains at the shops along the sides of that bridge."

"The Ponte Vecchio? Okay. Let's each do our own thing. Shopping bores me and the museum would bore you." I tried to sit up. My head felt like a tennis ball at Wimbledon, but at least the match was nearly over. "Oh! Guess what? Before I passed out last night, I saw Tessa in the parking lot down below. She gave an envelope to a man who left in a Fiat."

"Gianni?"

"Could have been."

"Mrs. Lamb, I'm happy to see you are awake now." The man in a white lab coat extended his hand.

I didn't catch his name, but it had to be my doctor. He explained what they had done to me last night and cautioned me in the strongest terms not to run such a risk again. He spoke very halting English. I assured him that I would be careful and he would not see me again. A nurse stood behind him. She made notes on a clipboard.

"May I leave now?" I asked the doctor.

"The nurse will take your vital signs, and then you may go."

The nurse jotted that down.

"One more thing," I said. I begged a pen and paper from Lettie and wrote SYNE, crossed that out and wrote SYNTOME-TRINE. I hoped I remembered correctly the word on Amy's little slip of paper. The doctor looked at it and frowned. "What kind of medicine is that?" I asked.

"After the birth of a child," he said, "It is used to make the uterus contract."

"What if it was given to a woman who was in early labor?"

He shook his head energetically. "Never!"

"What if a woman wanted an abortion?"

"That would do it."

I didn't pursue it any further. He was obviously uncomfortable with the whole conversation. I didn't have any belongings to gather up, but Lettie looked around the room anyway, while I signed a couple of papers the nurse gave me and changed into my own clothes.

"Oh, I forgot to tell you," Lettie said. "Marco Quattrocchi is downstairs. I guess we'd better sneak out another door, right?"

I didn't need an ugly confrontation. I thought about last night and about the pity party I had held in my own honor on the roof. *Time to grow up, Dotsy. So it all fell apart. So what? He's the man in charge of finding out who killed Meg and quite likely, who killed Amy too.* It occurred to me that it was much better to be on speaking terms with him than to be "out of the loop."

"Do me a favor," I said. "Go downstairs, find him, and think of some reason to mention that I'm here and I'm on my way down. If he wants to leave before I get there, he can."

"Why do I have to do all the dirty work?"

I waited at the window. This hospital was in a part of Florence I had never seen before; nothing medieval or charming here. The scene out my window could just as well be Richmond.

Lettie came huffing in. "I found him. I told him. He turned a funny color, but he didn't say anything. He's waiting for you at the elevator on the bottom floor."

I found Marco talking to a man in a lab coat—not my doctor—when Lettie and I stepped off the elevator. Marco cut his conversation short and walked over to me. I said, "Good morning."

"How are you feeling?"

"Fine." He looked good enough to eat, so I concentrated on the wall behind his shoulder.

"We have traced that blue Fiat. It does belong to Gianni Diletti. Now, he is missing. I have sent men to his address, but we have not found him yet."

Why was he telling me this? We had already established that I couldn't be trusted.

I told Marco about what I'd seen in the parking lot last night, but didn't allow myself to look straight into his eyes.

"Very strange," he said. "I will ask Tessa about that. I have not seen her since last evening."

"Why don't you call her cell, I mean her mobile phone?" I hadn't heard the term cell phone used in Italy. They seemed to always say mobile.

"I do not know her mobile telephone number."

"But you called it yesterday, didn't you? When you arrested Beth?"

"No. I called Tessa at her room. First I called the home number that we had on record, her apartment telephone. Then, when I had no answer, I called her room at the Hotel Fontana."

I glanced at Lettie and wondered if she was thinking the same thing I was thinking. If the call Tessa had gotten when she left our room in such a hurry yesterday wasn't from Marco, then who was it from? It had upset her so much she hadn't been able to tell us good-bye.

Marco lowered his voice and motioned Lettie and me closer. "I talked to the doctor who did the autopsy on Amy Bauer. He told me he cannot be sure, but it looked to him as if Amy may have been dead before she hit the ground."

"You mean somebody killed her," I said, "and then tossed her over?"

"He cannot be sure. She died from a compression fracture of the vertebrae in her neck." Marco put his hand on the back of his own neck as Lettie and I moved in closer. "That could have happened," he said, "because she hit the ground face first and pushed her head backward, or it could have been done by something that quickly snapped her head backward." Marco demonstrated with his palm against his forehead. "And then she would, of course, have fallen. There is probably no way to determine which way it happened, but the doctor did point out, as I had already noticed myself, that the hillside was steeply sloped where she landed. If she had been conscious as she fell, it is unlikely that she would have turned her head so as to land face first."

"Absolutely not." To me, this sounded like proof positive that Amy had been attacked and then thrown over the balustrade. But without any other hard evidence, it wouldn't count for much in a court of law. Why was Marco telling me all this? Maybe he was demonstrating how one goes about being open and forthright. Or maybe he was over his anger. Ah, the Italian temperament.

"So I need to find Gianni Diletti," he said. "I have been informed that I cannot keep your group here in Florence any longer. Your tour company is taking you to Rome tomorrow, and there is nothing I can do about it. Just like Ivo the Gypsy, all my suspects will now be out of my control."

"What about Beth?" Lettie asked.

"Her brother has hired a lawyer and they have arranged for her release. She will be free to go this morning, but she will have to stay in Florence."

I NEEDED AN EXCUSE to talk to the desk clerk—the young woman with the tight curly black hair—and I suddenly remembered the Bible I had borrowed. Perfect. Lettie talked me into getting some breakfast before we hit our room. We asked for a table on the patio and were seated between the oleander hedge and the gruesome…threesome? I checked their place settings. Walter, Michael and Elaine. There was no place setting for Dick.

Nodding discreetly in their direction, I mumbled to Lettie, "No Dick. Might that be the reason Elaine was crying last night?"

"Oh, yes. I forget to tell you because I only found out about it last night when you were…out." Lettie grinned at her accidental double entendre. "Dick has gone off somewhere," she whispered. "They don't know where he's gone, exactly, but he called Tessa just to let her know he's still in town and she needn't tell Pellegrino Tours that she's lost another customer. That would make three, no four counting Crystal. No, five, because for a while there Shirley was also missing. But two came back, and five minus two—"

"I get the idea, Lettie."

"Apparently, Dick is getting in touch with his inner self somewhere in Florence. Elaine is—well, she's in a rather odd situation now, isn't she?"

Lettie, having already eaten, ordered coffee, but I ordered a full breakfast. I checked my blood sugar. It was okay, but after last night I planned to check it every thirty minutes. I glanced at Elaine. Her dark sunglasses obscured eyes that I suspected were red and puffy.

"Look at them," I whispered. "Each is playing a different charade. Elaine has to pretend the guy next door has gone walkabout, but there's no reason for her to be upset about that, so she has to pretend she's not upset. Walter has to pretend the guy next door is gone, but it's his boss, the man who's paying for his trip, for heaven's sake, who's gone. And Michael has to pretend his boss-roommate has disappeared on him, but it's the guy next door."

"You're making my head spin, Dotsy."

"Lettie," I said, buttering a croissant, "supposing Amy was murdered. Can we assume the murder was committed by the same person who killed Meg?"

"No, I don't think we can."

"But then we'd be talking about two murderers occurring in one small group. That sort of defies the laws of probability, doesn't it?"

"Not if Amy was the one who killed Meg, and somebody found out and sought revenge by killing Amy."

"Okay, that's possible. But wouldn't it make more sense to give whatever proof you had to the authorities?"

"Not if you had no confidence in the Italian authorities. Not if you had a personal reason for not wanting your evidence to become known. Not if you just lost control of your anger. Not if—"

"Stop. I forgot to take my ibuprofen. I really do have a headache, and you're making it worse." I shook two pills from my little bottle and swallowed them with orange juice. "I lean toward the one killer hypothesis, myself," I said.

"One killer with one motive, or one killer with two motives?"

"Good question. You do amaze me sometimes, Lettie. It could be either, couldn't it? Perhaps he or she killed Meg for whatever reason, and Amy discovered the killer's identity. Amy could have been murdered to keep her from talking. But your idea about Amy killing Meg and someone killing Amy for revenge won't work. We already know that Amy couldn't have killed Meg because she and Tessa have given each other alibis, and they have an ATM receipt to back them up." I paused a minute and thought. "Or both Meg and Amy could have been killed for the same reason. They were sisters, after all."

"I think that's Captain Quattrocchi's idea," Lettie said, "but I don't buy it."

We spoke to Elaine, Walter and Michael on our way out. They said they were still undecided about their day's plans. Walter said he was eager to go to Siena, and Michael concurred.

"I don't much feel like another bus trip today, especially if we're going to Rome tomorrow," Elaine said.

This would allow Michael and Walter a day to themselves, and I saw Michael glance at Walter.

"I'm going to the Ponte Vecchio to look at some gold neck-laces in a little while, Elaine," Lettie said. "Would you like to go with me?"

Elaine appeared startled by the offer. Her head jerked up, and she offered a weak smile, from the lips only. "How nice. Yes, thanks. I'll walk down with you. Call my room when you're ready to go."

I placed my hand on Walter's shoulder. "I'd like to see the rest of your pictures from the plaza. Could you help me hook your camera up to a computer? I'll pay for it. If you could download them, I could do the rest myself."

"I'll meet you in the lobby," he said. "Say, nine-thirty?"

Assuming the bus departed for Siena at the same time as yes-terday, that would give us plenty of time. Especially since we now knew which computer to use.

I left Lettie in our room and carried the borrowed Bible to the front desk. I needed to speak to the girl with the little black curls, because, by process of elimination, I knew she had to have been the one who told Marco she had not delivered any urgent messages last Friday.

Lettie recalled seeing Ms. Black Curls behind the desk, but neither of us remembered seeing her in the group of hotel em-ployees who'd dashed upstairs after Beth called to tell them about the dead body on the third floor. Neither Lettie nor I could recall Black Curls behind the desk Saturday, Sunday, or Monday. If she'd been there, Lettie would have recorded it in her data bank. I can depend on her for things like that.

A night clerk with blonde hair had loaned me the Bible. I didn't see her. Good.

"*Scuzi? Ritorno…*" I made some deliberately confusing hand gestures while edging toward the swinging half-door at the end of the counter. Just then, I spied the girl I needed, retreating down the narrow hallway behind the desk, and I dashed through, mut-tering, "Ah, there she is. *Un momento.* I need to give this to her."

After explaining to the girl with black curls that this was the hotel's Bible and I was returning it, I prolonged the conversation with, "I used this Bible for the memorial service we gave for Miss Bauer. Margaret Bauer. You know?"

"Ah, yes." She adopted a suitably sympathetic expression. "So sorry."

"You were here the day she died, weren't you?"

"I was here earlier, but not when the body was discovered."

"Were you here when Miss Bauer's sister was called down to the desk? She told me she received an urgent phone call."

"That is very strange. I was here, but I made no phone call to her room. There was no urgent message. I would remember."

"Was there any message at all?"

"There was a note in her box. When she came to the desk, she was all…" Black Curls puffed her cheeks out and scowled. "She was upset. I gave her the note that was in the slot for her room and she said, 'This is urgent? This is not urgent.' Like it was a big deal. Then Tessa D'Angelo, your guide, came over and talked to her."

So, there had been no phone call, but there *had* been a note.

I had fifteen minutes to spare before meeting Walter in the lobby, so I hurried up to Paul's room. Lucille answered my knock.

Damn, how can I talk to him with her here?

"Are you going to Siena, Lucille?" I asked.

"Come in, Dotsy." Paul pulled a yellow T-shirt over his wet hair, then whacked a pair of socks against the dresser. "I've told Lucille about my assignment, so we can talk in front of her. Doesn't make much difference now, anyway. It seems our man, Dick Kramer, has decided to…well, I don't know what he's decided, but I have enough stuff on him to write a book. I'm finished."

Which assignment had he told Lucille about? The assignment given to him by Dick Kramer's wife, or the one I gave him, the assignment to find out all he could about Meg Bauer's past? I had already accepted the fact that if his sources back home discovered a connection between Meg and Paul, or Meg and Lucille Vogel, Paul wouldn't pass that information along to me. Therefore, I might as well talk freely.

"Something Captain Quattrocchi told me this morning makes me think that this may be our last day in Florence," I said. "Beth and her brother will have to stay, but the rest of us will go, so time is of the essence. What did your resources back home find out?"

"Have a seat," Paul said. "I talked to them yesterday. Hospital records and legal proceedings are hard things to get hold of, you understand, but my man thinks he'll have something on that today. Up to now, the information has come from public records, tax records, talking to nurses. Meg was straight with the IRS. No criminal record, no hard evidence of pilfering drugs. I say 'no hard evidence' because Meg Bauer did have a suspicious amount of money for a nurse from an average middle-class home. My sources tell me that, when the bean counters get finished, they wouldn't be surprised if her net worth doesn't come to three million, or more. Real estate, municipal bonds, blue-chip stocks. She didn't get that by clipping coupons.

"The hospital personnel she's worked with are unanimous. They all say she was a bitch. They all seem to know of one incident or another where Meg was negligent, managed to get somebody else blamed for something she did, made mistakes with medications, or didn't follow doctor's orders. But we need names and dates, and that information would be recorded on the hospital records."

"Which you think your contact will be able to get today."

"Entirely off the record, of course. Anything we find out from hospital records will have to be kept confidential because it's strictly illegal. You could use the information to shed light on this murder, but you couldn't use it in court. You could allude to it if you're working with Quattrocchi, but you can't tell him where you got it. Understand?"

I nodded, but other than the possible size of Meg's estate, he hadn't told me anything I didn't already know.

TWENTY-SIX

POOR LITTLE BETH shuffled into the lobby between Marco and Tessa. Joe Bauer and a gaunt man—Beth's lawyer?—followed. I was five minutes early for my appointment with Walter, so I joined them. I told Beth that Lettie was in our room and would love to see her. I asked Tessa about our plans for the day.

"The bus will leave for Siena at ten o'clock and should be back here by three-thirty or so. Then at five we'll go to the hill country, to Cesare's party and festival. I'll join the group for that trip, but not the one to Siena."

"And tomorrow?"

Tessa looked at Marco, as if asking permission. "Tomorrow we go to Rome. Pack your bags tonight."

Marco said, "I have your itinerary, if I need you."

"Ready to do the pictures?" Walter asked, having walked up behind me.

While I rented the good computer, Walter told Marco what we planned to do.

Marco hustled a key from the receptionist and set us up in the small conference room.

As Walter plugged in his camera and clicked on some icons, Marco pulled up a chair beside me. He was so close I could smell his toothpaste.

"Are these in the same order they were taken?" he asked Walter.

"Yes. They'll include the date and time."

Walter scrolled through the shots. There were several that preceded the three I had copied yesterday, but only two pictures taken after those. The first was a shot of all of Florence, with the Duomo and the Church of Santa Croce looming above hundreds of rooftops. For the last photo, Walter had apparently swung his camera down and to the west, across the overlook where Lettie and I had been standing. Both pictures were labeled 17:47, so they had been taken in rapid succession.

The last shot showed the top of Lettie's red hair and the front end of a blue Fiat.

I said, "Wow! Do you see what I see?"

Walter downloaded all the photos from the piazza, unplugged his camera, and left me alone with Marco. I could feel his breath on my neck.

"We can get this blown up," he said. "We might be able to read the license number, but first let's make a print of all of the pictures, just in case."

Marco took the computer with him when he exited. He still didn't trust me. I'd have to earn his trust. But the smile he gave me was as soothing as a hot cappuccino on a cold winter day.

JIM KELLY WAS LEAVING my room when I arrived. He tipped a non-existent hat, then stepped back to let me pass through.

"I expected to find you in bed, recuperating," he said. "I dropped by to see if there was anything I could do for you and found, much to my amazement, that you're already out running around. How are you feeling?"

"I'm fine. A little embarrassed at having put you all to so much trouble."

Beth lay on my bed, staring at the ceiling, and Lettie sat at the desk, her bare feet crossed on top of the morning newspaper.

"Jim and Lettie were catching me up on everything that's happened since I was so unavoidably detained," Beth said with a wry grimace.

"But now, if you'll excuse me, ladies, I have to hurry if I'm to catch that bus." Jim backed out of the room.

"Jim had an interesting tidbit of information he just happened to throw out," Lettie said, as soon as the door closed. "While most of us were running around looking for you, Jim saw Cesare in the lobby. Jim spoke to him, but Cesare ignored him and strolled over to the bar next to the restaurant. Jim says Cesare handed Tessa an envelope and left. Didn't stay for a drink, or anything, as if he was in a big hurry, or he was ticked off."

"Well, well, the plot thickens," I said. "Beth, what are your plans for the day? Lettie and Elaine are shopping for gold, at least I think Elaine plans to join Lettie, and I plan to visit the archaeology museum. Any of that interest you?" I figured Beth would be happy to have something touristy to do for a change.

"I'm washing the cigarette smoke out of my hair," she replied, "and then I'll take a short nap. I almost had to take up smoking myself last night, in self-defense. But that jail puts out a good breakfast, Dotsy. I have to give them credit for that."

"Did they treat you okay?"

"Oh, they were quite nice. I can't complain. But I'm not out of the woods. I can't leave town, and they'll probably call me in again."

"I've been downstairs with Walter, looking at the pictures he took up on the plaza. We hooked his camera up to a laptop."

"Oh, please don't tell me he took one of Amy." Beth sat up quickly, her face slack. "I couldn't bear to see that."

"No, no. He didn't. But apparently he shot a picture immediately before Amy fell. Did you say you heard her scream, but didn't see her fall?"

"That's right. I walked up those steps and was looking for a water fountain when I heard the scream."

"Are you sure it was Amy?"

"Yes."

When Beth left for her room, I thought about her certainty that the scream she had heard was Amy's. A voice is distinctive, and one would recognize one's sister's voice in a normal conversation. But a scream? If you could tell anything more than whether it was male or female, you'd be lucky.

Lettie slid her feet off the desk and tied her shoes. "What do you and Walter think you'll find out from those pictures? I mean, if he didn't actually get a shot of Amy falling, what's the use?"

"We hoped we'd see where the other people were. His camera puts the time on the pictures."

"Okay, so who can we eliminate from our list of suspects? If we are, as you suggested, looking for one killer, who can we say for sure did not kill Amy?"

"Absolutely nobody."

"Except you and me."

"Except you and me."

chimera (ki-meer-a) n. (pl.-ras). 1. Greek Mythology, a fire-breathing she-monster usually represented as a composite of a lion, a goat and a serpent.
2. an illusion or fabrication of the mind.

I FOUND A SEAT NEAR the Etruscan bronze sculpture called the *Chimera* and studied it. The word itself was strange because I remembered a biology teacher in college using it to refer to something like a hybrid, inferring that it should not even exist. I had seen the famous sculpture in a dozen books, but because I had known, before I left home, that I would be visiting this museum and viewing the real sculpture, I had looked up the word "chimera."

The statue was beautifully wrought. A lean and hungry she-lion with paws splayed and mouth agape, she had a goat twisting, writhing, emerging from the middle of her back. Her tail was a snake. Like most of mythology, the legend probably grew with time and retelling. Etruscan civilization had always been hard for me to teach, because I didn't understand it myself. The civilization flourished in Italy, in Tuscany—in fact the word Tuscan comes from Etruscan—before and during Greece's golden age. Obviously, the

Etruscans were influenced by the Greeks, but in my mind, they were strangers while the ancient Greeks were my friends.

This last semester I had taught Ancient and Medieval Civilizations, and was rather proud that enrollment in the course had doubled since I started teaching it. I wanted to give my students their money's worth.

But the problem with the Etruscans was their writings. A people became "real" to me, like the Velveteen Rabbit, when they spoke to you through their writings. That's called being *historic* as opposed to being *prehistoric*. The Etruscans didn't write down nearly enough stuff. They used the Greek alphabet, sort of, but we don't know enough of their words to read what little they did write.

Now I looked around the hall and thought: *Speak to me!*

But the ancient Etruscans were an enigma. To me, they were an illusion, a fabrication of the mind.

Hey, I thought. Do I perceive a theme here?

A fabrication of the mind brought to mind Meg's murder. On the face of it, we had a number of possibilities and a number of solutions to our mystery, but none of them satisfied. None of them felt right. On the other hand, if there was a satisfying solution, we would have to twist something to reach it. So if I could figure out which assumption or "fact" was false, I could twist it and everything would fall into place.

I could assume with some certainty that the murderer lied. But there were so many people saying "I was here" or "I was there," if one person lied, the whole thing made no sense.

When I have a problem like this, I find the best thing is to sleep on it and let my mind wander freely around it, but it was a little past noon and I didn't need a nap. So I wandered around the Museo Archeologico, enjoyed the Egyptian mummies and sarcophagi imported by Leopold II. I bought a little replica of the *Chimera* and did *not* think about murder until the museum closed at two.

TWENTY-SEVEN

THE BUS WAS HOTTER than the hinges of hell. Achille had let it sit in the blazing sun in the middle of the parking lot, ever since the Siena group returned. I was the first one there, but changed my mind about waiting on the bus until everyone else arrived, and took up my vigil in the shade of a stone wall. Victoria and Geoffrey Reese-Burton joined me while Achille cranked up the bus's air conditioner.

"Hop hafstar...bisk some, eh?" Geoffrey burbled, as he mopped his brow.

Victoria translated. "He says, 'I hope they have some starters, biscuits, or something at this party.' I told him already, I said, 'You'd better grab a bite of something, because we won't get back here before half-nine or so,' I shouldn't think."

There was that funny British expression again. "Half-nine." She meant nine-thirty.

We watched as the group members convened around the bus, but avoided climbing aboard until the last minute. Lettie popped over to show me a gold box-chain necklace she had just bought for her daughter.

"I couldn't resist," she said. "The price was too good, at least I think it was a good price, hard to tell, isn't it? When you go from dollars to Euros, and this is fourteen karat, and they use millimeters instead of inches, it's hard to tell. I may have paid too much. Oh, look, there's Beth! Are you going with us, Beth? Oh, I'm so glad."

I was surprised to see Beth, too. She crept over to our little group by the wall like a kitten at the Westminster dog show.

"But I didn't think…" Lettie,face flushed. "I mean, I thought the Captain said you couldn't—"

"Leave town? I asked him about this little outing. He said I could go. I don't think he considers this 'leaving town.'"

I watched Beth walk to the bus, to Achille, and slip her hand in his. He gave her a quick peck on the cheek before she climbed aboard.

Shirley Hostetter shuffled across the street from the hotel. She walked almost normally now. "Have you seen Crystal? Oh, my Lord, I told that girl. She promised me she'd be here by quarter to five. If she's not here by the time the bus leaves, I'll have to stay here. I am *not* going to leave her to her own devices all evening. She'll run right out to that Gypsy camp again."

But Shirley needn't have worried. Crystal tramped toward us, across a flowerbed.

Shirley heaved a deep sigh, then said, "I told you to be here by quarter of five, young lady!"

"So, I'm a little early. Is that a problem?"

"It's five after five."

"Wait a sec. What does 'quarter of five' mean? Fifteen minutes after five, right?"

I quickly stuck my head in my purse to hide my laugh. Victoria and Geoffrey were less discreet.

Shirley arched her back and looked skyward, imploring the heavens. "Oh, my God! What are they teaching in schools these days? 'A quarter of' means fifteen minutes before, not after."

"Then you should have said four forty-five. I'm from the digital age, Mother." A little grin wiggled out the corner of Crystal's mouth.

Shirley caught it, laughed out loud, threw her arm around Crystal's shoulders, and steered her toward the bus.

Lettie took a seat beside Beth in the front, just behind Achille. Looking back through the bus, I made a quick assessment and saw that Elaine was alone. Walter and Michael sat together on the row in front of her. I supposed they felt less compelled to maintain the façade, with Dick gone.

"May I sit with you?" I asked Elaine. She smiled and moved her bag to make room for me.

Across the aisle from me, Lucille sat by herself. Victoria and Geoffrey took the seats in front of her, with Crystal and Shirley in front of them. There were a few empty rows on that side, behind Tessa's jump seat. On the left side, in front of Walter and Michael, were Wilma and Jim Kelly, then Lettie and Beth in front of them. Paul Vogel hopped on, panting, just as the bus pulled out. He took the seat behind Tessa.

"Poor Beth." Elaine peered down the row of seats, her head against the window.

"You knew her before this trip, didn't you?"

"Yes. It was Beth who told me about the tour. She works for a lawyer who's handling a case for my firm. Beth and I had a working lunch one day last winter and we talked about how desperate we both were to get away. She's had it rough the past year or so. Do you know about her—what her husband did?"

"Lettie told me."

"Of course. Well, Beth said her sister Amy had run into Tessa at a travel convention. They knew each other in college, I believe. Tessa said she was a travel guide in Italy now, and she told Amy about this tour. So Amy talked it up with Meg and Beth, and they all decided to go. To me, in the dead of a Washington, D.C. winter, Italy sounded like paradise. So I told, um, Walter about it, and, um …"

"I know, Elaine," I whispered. "You needn't pretend with me."

Walter's head snapped around. He peeked through the crack between the seats. Elaine seemed to tense up, then relax, as if glad to drop the charade for a little while.

"How did you find out?" she asked.

"I guessed. Combination of things, like you and Dick at the museum, and some other little things I noticed. Hey, I raised five kids. I can pick up on non-verbal stuff like gangbusters."

I certainly didn't want to tell her that Paul Vogel filled me in, but the whole fake show exhausted me and I didn't want to ride all the way to Cesare's village listening to Elaine filter her every word through a veil of deception.

"Then you know that Dick has left me. Not the group. Me."

Achille veered onto a country road off the main highway east of town, into the Tuscan hills where patchwork farmland in a hundred shades from amber to emerald green receded into rows of blue hills, then pale blue mountains, then sky. Silver-black olive groves, dark green vineyards, and medieval walled towns with watchtowers. Tall, thin cypress trees, like exclamation points between fields. It was as if man and nature had worked from an idealized dreamscape design.

Elaine was so relieved to be able to talk honestly for the first time in a week, she gabbed on and on the entire ride. I shut her out after a few minutes so I could enjoy the trip. The gist of Elaine's tirade was that Dick was her soul mate, but she wanted him to be sure he knew what he was doing before he left his wife, and he probably needed a few days to think, and so on.

At some point, when I wasn't listening, her monologue morphed into the subject of Beth.

"So, as horrible as all of this is," she said, "I'm glad Beth will be well-off financially. With lots of money, she can give the finger to any man who doesn't treat her right. I mean, I don't want to sound like money is all that important, but not having money is what has made Beth so vulnerable. She put up with trash from that husband of hers, and she put up with trash from Meg, too, according to Amy. But she's going to be filthy rich now, from what I've heard."

Lettie careened down the aisle of the bus, toward me. Bouncing off people left and right, she said "Excuse me" to each and every one she jostled. "Stand up, Dotsy. I've got something to say, and I have to whisper. Excuse us, Elaine, don't mean to be rude, but—"

"Oh, for heaven's sake," I said, grabbing the handgrip on the seat back and hauling myself up.

Lettie pressed her mouth against my ear. "Achille has asked Beth to marry him."

"You're kidding."

"And Beth said yes." Lettie started a little happy dance in the aisle, but it was cut short by Achille slamming on his brakes. I do believe Lettie would be ecstatic if her own daughter told her she was engaged to a cobra. "But we can't say anything about it yet," she added, grabbing a seat back with both hands.

Tessa flipped on the microphone. "We'll have a bit of a walk from the bus to the festival. This little town, like most medieval towns in the region, was not built for motor traffic. The streets are much too narrow for a bus, so Achille will drop us off in a car park near here, and you can follow me to the center of town, where we will meet Cesare and he will explain the festival to you."

We stepped off and gathered into a ball so Tessa could herd us downtown. I expected a collie to snip at my heels any time. Beth, I noticed, had lagged behind with Achille while he locked up the bus. The air here was so clean. Without realizing it, I'd grown used to the oppressive, stagnant and exhaust-fume-laden air of Florence.

Tessa stopped us at the edge of the car park. "It's ten minutes to six right now. Let's synchronize our watches. In case you wander off, and in this town that's a safe enough thing to do, make note of where we are now and be back here no later than eight-fifteen."

Achille called to her from the door of the bus. *"Che ore?"*

"Alle otto e un quarto," she yelled back.

"No. Adesso."

"Sono le sei meno dieci."

Amazingly, I understood that exchange—sort of. *Otto e un quarto* would mean "eight and a quarter" whereas *sei meno dieci* must be six minus ten, or ten to six. Or, to Crystal and her generation, five-fifty. What a lot of ways there were to say the same thing.

The marbles in my head made a sudden seismic shift. The puzzle—that fabrication of the mind I had worried over while sitting in front of the Etruscan *Chimera.* Suddenly, I thought I could see a way to change one little lie, maybe more than one, and it would all fall into place. It reminded me of my cordless drill at home. The drill had a carrying case that was form-fitted on the inside to hold the drill, the charger and the bits. If you tucked the drill in wrong, the top wouldn't close. There was only one way to do it and shut the lid.

While pondering, I had lagged behind. I hoped Lettie wouldn't ask me what I was thinking, because I'd have to say, "Cordless drills."

The town was lovely. Victoria said it wasn't any prettier than San Gimignano, which she had visited earlier in the day, but this was my first Tuscan hill town and I was entranced. The narrow streets were paved with flagstones, set in a herringbone pattern. Ancient stucco buildings were on both sides. As we traipsed along, we passed a produce market with a sign that said ALI-MENTARI and I steeled myself for Lettie to add, "my dear Watson," which she did.

Tessa led us around a corner, up a hill, and under a series of stone archways, which opened out into a broad plaza with a huge fountain in the middle. Water poured from the mouths of various wild animals and into a stone trough, worn down at intervals along its edge by centuries of peoples' arms and animals' necks. Around the perimeter of the plaza, stalls were set up with brightly-colored banners, sweets, sausages, trinkets, pottery, you-name-it, for sale.

"They're trying to keep the center cleared out!" Tessa shouted over the din of revelers. "The parade will come through here and around the fountain."

"Lettie, look." I elbowed her.

"What?"

A young man in a dark green shirt and jeans browsed a table of lace tablecloths and napkins. I would have missed him but for the aviator sunglasses. "That's Gianni," I said.

"What's he doing here?"

"I can't think of a single good reason. He's not from here, is he? He's not here to be with his old buddy Cesare or his old buddy Tessa, because we've already established that he only met them last week. He's not here to meet Amy, because she's dead. So why?"

"Maybe he's looking for some nice lace for his mother?"

We watched him until Tessa waved us through a pair of giant wooden doors on one side of the plaza. Gianni ambled on past a gelato stand and slipped around a corner.

Lettie and I found ourselves in a large room with exposed wood beams and stone walls. There were several doors and a couple of halls leading off in various directions. One of them led to what was obviously a kitchen, with clinks and rattles indicating that food preparation was in progress. Cesare, gorgeous in designer slacks and a pinstriped shirt, welcomed us with his arms spread wide.

"I'm so very glad you have all come." He smacked his hands together. "This is the place, the room where we hold our town meetings. The other council members have been kind enough to let me have a few of my friends here today. While you are here, please have some wine, enjoy our delicious food. Everything has been prepared from what we ourselves have grown, and if you want something to drink that you do not see, ask one of the waiters. They can service you."

"Accommodate you," Tessa muttered over his shoulder, and there were some titters.

Unfazed, Cesare said, "This building was built in the sixteenth century and has been changed into many hands. It has been a palace, a fortification, a market, and now, a meeting place. Unlike Americans, we do not tear a thing down when it gets a few cracks in the wall."

"He's right," I said. "We do tear things down as soon as they start to show their age."

I checked my blood sugar and grabbed a glass of Chianti. We were not Cesare's only guests by a long shot. I estimated there were about two hundred people, all drinking Cesare's wine and eating his food. Some were in work clothes, some in suits. It looked like a political fundraiser in Little Italy back home, only no one asked for money.

Jim Kelly sidled up behind me and said, "How does the son of an olive farmer, with no known job other than 'he helps his father,' afford a 'do' like this?"

"A little graft and corruption on the side," I guessed.

Before long, ruffles and drumbeats echoed into the square from somewhere beyond the arches, and we all drifted outside, drinks in hand, lining the north side of the plaza.

The marchers were in medieval costume. Each family paraded its banner and crest. Men in tunics, velvet chaperons, and multicolored leggings—some on decked-out horses, some on foot—marched to the drumbeat. Fascinated children had to be dragged out of their path. I let my eyes scan the crowd around the plaza and spotted a few men who didn't fit. Plain-clothes police, I'd bet, or hired security men. They stuck out because they were alone, and they weren't watching the parade. They were scanning the crowd, and I felt pretty sure they weren't here for the homemade sausage.

Lettie nudged me. "Dotsy, guess who? Look!" She pointed toward the opposite side of the plaza. "Just to the right of the lion on that fountain."

Marco Quattrocchi! What was he doing here? Keeping Beth under surveillance? Checking out our party? I wondered if all four of the men I had spotted were his. I edged my way around, slipping behind spectators wherever I could. When people were backed up against a wall, and I had to walk in front of them, I endured the dirty looks. Marco jumped when I came up beside him and touched his arm.

"Aren't you a little out of your jurisdiction?" I asked.

"I am on vacation. Is there any law against that?"

"Looks like you've brought some of your men with you."

"They are on vacation, too. But when we go back home I

may have to give them some more training in how to not look like carabinieri."

"Are you watching Gianni Diletti?"

"What? He's here?" Marco's whole body turned rigid. "Where?"

"He was over by the lace napkins a little while ago."

"You must help me, Dotsy. You forget; I have never seen Gianni Diletti. I have only seen an old driver's license photo."

I hadn't thought of that. Marco's men were looking for Gianni, but Marco hadn't met him. After thoroughly searching the faces around the plaza, I led Marco down a side street with more vendor stalls. The street itself was so narrow, the stalls lined one side only, with barely enough room for browsers to walk by, in single file on the other side. The smells of baking bread and sautéed onions filled the narrow passage. Thankfully, I spotted Gianni's green shirt when we were still fifteen yards or so behind him.

"There he is," I told Marco. "The guy in the green shirt."

Alone, I fought my way back to Cesare's party and told Lettie what had transpired. The parade passed on, but our party walked back inside the meeting hall. I made several trips to the long row of food tables that extended across one end of the room, and poured another glass of wine. I joined Tessa and Cesare in the middle of the room. They were explaining to the Kellys and the Reese-Burtons how to find the best local olive oils. Elaine King followed me, standing somewhat uncomfortably outside the circle. She seemed so terribly alone. Cesare noticed that Tessa had no wine and left to fetch her a glass. He disappeared into the room I had already decided was a kitchen.

"Most of the families here have their own olive presses," Tessa said. "And people like me, who live in Florence, come out here to buy our oil, usually from someone we know."

Cesare returned with two fresh glasses of dark red wine. I wondered if he and Tessa were drinking the same wine they served their guests, or if they dipped into a private stock. Actually, my Chianti was quite nice. I couldn't wish for better.

Paul Vogel, sweating, slipped up beside me and shoved a piece of paper into my hand. "I called the hotel…and asked them to read my messages," he panted. "This is from the guys back home. Remember, you promised. Background only. No quotes."

I read the note quickly; it was short but succinct. I wanted to compress it with my hand. Instead, I slid it into my pocket. As I did, I remembered the piece of paper in Amy's pocket. Poor Amy.

"If you never visited the Bauers," I said, as soon as there was a pause in the olive oil lecture, "you wouldn't realize Meg, the sister of Amy Perez, and Nurse Margaret Bauer were the same person, until you saw the name on the tour group list. Would you, Tessa?"

She turned toward me, sipping her wine as she did so. Suddenly, she gasped. Her eyes rolled back in her head and her mouth curved down in a horrible grimace. I started forward, but collided with Wilma Kelly as Tessa dropped to the floor. Her glass hit the stone floor and shattered, sloshing wine across Wilma's legs.

Cesare let fly a long string of orders in Italian. He knelt beside Tessa and waved everyone else back.

"Find a doctor!" I called out, probably repeating what Cesare had said. "It's too hot for her in here. Is there a room where we can put her until a doctor arrives?"

Shirley Hostetter dashed through an open door at one end of the room. "There's a sort-of bed in here. The room looks like an office or something, but there's a big window. We could get a breeze."

Cesare picked Tessa up and dashed across the room with her. He pushed Shirley aside and disappeared into the little room.

I heard Jim Kelly say, "Don't touch the wine glass. Don't mop up the wine. It may need to be tested," as I followed Cesare and Tessa through the door.

Carefully, Cesare placed Tessa on an upholstered chaise longue while I hefted a huge window as far up as it would go. Tessa didn't appear to be breathing and her face was bright red.

Cesare slapped her hand and moaned incoherently, great tears flooding his face.

"Shirley, take her pulse," I said.

Shirley lifted the hand Cesare did not have and looked at her watch. After a few seconds, she gave me a very puzzled look and said, "There's bound to be a doctor around here somewhere. What's keeping those guys? Cesare, you know everyone in town. Find a doctor! Now!"

She virtually led him out the door.

I said, "I'll stay with Tessa," but I'm sure they didn't hear me. I didn't shut the door the whole way because we needed the cross draft, but I wanted to keep the crowd out. I pulled up a chair near Tessa's inert form and talked to her softly.

TWENTY-EIGHT

"YOUR BROTHER WAS horribly brain damaged at birth because of Meg Bauer's carelessness, wasn't he? I can certainly understand why, over the years, watching your mother grow old caring for him, you would have built up a seething hatred of Nurse Bauer. I'd bet that name was never spoken in your home without a curse to go with it.

"I had already considered that it could have been Meg who gave your mother the syntometrine while she was still in labor. The doctor at the hospital this morning told me it is only given *after* birth, to make the uterus contract. Given during labor it would crush the baby's skull, I think."

I shuddered as I recalled those same words on the little piece of paper Amy had dropped in the Milan airport. Tessa's face had gone from red to purple.

"The thing that threw us off, of course, was the time. I eliminated both you and Amy from my list of suspects early on because you had an alibi for the time of Meg's murder. What nobody understood was that you, acting as translator between all of us and Captain Quattrocchi, were easily able to translate the times wrong. It's easy to change 'quarter to' or 'quarter of' to 'quarter after.' The Captain wouldn't notice, would he? The English-speaking person wouldn't know the difference, would he? But the interviews were taped, remember? All Captain Quattrocchi has to do is play back those tapes."

Like a shot, Tessa was up and out the open window. By the time I could crawl across the chaise longue and stick my head out, she was past the fountain and heading for a side street.

"Catch her! Catch that girl!" I yelled to whomever might understand me.

Tessa ran fast, but Marco had a man on every corner. I rolled my aging butt over the windowsill and dropped to the pavement below. It was a bit more of a drop than I was prepared for, but on twisted ankle, I dashed across the plaza in time to see two of Marco's men grab Tessa. With carabinieri on each arm, she hung, suspended, while her legs pumped away at thin air.

In less than a minute, the men had her in the back of an unmarked car. She glared through the window at Gianni, who was already in the back of an adjacent car.

Good thing Marco and his men had brought two cars.

I ANTICIPATED THE BUS RIDE home would be a grim affair, but was I ever wrong. Tension relieved, it was party time. Well, that plus the fact that most of our group had had a snoot full.

Beth was relieved and therefore Achille was relieved. For them, it was the best possible outcome to a horrible situation.

Lettie happy-danced in the aisle until I made her sit down. I hadn't realized how heavily the suspicion surrounding Beth had been weighing on Lettie, too.

I carefully avoided saying anything that would betray my promise to Paul. I took an aisle seat so I could prop my swelling ankle on the seat arm in front of me. There, I held court. People knelt with their knees on the seats and faced me, while those behind me formed a solid line of standees, all leaning over the seat backs.

Jim Kelly said, "So there was nothing wrong with the wine?"

"Apparently not. Shirley took her pulse," I replied.

"It was perfectly normal," Shirley said, "but she wasn't breathing. I guess she was holding her breath."

"Which would account for the purple face. I didn't know when she first fell, if she'd fainted, been poisoned, or was faking," I said. "Then it became obvious that she was faking."

"How did you know she killed Meg, Dotsy?"

"I've raised five kids. I know when someone's playing possum, so I merely suggested that this whole mystery made sense if one assumed the alibi times she translated had been translated wrong. Tessa and Amy had an ATM receipt marked with the time, and it established that they were downtown at five-thirty. Tessa created the false impression that Meg was killed at about that time by changing the times she was translating to Quattrocchi and, I suppose, changing them back the other way when she translated his words to us. Meg was dead by five o'clock, I'd bet."

Wilma Kelly held up her hand like a school kid. "So when I said I had seen Meg at quarter to five, Tessa translated that to the Captain as...what? Quarter after?"

"Yes. Something like that. But it'll all be on the tape."

TWENTY-NINE

"AMY BAUER WAS dead before her feet went over that balustrade," I said, looking out at the Gulf of Naples from a sunny terrace or the Isle of Capri. "Tessa's father was in the U.S. Army, a Greer Beret. He probably taught his daughter twenty ways to kill a mar with a sock—green berets know that stuff—and she used those skills to kill Amy by vertebral compression."

More precisely, Lettie and I were sitting at the top of the Isl of Capri, having taken a funicular train from the harbor dow below. Walter and Michael had taken off for the shops to do a little celebrity spotting. Famous faces were as ubiquitous as tan and sandals around here.

Dick Kramer was no longer with us. He had gone home t straighten out his life. He confided to me before he left Florenc that his first step would be to end his marriage, and then he woul work on saving his business. He didn't mention Elaine.

Joe Bauer would be leaving for the States soon. He and Bet planned to have a large memorial service for Amy and Meg. Bet and Achille told him of their plans to marry. Joe hadn't bee overjoyed. But he accepted it, rather than alienate the only siste he had left. Achille and our new guide, Sophia, had brought u to Capri, bypassing a couple of other places on our itinerary.

Jim Kelly had drawn me aside on the boat, after we left th mainland. "Wilma and I didn't tell you the whole truth," he sai His words were blown back, and it was hard to understand hin

"We weren't together during Amy's murder," he continued "I had gone down to the lower level and she had stayed u above. But I'm afraid neither of us was absolutely sure the oth one hadn't done it. We both hated Meg Bauer. She had, on more than one occasion, told some vicious lies about Wilma. Two lies even made it to the newspapers. I knew Wilma had been the last person to see Meg alive, but I didn't question her and she didn't question me. When Amy was killed—poor dear girl—we both thought it was because she knew who murdered Meg. Since Wilma and I weren't really together, I thought Wilma might need me to cover for her, and she thought the same thing about me."

"So you were both covering for each other," I said.

Now Jim and Wilma stood at the terrace rail, his arms around her waist. Geoffrey, Victoria, Lettie and I sat at a table. We all sipped red fruit things.

"How much trouble is Gianni in?" Victoria asked. "Is he guilty of anything other than a little blackmail?"

"Harrumph," Geoffrey said.

"A little blackmail is all it was," I said. "That young man was out of his depth when he tried to blackmail Tessa. He drove up to the Piazzale Michelangelo in hopes of meeting up with Amy because he'd gotten off work early. Of course, he was horrified when he saw what Tessa had done, but he figured he might as well make a little money out of the murder. What he didn't know was that Tessa had no way to get blackmail money except from Cesare. Cesare gave her an envelope full of cash and she took it out to Gianni in the parking lot. I saw that part from the roof."

"Given the looks of Cesare's associates, the ones I saw at the festival the other night, I wouldn't bet a whole lot that Gianni would have lived long enough to collect another installment," Jim Kelly said.

Shirley leaned against the terrace railing. "If he's lucky, they'll put him in jail until the heat's off."

"What kept throwing me off were all the other things that were going on at the same time," I said. "Things that had nothing to do with Meg's murder. But I started seeing motives and mysterious behavior everywhere I looked. I hate to admit it, but

I suspected Paul because he was asking odd questions. I suspected Wilma when Amy showed me a photo of Meg in a white fur coat, because I knew how Wilma felt about the slaughter of baby harp seals."

Wilma winced. "If I'd seen that picture, I probably would have killed her!"

"Then there was that note," I said. "When Amy dropped it in the Milan airport, the only words I saw were 'crushed the baby's skull' and that fit right in with the clubbing of baby seals. I saw the note again when we were waiting for the ambulance. The word 'seal' was on it."

"I would have thought the same thing," Shirley said.

"I suspect that word referred to the malpractice case being sealed after the hearing," I said. "But we'll never know for sure, because we'll never see that note again. Tessa must have seen me reading it and slipped it out of Amy's pocket when they were loading her body into the back of the ambulance."

Shirley cringed. "Too many things Meg did were sealed. Our lips were sealed."

"And you, Shirley. I heard that you had left your post at Meg's hospital some years ago, before Crystal was born, because you were blamed for a mistake Meg herself committed."

"But that's ancient history. If I were going to kill her over that, and I'll admit it crossed my mind, I'd have done it long before now."

"When Crystal disappeared, and you disappeared too, I began to imagine—"

"I was trying to save my daughter, that's all." Shirley looked at Crystal, whose hair color today was aqua.

"And all I was doing was furthering my education along nontraditional lines." Crystal leaned over the terrace railing far enough to elicit a quick shirt-grab from Victoria. The drop on the other side was at least a hundred feet.

"Furthering your education? The sort of education you received at that Gypsy camp is the sort you can do without," Shirley fired back.

"I learned some good stuff, Mom. Useful stuff." Crystal had a strange half-smirk around her mouth.

"So," Shirley said, "Amy put two and two together and discovered the awful secret about her college friend and her sister."

"Right," I said. "We'll never know who Amy got her information from, but the way it was written, with words scratched out and misspelled, I suspect she was on the phone when she wrote that note. She may have seen something in Tessa's face when Tessa saw the name 'Margaret Bauer' on the list. We know that Amy and Meg had a big argument after they reached Venice. I'd bet it was over what Amy had learned. The knife was pure luck. Tessa could have used another knife, but since Beth happened to buy that one and showed it to everybody, it fit Tessa's plan beautifully."

"How cruel," Lettie said. "What had Beth ever done to hurt Tessa?"

"Nothing. But Tessa knew that Beth would be blamed. My guess is that Tessa rubbed her prints off the knife, although she tossed it out the window and it landed in the fountain, so the prints would have washed off anyway. She had one of those thin disposable raincoats and a pair of latex gloves, which she probably donned when Meg wasn't looking. She killed Meg, emptied Meg's purse on the bed, and tucked her plastic coat and gloves into the purse until she could get out the side door of the hotel. She dumped the bloody coat in a large industrial-sized dumpster behind a butcher shop—Quattrocchi's men found it on Thursday—and a few blocks farther on, she dumped the purse."

"But she forgot to wipe off the gelato," said Lettie.

"She ordered flowers using Meg's credit card number," I continued, "which she copied from the extra excursion form Meg filled out for the gondola ride. Using a thick Italian accent, she called Beth's room. She pretended to be the girl at the reception desk and said there was an urgent message. She then walked by as Beth was reading the message about the flowers and suggested Beth could pick up the flowers. She led her to believe the florist shop was close by, but it was almost a mile away. Next, Tessa asked Lettie to sit by the elevator and pass along a message to everyone she saw, telling them we would be leaving an hour later. That gave Tessa a witness to her own departure, and to the comings and goings of others as well. She went out the front door and in the side door to the stairwell. She dashed upstairs and killed Meg. Then she exited through the side door and visited the ATM machine in order to establish her handy-dandy alibi."

"Amy was with Tessa at the ATM, wasn't she?" asked Victoria.

"I don't know if Tessa planned to meet Amy or not," I said. "But it served to strengthen her alibi, didn't it? Oh! Those green bridesmaids' shoes. I would bet Tessa had already purchased or ordered the shoes in all the right sizes from the shoe store. She had one pair in her closet, which she showed to Lettie. I'm sure her story about postponing our departure so she could run downtown was pure fabrication.

"And then poor, poor Ivo. What luck. He had Beth's room card, so he breaks in to do a little burglary and sees a corpse on the floor. And a bunch of stuff on the bed, including a nice wad of cash. If Ivo had looked more like a hotel guest, more like a tourist, I'm sure he would never have been noticed or caught."

"And if it hadn't been for me, they'd have convicted him of the murder," Crystal said.

"Yes, dear, I'll admit that was one good thing that did come from your little disappearing act," Shirley said, "but it was the only good thing. And don't you ever do that again."

"Oh, my God! My passport!" Lettie, who had opened her bag, had lost every stitch of color in her face. "My passport's gone, Dotsy! How will I ever get home? What can I do?" She was shaking and her eyes were teary. "I saw this man on TV. He had to live at the airport in Paris for ten years because he lost his passport and they wouldn't give him another one."

"I'm sure there was more to it than that, Lettie," I said.

"Think, darling," said Victoria. "When did you see it last?"

"When I bought my ticket for the funicular, at the bottom of the hill. Oh, I remember now. There was a man behind me and he was standing uncomfortably close. He wore a red and white striped shirt and he had short brown hair, but he didn't look like a Gypsy. He looked like an ordinary tourist."

I grimaced. "What makes you think a tourist can't be a pickpocket?"

Crystal drew her own string bag open. "That particular tourist was definitely a pickpocket," she said, "because I *saw* him take the passport. Don't forget, I've had lessons in that stuff and know what to look for." Pulling out a dark blue passport, she handed it to Lettie. "And I also know how to pick a pickpocket's pocket."

ABOUT THE AUTHOR

Maria Hudgins is an avid traveler and mystery lover. Until her recent retirement, she taught oceanography, earth science, biology and chemistry at the high school level. She holds a bachelor's degree in natural science education and a master's in plant physiology. Like Dotsy, she is an empty nester with a grown daughter. She lives in Hampton, Virginia with her dog, Skippy, and her cat, Elvis.